Much Ado About Persuasion

BARBARA CORNTHWAITE

ISBN: 978-1-951839-58-1

Celebrate Lit Publishing

304 S. Jones Blvd #754

Las Vegas, NV, 89107

http://www.celebratelitpublishing.com/

Chapter One

S ir Walter Elliot of Kellynch Hall in Somersetshire was a man
who had long admired the British Navy. He was well aware,
of course, that other men whose names appeared in the Barone-
tage along with his own did not share his appreciation. His own
friend, Sir Basil Morley, had been known to scoff at the profession, saying that while it had its utility, it was objectionable
because it often brought men of obscure birth into undue distinction, and raised lowly men to honors which their fathers and
grandfathers never dreamt of. Sir Walter felt the force of this argument, but he could not get over his youthful admiration of
Captain James Cook's voyages of exploration. Cook's published
journals had been his constant companions during his final years
at Eton, and they had fired his imagination. Even Sir Walter's love
of rank and beauty could not quite suppress the thought that
although any profession at all would be something of a disgrace
for an Elliot, he wished he had been granted the opportunity to
command a ship-of-the-line and win the same honor and renown
as Admiral Nelson.

Still, Sir Walter placed a high value on his nobility and the
reverence that was owed to him as a baronet. He was enamored
with precedence, and was fastidious as to taste and appearance.

He privately acknowledged that his admiration for the Navy was somewhat beneath his dignity, and he kept his veneration to himself. A keen observer might have noted that he never criticized the appearance of naval officers (a fate from which no one else was excluded), he allowed his daughters to dance with sea captains at public balls, and he cultivated the acquaintance of one Admiral Croft, who had been slightly injured in action and was recuperating in London one winter when the Elliots had hired a house there. Admiral Croft told him—in jest—that it was a loss to the Navy that Sir Walter had never become a captain, as he surely would have risen to the very highest rank in the fleet. Sir Walter, on whom subtlety was lost, took this as absolute truth, and from that day forward he felt he owed a debt to His Majesty's Navy for not joining it and becoming its most honored son. There was no doubt in his mind that the Navy's loss had been severe.

During those weeks in London he frequently invited Admiral Croft and his wife to be his guests at dinner, and the Crofts introduced Sir Walter to other officers who were at that time in London; these men were likewise asked to come and dine. There had been Croft's brother-in-law Captain Wentworth, as well as Admiral Baldwin, Captain Harville and Captain Benwick; all of them masterful, dashing, and brave—exactly what Sir Walter fancied he would have been as an officer.

Had Sir Walter's wife still been living she might have objected to the frequent visits of these gentlemen, in case her daughters might succumb to the fascination of men in uniform, but she had been dead for more than a decade. To be sure, Elizabeth and Anne were past their girlhoods—twenty-seven and twenty-five years old during that winter—and not prone to giddy infatuations. Sir Walter did not perceive any danger in that quarter. Indeed, he would not have minded if Admiral Baldwin had made a match with Elizabeth. They seemed to like each other very well, and whether at the dinner table or in the drawing room, their wit and repartee never seemed to flag. However, the Admiral went back to sea without making her an offer.

Captain Wentworth, Captain Benwick, and Captain Harville went away unlamented by Sir Walter: Harville was married, Benwick was engaged, and Wentworth, though a good-looking young fellow, was only the captain of a worn-out sloop called the *Asp*. Sir Walter could not think him an eligible match for either Elizabeth or Anne. Wentworth might have done for Mary, the youngest, but she was already married to the son of a nearby squire, and now resided three miles from Kellynch at Uppercross.

Elizabeth had inherited the vanity of her father. She had expected a proposal from Admiral Baldwin—who ought to have been elated at the prospect of wedding an Elliot—and had been disappointed when it was evident that he meant to go away without offering his hand. She had made a cutting remark to him at their last meeting and he had responded with something equally sharp. Her pride kept her from acknowledging her heartache, and in the two years since he had gone, the sting festered into bitterness. She disclaimed any interest in marriage and her waspish remarks on the inferiority of men made no one wonder why she was not yet married. She read the newspaper daily to see the list of Navy casualties in hopes, as she told herself, that Admiral Baldwin's name might be among them. It never was, and she was always unaccountably relieved.

Anne had a sweeter temper and a more humble cast of mind, and although she had felt herself drawn to Captain Wentworth when they were in company together, she had not expected any attention from him before he went back to sea. The Elliots had returned to Kellynch in the spring and resumed their usual activities: Sir Walter and Elizabeth spending more money than they ought, and Anne doing most of the household management and visiting the tenants.

When Napoleon was defeated, Sir Walter resumed correspondence with Admiral Croft, and invited him, his wife, and any other officers requiring a rest to come to Kellynch for as long as they pleased. Anne, when informed of this, worried about the expense of a house party. Sir Walter was a lavish host who believed his rank demanded that everything should be of the finest, especially when there were visitors. "A baronet must be seen to live as a baronet," he was fond of saying. This held true even if the visitor was not distinguished: he was extravagant even if the guest was only Elizabeth's friend Mrs. Clay, the widowed daughter of his man of business.

Every day, Sir Walter expected a letter from Admiral Croft accepting this invitation. None came until one summer morning while the family was at breakfast. A servant handed Sir Walter an express that had just arrived, and he opened it eagerly. His face darkened as he glanced at the signature at the end of the missive.

"What is it, Father?" asked Anne.

"A letter from our cousin, William Elliot."

"What can *he* want with us?" said Elizabeth. "After the letter you wrote, repudiating him for his disreputable actions ..."

"Scoundrel! Traitor!" Sir Walter growled. "It is bad enough to have the heir presumptive to the Kellynch estate engaged in trade —owning merchant ships! But to use one of those ships to smuggle captured French officers back to France for an exorbitant bribe ..." He shuddered.

"Dreadful!" agreed Elizabeth. "You were quite right to disavow him."

"He did say it was none of his doing, Father," ventured Anne. "You remember—he said the captain of the ship had done it of his own accord, and as he was only the owner of the vessel, living in Surrey, he knew nothing of it."

"Bah!" said Sir Walter. "He would be bound to say that, whatever the truth may be. Well, I suppose I must read this." He turned to the beginning of the letter and read it silently.

"Well!" he said when he reached the end of it. "One hardly knows what to think."

"What does he say?" said Elizabeth, and in answer Sir Walter gave the letter into her hand.

"Oh, he intends a visit," said Elizabeth as she skimmed the page. "He regrets that his ship should have been used for such a purpose, and that a naval vessel should have been distracted from carrying out its orders to apprehend his ship and send the French officers back to England. He says he is retiring from the merchant trade, and hopes this visit will heal the breach with his family." She put the letter down on the table. "What shall we do? Should we allow him to stay at Kellynch?"

Sir Walter deliberated. Every feeling revolted at the idea of giving hospitality to one who had proved himself an enemy of the Navy. Moreover, the French were hostile to aristocrats like himself, and anyone who aided the barbaric French in any way must be considered a foe.

On the other hand, his idol, Captain Cook, had generously taken back the deserter, Mr. Marra, who had been a kind of traitor, and Sir Walter would like to feel he had something in common with the great man. All he said aloud was, "It would be a public snub, I suppose, if we were to refuse to have him. Gossip would circulate."

"I daresay it would," said Elizabeth. "And it would probably paint us in an unflattering light. Mr. Elliot's connection to that ship is not widely known, so that we would no doubt be under much censure from the gentry of our acquaintance if we refused to have him."

Sir Walter stirred his cup of tea moodily, swirling the spoon around with a frown on his face. "Indeed, we would have to turn him away from our very door, as he is traveling toward us now, and there is no way to warn him off before he gets here. I suppose he will arrive the day after tomorrow."

After very little more conversation, it was decided: Mr. William Elliot would be allowed to come. Reluctantly, Elizabeth gave orders that a room be prepared for their cousin, and quarters arranged for his valet, coachman, and groom.

The very next morning, happier news arrived by way of the post.

"Captain Croft will be here the day after tomorrow!" Sir Walter waved the letter gleefully. "And he brings with him a party of friends: Admiral Baldwin, Captain Wentworth and Captain Benwick. The defeat of Napoleon has set them all free from their naval duties."

Most welcome news to Sir Walter! Elizabeth could have wished Admiral Baldwin back at sea, but she was pleased that the tedium of entertaining Mr. Elliot—a man they must be civil to despite harboring grave suspicions about his character—would be diluted by the presence of so many other guests. And even Anne, whose apprehensions about the cost of this hospitality were amplified significantly by the idea of so many coming, could not but rejoice at the thought of Kellynch being filled with such intelligent, brave, and honorable men.

"Does Mrs. Croft not come?" asked Anne. During her time in London she had found in Mrs. Croft a kindred spirit and she looked forward to renewing her acquaintance with her.

"No, no," said Sir Walter. "She is visiting her brother—not Captain Wentworth, but the other brother—and his wife." Sir Walter could not be in the least disappointed by this omission from the list of guests. Mrs. Croft had no rank or distinction in herself, and her only worth to him lay in her connection to the admiral. If she had been extremely beautiful she might have served a decorative purpose, but she was only passably good-looking. Only Anne would miss her.

If Sir Walter had but known, it was only this visit of Mrs. Croft's to her brother that had prompted the admiral to respond to the invitation from Kellynch. His brother-in-law's house was too small and his wife too ill to make the admiral a welcome addition there, and he did not want to stay in his own home without his beloved Sophie. He needed a distraction, and an excursion to Kellynch was the first opportunity that presented itself. Moreover, he knew an officer who needed a rest, as Sir Walter had suggested, and so made up the party with those he knew would enjoy the visit.

While Sir Walter made elaborate plans for the entertainment of his guests, Anne determined to apply to Lady Russell, her mother's old friend and their near neighbor, for ideas about miti-gating the expense. A note was written and within two hours of its receipt Lady Russell appeared at Kellynch. Unfortunately, Anne could not talk to her about her trouble immediately; no discussion about reducing expenses could be embarked upon in the presence of Sir Walter and Elizabeth. Sir Walter dominated the conversation by describing the coming party in the most glowing terms—he felt the need to justify himself for hosting a group of men who had no connection at all to the peerage.

"Well!" said Lady Russell when at last he exhausted the topic. "This will add considerably to the gaiety of the neighborhood. I suppose you will give a ball after they arrive? I know Admiral Croft has a wife, but I assume the others are not married. I consider this visit a very good thing." She glanced at Elizabeth and Anne and said nothing more, but no one had any doubt about what was in her mind.

"I do not consider any of them eligible," said Elizabeth. "Two of them are merely captains, and the single admiral is forty—well past the age of wanting to marry."

"Nonsense!" said Lady Russell. "It is Admiral Baldwin, is it not? I have known of several men who did not marry their first wife until the age of fifty! I consider Admiral Baldwin to be quite eligible for either you or Anne. Only eleven years older than you, Elizabeth, and completely respectable. I hear he made a fortune in the war."

"He is unamiable enough that he has not found anyone willing to wed him," countered Elizabeth. "For my part, I would rather never marry anyone than be forced to abide *his* company all my days!"

Lady Russell held her peace. Elizabeth and Sir Walter had the same flaw: to argue with them was to entrench them more firmly in their opinions. They might be manipulated, but they would not be persuaded. It was pointless to continue discussing the topic now, but she by no means gave up hope of an eventual alliance between Elizabeth and the admiral.

Mr. William Elliot arrived on a Wednesday. He had not been a frequent visitor, even before his lapse in judgement, and it was hardly a convivial family atmosphere. Mr. Elliot did his best to live up to his reputation as a charming and witty guest, but one talkative person is not enough to make an enjoyable gathering. The Elliots of Kellynch were distantly civil, and only soft-hearted Anne cared enough to ask him any questions and listen to the answers.

He pretended not to notice the constrained atmosphere, and professed himself charmed to discover a group of naval officers about to descend on Kellynch.

"They come tomorrow, do they?" he said. "I will be delighted to know them! Such distinguished fellows! One cannot praise them too highly."

"An admirable opinion," said Sir Walter. "Particularly when it was a naval officer who intercepted your ship with its cargo of French officers, bound for France."

A shadow flickered across Mr. Elliot's expression. "Yes, I might be supposed to harbor some kind of grudge. The captain of my ship, you know, did his bit of smuggling without my knowledge, and my lovely ship, the *Don John*, was confiscated by the Navy. No doubt they have found her to be an excellent supply ship." He sighed.

Elizabeth coughed. "I daresay they felt justified in doing so."

Mr. Elliot summoned a smile. "Of course. And I may say there was some punishment due me for choosing a captain who was so very unprincipled."

"He says he was acting under your orders," Elizabeth reminded him.

"Well, a man who would behave so traitorously would say anything, wouldn't he?" Mr. Elliot smiled deprecatingly and turned the subject.

At noon precisely the next day, the naval party arrived. Sir Walter was all graciousness.

"My dear fellow," said Admiral Croft, as he alighted from the carriage and saw his host standing on the steps of Kellynch Hall to greet him, "your kind invitation is all that is generous! To take so much trouble upon yourself for our sakes!"

"No indeed, no indeed, no trouble at all! It is the very least I can do—certainly no more than what I owe to the Royal Navy!"

The assembled throng assumed he meant that he owed the Navy gratitude for protecting England from Napoleon, but such an idea was far from Sir Walter's thoughts. He meant that he owed them every kindness because he had neglected to join the Navy and lead them on to victory. It had fallen to Admiral Nelson to do his poor best and lose his life in the process. It was sad, very sad, that the Navy had had to fight the war without Sir Walter.

There was warmth in his tone as he bid the other officers welcome and invited them to come into the house. Elizabeth and Anne were in the drawing room along with Mr. Elliot, and introductions and greetings were gotten through. Anne thought there was a little constraint on the part of Mr. Elliot as he was introduced to Captain Wentworth, but she could not think why that should be so and decided that it was probably mere fancy. It was *not* mere fancy that Admiral Baldwin and Elizabeth were distinctly unfriendly to each other. His bow in her direction was very brief, and her curtsey was so delayed that Anne wondered if Elizabeth meant to curtsey at all.

They were not all together long. After no more than five minutes, the butler and housekeeper appeared, and there was the usual bustle of guests being shown to their rooms, menservants carrying trunks and boxes up the back stairs to the bedrooms, and housemaids bringing water for washing the dust of the road away.

Her guests disposed of for the time being, Elizabeth went out to the terrace and then down the steps to the formal garden where she could be alone with her thoughts. Her feet crunched the gravel paths amid the neatly trimmed shrubs until she reached the further edge of the garden. Beyond it was the park with a small lake and a folly in the shape of a small columned temple, just visible from where she stood. It was nothing to the gardens at the

Great House at Stowe as described in Seely's guidebook—a copy of which was in the library at Kellynch—but it was still a lovely place. There was a wilderness behind the temple that contained more walks, but Sir Walter no longer had enough gardeners to keep it in good order, and the paths were full of weeds.

Two years had passed since Elizabeth had last seen Admiral Baldwin, and though she was reluctant to admit it, his personal attractions had not diminished. He seemed to be more handsome, more powerfully built, and more masterful than she remembered. She found herself, for a fleeting moment, wishing she could see again what he looked like in uniform, but of course officers did not wear uniforms when they were not at sea. It would be all too easy, she knew, to fall in love with him again. The only way to safeguard herself would be to be on the attack. If she made her disdain plain, he could not scorn her first.

Chapter Two

S ir Walter had expected his guests to take several hours refurbishing themselves after their journey; it was what he himself would have done in their place. These, however, were men of action, not given to devoting more than a few minutes to their personal appearance. Admiral Croft, after spending very little time in his room, made his way out of the house and onto the terrace, where he found Baldwin and Wentworth already in conversation.

"Benwick not here?" he asked.

"He said he needed rest," said Wentworth. "I only hope he *is* resting and not sitting in his bedroom, brooding."

"He will come about in time," said Croft. "But the shock of Fanny's death cannot be got over all at once. They would have been married by now if that fever had not carried her off."

"Aye, it was a sad homecoming for him," admitted Baldwin.

"Well," said Wentworth, looking from the terrace out toward the gardens, "this is a pleasant spot in which to spend a few weeks. Perhaps a change of scene will help poor Benwick revive his spirits a little."

"It had better," said Baldwin. "His recovery was the only reason I agreed to come. As you said, Croft, a party of good friends in congenial surroundings is the best way to mend a broken heart. My duty to a brother officer required that I come to join the effort. Otherwise, I would never have consented—" He broke off and cleared his throat. "Well, Sir Walter is generous in his hospitality, but his conversation is ... tedious."

Wentworth and Croft smirked at the understatement, but they were too loyal to the dictates of politeness to criticize their host.

"The truth is, you had nothing else to do," countered Croft. "You were at a loose end, and could not face hanging about your brother's estate for weeks on end with nothing to do. Coming to Kellynch was the only sensible alternative. The visit won't last forever, though—you will have to make some plans before long. You must face facts: you are on land now and there are no more battles to fight. You don't want to live in your brother's house for the rest of your life, so the only solution is to settle down. Find a wife and buy your own estate—you have enough prize-money from the war for a very good property. Raise a brood of little Baldwins. Enter Parliament if you must fill your time with something."

Baldwin rolled his eyes. "Find a wife? Of all the idiotic notions! I am forty years of age, Admiral. I will live and die a bachelor—it suits me. No one to worry over you when you go to sea, no chance of losing someone near to you, no one to consult if you want to travel to, say, the West Indies—there is just yourself, unattached and easily maneuverable. Like a Cruzier."

"If you're going to compare yourself to a ship—!" said Wentworth. "I daresay I know what the trouble is. You think no one will have you. You're wrong, you know—what about that girl at Gibraltar? Colonel Crabb's daughter. I'll wager she would take you, in spite of your forty years."

Croft gave a crack of laughter. "Lavinia! Aye, she was very much attached to Baldwin. And yet he was unappreciative—he hastened our departure by a full two days!"

Baldwin snorted. "I don't like sentimental, clinging girls.

Much better to leave before she convinced herself I was on the verge of making her an offer. And she was the sort that would!"

"You have this trouble often, do you?" teased Wentworth. "Enough time in your presence and a woman inevitably falls in love with you?"

"Oh yes, inevitably," said Baldwin in the same spirit. "The trouble is, you see, I am too gallant. If I were ugly, cowardly, and dull, I could be as polite as I liked without being a danger to anyone. As it is, when a woman is confronted with such a combination of wit, bravery, and handsomeness, a polite compliment is all it takes to completely overset her."

Croft heaved a dramatic sigh. "I suppose there is no help for it but for you to counterbalance all your good points by being rude. Otherwise both Sir Walter's daughters will be languishing for you inside of a week."

"Not Miss Anne," said Wentworth quickly, and then, as Baldwin looked at him curiously, added, "I think she is not the sort to languish over a new acquaintance."

Baldwin waved his hand dismissively. "Now then, I have done talking about this subject. I have the utmost reverence for the fair sex, but my heart will not be touched by any of them. I am now going to explore this delightful garden spread out before us. You may accompany me if you choose, but if either of you mention marriage to me again, I will challenge you to a duel."

Croft feigned a gasp of horror and Wentworth chuckled, but they followed him down into a path among the flower beds. For a little while no one made any remarks, but suddenly Wentworth said, "Speaking of the fair sex, there's Miss Elliot now." He nodded toward the south end of the formal garden where a gap in the shrubs showed a vista of the park beyond. Elizabeth was standing there, gazing out toward the lake.

A groan escaped Baldwin. "Quick! Down that way before she sees us." But even as he spoke, she turned and saw them.

"Too late, Baldwin," murmured Croft. "You must bear up as

well as you can. Remember to hide your attractions! We cannot have her falling victim to your charms."

"No danger of that," said Wentworth, seeing the rather frozen look on Miss Elliot's face.

"A lovely garden, Miss Elliot," said Croft when they were near enough to speak.

"I am glad you approve, Admiral Croft," said Elizabeth graciously, "you, who must have seen a great many gardens in your travels."

"I haven't seen so very many," Croft replied with a note of regret in his tone. "I have traveled much, as you say, but my journeys rarely brought me to carefully cultivated gardens. Now, if you had a sea port I could compare to others, I would judge that with a much more practiced eye ..."

Elizabeth smiled—a rare sight. She had not meant to smile; she had meant to be nothing but civil. But in the presence of these officers she recalled the weeks in London when they had been frequent dinner guests. She remembered how often these men laughed and how much she liked their good spirits. Hilarity was a quality missing from the Elliot household. Her father had no sense of humor and thought laughter merely prompted the formation of wrinkles around the eyes. Anne was too serious and gentle to make witty remarks or laugh much at the quips of others, and Mary was too stupid to laugh at anything but the simplest and most obvious of jokes. Elizabeth had not laughed for a long time.

"No," she said, "I'm afraid we have no sea ports hereabouts. The only water nearby, in fact, is the lake." She gestured toward it.

"I approve of it," said Wentworth. "Very calm and not a French frigate in sight. Just the thing to appeal to a man tired of storms and sea battles."

"Indeed," agreed Croft, "it is all very pretty. I do wish Mrs. Croft could see it—she loves gardens."

"I am sorry she was not able to accompany you."

"No more than I, Miss Elliot. The one disadvantage to a happy marriage is the misery suffered when you are separated."

"You have not been miserable very often, then, for as I remember, your wife sailed with you on almost every voyage."

"Aye, we have crossed the oceans together, and she rarely saw anything as tranquil as this."

"I hope she may come another time." Elizabeth said this with more sincerity than usual.

"Thank you, Miss Elliot. On this visit I will have to put up with the society of these two fellows, who have no sympathy for me, as they have no one to miss."

"And I never shall." Baldwin spoke for the first time. "I will stay single all my days and so never feel the pangs which Croft here is enduring."

"A dear happiness to women, as they shall be spared a pernicious suitor," retorted Elizabeth, and was pleased to hear Croft chuckle at that. She had a feeling that Admiral Baldwin had thrown that statement into the conversation to warn her that he had no intention of pursuing her. He need have no fear: she would not be pining away after him. "I myself am of the same mind," she said coolly. "I have no desire to marry."

Baldwin raised an eyebrow. "I pray you may hold firm in that decision, though I fear the fabled fickleness of women might prompt you to change your mind."

"You fear?" challenged Elizabeth.

"Yes, I fear for some poor soul who will marry you and get a scratched face!"

Elizabeth smiled serenely. "Scratching could not make it any worse, if he had a face like yours." It wasn't a very good rejoinder, as Admiral Baldwin had a very handsome face, even if he was slightly weather-beaten, but it was the only answer that came to Elizabeth's mind. Croft and Wentworth were both grinning now.

"Oho, I think she's got the better of you, Baldwin!" said Croft. "Miss Elliot can give measure for measure. It would be safer to give her compliments instead of insults."

Baldwin grimaced and bowed. "I beg pardon for my discourtesy, madam; I should indeed praise what is admirable in you. Let me say, then, that I wish my horse had the speed of your tongue."

Elizabeth's flush was barely perceptible as she said, "And I would that *my* horse had the wind of your lungs—it is a true gift to be able to prattle on so without drawing breath."

Croft and Wentworth laughed, and Elizabeth felt triumphant. "I beg you would excuse me, gentlemen, as I need to speak with the housekeeper." She curtseyed and left them without a backward glance.

She was hardly out of earshot when Wentworth commented, "You seem to have met your match in Miss Elliot, Baldwin. What very good luck for you—now you need not be bored at Kellynch. You may spend your hours in verbal combat with her."

"Hours spent with Miss Elliot? What torture that would be! Heaven deliver me from all such women!"

"I thought you didn't like sentimental, clinging girls," said Croft, trying to preserve his gravity.

"I don't, but I would not object to the odd trickle of civility, either. And speaking of civility, I think I have reached the end of mine with the two of you for the afternoon. I believe I will walk in this fine park here before us." He stalked off with dignity, leaving two amused companions behind him.

William Elliot sat at the little writing table in his bedroom, gazing out the window and brooding. He had not been given the best of the guest rooms in the house—that had gone to Admiral Croft. The second best had gone to Captain Wentworth.

Wentworth. He knew exactly who he was—the captain who had intercepted the *Don John* with its smuggled cargo, commandeered the ship, and caused charges to be filed against him. Wentworth was the hero of the hour while Mr. Elliot was the disgraced merchant. He doubted that anyone at Kellynch knew how the two men were connected—all that was generally known of the business was that "the Navy" had intercepted his ship—Captain Wentworth's name had not been mentioned. Further, he doubted that Wentworth knew him as the owner of that ship—he'd only been concerned with the captain ... that fool, Captain Conrad. Mr. Elliot shook his head. He ought never to have trusted him to get those officers back to France safely. Not that their money hadn't already gone safely into Mr. Elliot's coffers—a much bigger profit than smuggling French brandy. Now, of course, he could no longer take the risk of smuggling anything; the authorities would be keeping an eye on any business his ships might do. He really had no choice but to leave the merchant trade altogether.

His deceased wife had not been of noble birth, but she had brought him a fortune, courtesy of her father's import business. It was through his connections that Mr. Elliot had bought his three ships and begun importing French textiles—legally at first, and then by smuggling when war with Napoleon had brought embargoes on trade. Well, it was all done with now. He had nothing to do but settle in for the long wait for his inheritance. Sir Walter was only fifty-three and disgustingly healthy, and barring an accident would probably live for twenty more years before he died and let Mr. Elliot become the owner of the Kellynch estate.

The door opened behind him and he turned to see his valet enter the room with an armful of freshly laundered shirts and cravats.

"Ah, Borlock. Tell me; what do you think of the house? You have not been here before, I think, for you were not in my employ during my last visit—it must be more than ten years ago."

"The house is very large, sir, and set in a very pleasant situation."

"And how do you find the servant's quarters?"

Borlock shrugged. "Much like any other. The grandeur of the public rooms is not extended to the rooms even for visiting servants. I suspect a leaking roof in my bedroom, and the plaster is coming down in the laundry."

"Yes, the old fellow is purse-pinched, but he'd let the servants feel the pinch before suffering anything himself."

"If I may say so, sir, it will be a comfortable property to inherit."

"Yes. Always assuming that Sir Walter does not take it into his head to marry again and produce an heir before he dies."

"Yes, sir." The valet began laying the stacked cravats neatly on a shelf in the wardrobe, ready to be used.

"Did you recognize the name of one of the captains staying here?"

Borlock glanced at his master. "Do you mean Captain Wentworth, sir?"

"I do."

"He is the one who is responsible for the loss of your ship, and your commerce as well."

"Not he alone. Captain Conrad, however, has already been punished by the Navy." Mr. Elliot got up from his chair and continued in a conversational tone, "I wish to take my revenge on Captain Wentworth, Borlock. If you find a way to accomplish that without anyone becoming aware, you will tell me."

"Very good, sir." The valet's tone was every bit as dispassionate as his master's. He had finished his work in the room; he bowed and went out. A ruthless man, his employer, and one who had a particular talent for hiding a twisted character beneath a pleasant façade. Still, he paid well, and he had hired him even after he had been caught stealing from his former master. Mr. Elliot therefore had a hold over Borlock, and had long used this advantage to make him take part in various shady dealings. By this time, Borlock's conscience was well and truly seared—not that it had been very sensitive to begin with. His first task would be to win the confidence of Wentworth's servant. He made sure to sit beside him at the servants' dinner table.

Chapter Three

D inner that evening was a merry affair, or so it would have appeared to anyone looking on. Elizabeth was defiantly cheerful to all. No one was going to think of her as a drab, dull spinster who had been deemed unworthy of an admirable man's notice. She made certain that she was in her best looks, and her conversation with Admiral Croft and Captain Wentworth could only be described as sparkling. She was grateful that this was a house party, not a formal dinner party, so that rigid adherence to seating by precedence was not required—otherwise, she would have been seated between the two admirals. As it was, she had invited Lady Russell to dine with them and she put Admiral Baldwin next to her. She hoped he would be as rude to Lady Russell as he had been to her: that would remove all thought from Lady Russell's mind about Admiral Baldwin being an eligible suitor. Though Lady Russell had dropped the subject, Elizabeth suspected that she had not abandoned her opinion.

Anne ate her dinner with a smile, but also somewhat nervously. She had caught Captain Wentworth looking at her repeatedly, and when their eyes met she could feel herself blushing. She was annoyed with herself; she was much too old to behave like a girl from the schoolroom. Furthermore, she could find no reasonable explanation for her reaction. She had been admired before by various young men, and even Mary's husband Charles had wanted to marry her first. She had always borne such infatuations with equanimity, but there was something about Captain Wentworth that flustered her.

Mr. Elliot was not precisely jovial, but he did manage to converse sensibly with Captain Benwick. There was plenty of silence in their conversation, enough that Mr. Elliot had time to study the others at the table. Elizabeth tonight was a different creature than the haughty woman who had greeted him two days before. There had been nothing in her character then but cold, sullen pride, and now she was exchanging witty sallies with these navy men and laughing. What could have made the difference? Was she trying to attract one of the men? Admiral Croft was already married. Captain Wentworth was clearly fascinated by Anne, and Captain Benwick was seated nowhere near her—besides, he could not imagine Elizabeth condescending to marry a mere captain when there were admirals to be had. That left Admiral Baldwin, but he was conversing pleasantly with Lady Russell at the foot of the table, and not paying any attention to his hostess.

Mr. Elliot let the mystery go for the moment and turned his attention back to Captain Benwick, who was saying something or other about a poet. A poet! Word had been passed discreetly from guest to guest during the day that Captain Benwick had lost his betrothed to a fever just before he had come back to England. That was some excuse for the man's lethargy, but to be quoting poets at dinner! It took all Mr. Elliot's patience to endure his companion until they had finished their port at the end of the meal and could join the ladies in the drawing room.

❧

Sir Walter was extremely pleased with his house party. All the guests appeared to be enjoying themselves, and he was certain it was because of his skill as host. No one else, he thought, could have entertained the officers quite so well. At any other time he might have deplored the want of formality of these men, and their frequent laughter might have offended his sense that the grandeur of Kellynch demanded a more stately demeanor. But these men were a different breed than the ones common in Sir Walter's sphere. He was making amends to them for not joining their ranks, and he was prepared to tolerate much. Moreover, they were plainly admiring of his house, his land, and his table, and he was flattered.

It was particularly jarring, then, to receive a visit from Mr. Shepherd, his man of business, a few days after the officers arrived. One of Sir Walter's creditors (the butcher, in fact), had appealed to Mr. Shepherd to see what could be done about payment for the large orders of meat that had been delivered to Kellynch within the last week, for it seemed from the rumors in the village that there would be several weeks more of large, expensive orders.

"He is most appreciative of your custom," explained Mr. Shepherd. "Of course he is. It is only that he cannot continue to procure the articles of food in question if he has no money."

Sir Walter shook his head. "Times are not what they were, Shepherd. In days gone by, a butcher was so honored to be the supplier for a great house that he never thought of payment."

Mr. Shepherd almost smiled at the idea of a merchant in any era so willing to serve a lord that he was content to live on air and honor instead of hard cash—and Sir Walter was not even a lord, only a baronet. It would never do to say so, however, and Shepherd nodded sadly and told him that standards of service were slipping everywhere.

"The fact remains, Sir Walter, that Mr. Holcombe cannot go on without *some* payment. You mentioned at one time some jewels belonging to your late wife ..."

A pained expression passed over Sir Walter's features. "I told you, Shepherd, that they could be sold only in the most dire of crises. We are not yet to that point."

"Ah, but you are, Sir Walter. If you remember, I told you last month that the creditors could be staved off if you spent nothing beyond what was absolutely necessary for the rest of the year. You agreed with me, sir."

Sir Walter waved his hand. "But the situation is changed now. The officers—these noble fellows of the Navy—surely they deserve a little luxury?"

Mr. Shepherd blinked in surprise. Admiration for the Navy was the last thing he would have expected from Sir Walter.

"Of course, Sir Walter. But unless you want your guests to eat nothing but vegetables from your kitchen gardens, you must find a way to pay the butcher, as well as a few other creditors."

The thought of Admiral Croft sitting at his table and having a plate of nothing but turnips and asparagus set before him moved Sir Walter as the pleadings of his daughter Anne or the wise counsel of Mr. Shepherd never had. He sighed deeply. "Very well, Shepherd. I will have a few of the jewels sent to you tomorrow to dispose of as you will. I trust that will satisfy everyone?"

Mr. Shepherd was not prepared to agree that it would satisfy them. "It will be received with thanks," was all he could honestly say. "I must take my leave, Sir Walter—my daughter is awaiting my return."

Sir Walter thought of Mrs. Clay, always so fulsome in her praise of Kellynch, always so impressed with everything connected to the Elliots. She would be positively overwhelmed with the greatness of his visitors—and of course it reflected well on Sir Walter to have such heroic guests. It would be gratifying to witness her amazement.

"Shepherd, why don't you send your daughter to stay with us for a few days? Elizabeth would be glad of the company, I know— we have a very masculine assembly here. No doubt she would appreciate female companionship." Mr. Shepherd was all surprise and gratitude, and he hurried home to tell Penelope of the treat in store for her.

Mrs. Clay arrived that afternoon. The bedroom she was given

was one of the least used at Kellynch, and she looked discontentedly at the dark, dingy space. She was used to being given the best
guest bedroom when she stayed. It was not her place to complain,
however, and she must concentrate on the difficult task ahead of
her. Usually she could flatter Sir Walter and Elizabeth with no
competition for their attention. But with a houseful of guests,
and exciting ones at that, it would take all her wiles to get Sir
Walter to notice her at all.

As it happened, she had even more competition that afternoon than she had imagined: Charles and Mary Musgrove drove
over that afternoon to meet her father's guests. Charles, a good-
hearted, cheerful gentleman, was soon on friendly terms with the
officers. When they proposed exploring the wilderness beyond the
folly in the park, Charles enthusiastically endorsed the idea, and
they departed together. Mary had no desire to tramp about the
weed-infested paths listening to war stories, and she settled herself
to talk to Mr. Elliot, who sat in the morning room composedly
reading the newspaper.

"Well, Mr. Elliot," said Mary. "I have not seen you for this age!
You came once to visit when I was at school, and once before that,
when I was but a child. I would not have known you again, to be
sure."

"Nor I, you," said Mr. Elliot politely. "I hear you are happily
settled nearby."

"Oh, well—as to that—settled, at least. We live at Uppercross,
you know. Not the big house, of course—not *yet*—but the
cottage. It is excessively small. Not at all what I have been accustomed to." She looked around the morning room and sighed.
"*This*, of course, was once my home. This is my proper sphere.
But now I live in a pokey cottage with only a few servants and no
grounds at all to speak of. And I think it very likely owing to that
that the Musgroves are all too apt to forget whose daughter I am.
Mrs. Musgrove would never give me precedence if I did not
continually remind her."

Mr. Elliot put his newspaper aside. Here was a useful woman.

She would gossip freely, and with such a weak intellect—for Mr. Elliot could easily spot such vulnerabilities—she would be easy to manipulate.

"You do seem perfectly suited to this setting," he said smiling sympathetically. "I can always recognize those of noble birth— there are certain characteristic features, and you have them in abundance."

Mary preened a little. "I *do* have the Elliot countenance."

"And there are more indications than just your appearance. For example, I daresay you are a good judge of character."

"Oh, but I am! Charles always says I am mistaken about people, especially his family, but really I am *extraordinarily* gifted with insight into human nature."

Mr. Elliot nodded. "It does not surprise me. Such an ability is extremely common among those of rank. For example, if I asked you to tell me about Lady Russell, whom I only met for the first time a few days ago, you could summarize her character neatly in just a few words."

"Lady Russell! Has she been here?"

"Yes, to dinner a few nights ago and then for an afternoon visit yesterday."

"It is just like Elizabeth to invite her before me! Lady Russell is all very well, but I am *family*. Lady Russell is only the widow of a knight."

Mr. Elliot's eyebrows rose. "Indeed!"

"Yes. Of course, she was a friend of my mother's and has been devoted to all of us," Mary conceded. "And I will tell you this: she can see what that Mrs. Clay is up to, even if Father and Elizabeth cannot."

"Ah, Mrs. Clay. The delightful young woman who arrived this afternoon to stay for some time."

Mary snorted. "Delightful! Only if you like flattering, scheming women. I wonder that Elizabeth does not see through her."

"And for what does Mrs. Clay scheme?"

Mary leaned slightly closer to Mr. Elliot. "She wants to become the next Lady Elliot!"

"Does she?"

"Oh, yes. Although I think she is deluding herself about the possibility. Those freckles! Her low birth! She is a widow, you know, with two children already. Impossible that my father should align himself with her. And she must be over twenty years his junior."

"I am quite of your opinion, Mrs. Musgrove." Mr. Elliot smiled a little to himself. "Your father will never marry her."

Several hours later, as he was dressing for dinner, he found opportunity to talk to his valet.

"Have you seen the newest lady to join the party, Borlock—a Mrs. Clay?"

"I have, sir. I would not have termed her a *lady*, exactly."

"Just so," agreed Mr. Elliot. "I think she might prove useful."

Borlock paused briefly in the combing of his master's hair. "In your plan to revenge yourself upon Captain Wentworth, sir?"

"In any number of different plans. She has a weakness: an overmastering desire to become the next Lady Elliot. I feel there is little she would not do to reach her goal. She is also adept at flattery—which is to say, acting a part. Yes, I think she could be very useful. Cultivate an acquaintance with her, if you will."

"I, sir? A valet? If she is determined to be a baronet's wife, she would not look at me."

"Ah, but you will not be seeking her for yourself. You may, perhaps, suggest that the future Sir William Elliot is a much better possibility for her to pursue. I am younger and more attractive—whatever Sir Walter may think—and far more intelligent. Moreover, as you will no doubt inform her, I am a widower with a broken heart."

Borlock smiled briefly. "I see, sir."

"As she is a widow, she is no doubt suffering the same pangs of loss—or she will be as soon as she learns that I am."

"Very good, sir."

"She will no doubt do her utmost to make you admire her, since you will have informed her of your great influence over me. A recommendation from you will carry great weight, and it is entirely possible that I will fall in love with her on your suggestion alone. And it is not entirely out of the question that you also might fall in love with her, seeing as she is so beautiful and intelligent that she might be a good match for me."

"And if I have supposedly fallen in love with her, she may very well learn to be in love with me, too—the heart sometimes fixes on the most unsuitable objects."

"Exactly, Borlock. While the lady appears to be calculating, very few females can resist the ardent attachment of a personable and handsome man, even if he is a valet, particularly if they themselves are of humble birth."

"I will do my best, sir. There is one thing I was going to mention to you. Captain Wentworth's man told me that he has never seen his master so attached to any female as he is to Miss Anne. I do not know what opportunity this may present, but I thought you should know."

"Yes, there may be an opportunity there. I had noticed the signs myself, but of course it is good to have my suspicions confirmed."

Chapter Four

Penelope Clay stared into the mirror at her reflection, dissatisfied. She was dressed for dinner in her finest gown, but she had worn it so often that it no longer gave her the confidence it once did. It was not in the first stare of fashion any more, and the fastidious among her acquaintance, Sir Walter included, would soon be able to call it shabby without any exaggeration. She was satisfied with the arrangement of her hair, but the freckles Sir Walter had mentioned more than once were still plainly visible, in spite of her faithful use of Gowland's Lotion.

The sense of panic she had felt more and more often lately rose up in her again. Time was marching onward, and if she did not establish herself soon, it would be hopeless. She had married for love as a young woman, and five years later James was dead, leaving her with two young sons and no money. She and her children lived in comfort now with her parents, and so long as her father was alive, she was secure. But when her father died, the house would pass to her brother and she would have nowhere to live. No doubt Tom would make her a small allowance, but she wished to be his pensioner as little as he wished her to be. No, no, she *must* find a way to establish herself. She needed a husband,

and one with money. Sir Walter would do admirably, but her birth, her lack of fortune, her children, and her freckles were against her.

She thought she had one chance: if Elizabeth Elliot were to marry, it might leave a void at Kellynch that Penelope could fill. She had done her best to be thought of by the Elliots as necessary to their comfort. She was always agreeable, always available, and always willing to dispense the flattery that Sir Walter was particularly susceptible to. If Elizabeth were gone, Sir Walter might prefer to marry her rather than lose her company. He would not love her, of course; it was doubtful that he could be brought to love anyone but himself. However, his love of his own comfort and convenience might induce him to marry someone who provided that, even if she was of inferior birth. The only question was, had she become a necessary prop to him?

She looked into the mirror and saw her anxious countenance looking back at her. That would never do. She composed her features into an expression of grateful admiration, squared her shoulders, and went down to dinner.

Dinner, as Penelope discovered, was a larger gathering than she had anticipated. In addition to the people staying in the house, Charles and Mary Musgrove were dining with them, as well as Charles' two sisters, Henrietta and Louisa. These young ladies were full of lively spirits and a little awed to be dining with Admirals, Captains, and the wealthy Mr. Elliot. Penelope had met them all before, and they acknowledged her entrance with brief bows or curtseys, but then went back to talking. They had all gathered in the drawing room to await the summons to dinner. So full was the room, in fact, that Penelope had some little difficulty finding Miss Elliot in the crowd. She spotted her in a corner, slightly set apart from the rest of the chattering guests and looking aloof.

"Such a large party!" Penelope murmured to her, "So delightful!"

Elizabeth would not demean herself by rolling her eyes, but she gave a little toss of her head that meant the same thing. "It might be more delightful if Mary had not insisted on seating according to precedence! I shall be trapped between Admiral Croft and that odious Admiral Baldwin, while you, Penelope, will be seated with the Musgrove girls and the Captains."

"I am very happy to sit wherever I am placed," said Penelope, "Such agreeable company you always have around you! But then I have always observed that good people collect other good people around them. At least it is so with the Elliots." She would have preferred to sit near Sir Walter, to flatter him and laugh at his rather stale witticisms. However, she could not do it as openly as she could if there were not so many other guests, and it probably mattered very little where she sat tonight.

Captain Wentworth was well pleased with his place at dinner. He was seated next to Anne, and was able to draw her into conversation. He remembered that they had used to discuss books when they had been friendly in London. Although Wentworth had been too much occupied and too far from any booksellers to read very much, Anne had been steadily consuming poetry and prose in his absence. He asked her for recommendations of books he might enjoy, and they chatted very happily about that for some time.

When the next course was placed and Anne turned to talk to Admiral Croft on her left, Wentworth was forced to converse with Louisa. A nice girl, to be sure, and perfectly decorous, but having only an average understanding and an abundance of youthful spirits. She seemed to have a consuming desire for thrills and excitement and wished to talk of nothing but his adventures at sea, particularly tales where he figured as a hero. Wentworth was loathe to regale her with such stories and thought he would talk about books with her as well.

He asked what she had been reading, and she said, "Nothing of consequence. Since I have come back from school I have hardly read anything. Oh, yes, I read *The Castle of Otranto* once. It was very exciting, but Mama did not like me reading such things so I have not read any more. Did you ever find a cave in your travels? Like the one Isabella hid in? There is a cave near here, you know, just a small one. But ever since I read of Isabella being blocked up in the cave, I have nightmares about being trapped in it." Wentworth mentally commended Mrs. Musgrove for not letting Louisa feed her love of the sensational, and he was thankful when the next course arrived on the table and he could talk to Anne again.

Before he could say anything, however, Wentworth heard Sir Walter say to Baldwin, "Very interesting! And where did you say that happened?"

"That was when we were sailing off the Gold Coast," said Admiral Baldwin.

"The Gold Coast, eh?" said Sir Walter. "I thought you said you had never been to South America."

Wentworth saw Anne wince at her father's ignorance.

Baldwin covered up the blunder adroitly. "Oh, yes. But this is the Gold Coast that is in Africa."

Wentworth did his best to keep a straight face, not only to keep from denigrating his host, but because he could see that Anne did not find it amusing. His chivalry awakened and he knew a sudden impulse to take her away from Kellynch. She was a lovely, sweet, and intelligent woman, but she was dominated by her silly father and her strong-willed sister. If she were mistress in her own home, she would manage things capably and wisely; he could easily imagine her in that position. The thought took hold of him before he was fully conscious of it. Somewhere between the ham and the soufflé, he decided that he wanted to marry Anne. All that remained was to win her consent.

When the ladies rose after dinner and retreated to the drawing room to wait for the men, Anne also regretted leaving his company. Humble as she was, she could not deny that he showed a marked partiality for her. Was it possible he was only flirting with her? Men had been known to amuse themselves during house parties in that way. She pondered on this idea for some time, yet she could not quite persuade herself that it was so in this case.

She became aware then of the conversation around her; the ladies were discussing the idea of dancing when the men joined them. It was unclear to Anne who had started the idea, but it seemed likely that it was one of the two Musgrove girls. At the very least, it was their enthusiasm for the idea that enabled it to happen. Mary, always eager for a dance and rarely afforded the opportunity, championed the idea. "Might not the gentlemen like to dance?" she asked. Elizabeth's objection that there was no one to play was met by Mary's insistence that Anne could do it.

"There are too many ladies for the number of gentlemen, anyway. You would not mind, would you?" she said, turning to Anne. "The poor sea-captains, who have so few opportunities to dance with young ladies! And poor Mr. Elliot, too! He is just out of mourning, you know, and very likely has not had a dance in more than a year! Kellynch *ought* to provide entertainment for its guests."

The door opened then, and Charles Musgrove came in, closely followed by Admiral Baldwin and William Elliot, with the others trailing behind them. "Oh, Charles!" said Mary, jumping up and going over to him. "We ladies have all been settling that we shall have dancing now. Isn't it delightful? I have not danced for months and months—for I do not count that occasion at Uppercross as anything—and I have been *aching* to do so!"

Sir Walter might have deprecated the idea of an impromptu hop like this at any other time, but if the Naval men wanted to dance, it was his duty to oblige them. He glanced at Wentworth, who was closest, to gauge his reaction.

"Excellent!" said Wentworth. "Capital idea!"

This was good enough for Sir Walter. "But who is to play the piano-forte?" he asked. "If only we had had the foresight to keep Miss Adamson here for such occasions as this!" —as if the family's governess ought to have been kept on at Kellynch for the past ten years only to play the piano-forte for chance visitors.

"It seems a pity to ask any of the young ladies to play for us," said Admiral Croft. And then, recollecting that his words might be taken in another way, he added, "not because they cannot play well, of course, but because they must surely wish to dance. I'm sure Miss Elliot—" he bowed to her—"plays very well."

Baldwin snorted and said under his breath, but loud enough for Elizabeth to hear, "Well, if her fingers move as swiftly as her tongue, she'll play a jig at such speed we won't be able to dance to it."

"As it happens, Anne is willing to play for those who wish to dance," said Elizabeth civilly, and Anne nodded her acquiescence. Louisa and Henrietta waited no longer to begin moving the chairs and tables to the edges of the room, and Benwick and Charles helped them.

Under cover of all the bustle, Elizabeth turned to Baldwin and said, "It will comfort you to know, I'm sure, that Anne is a superior performer. Although, having no doubt learned your dancing from the natives of some far-flung island, you may prefer to dance to the howling of a dog, as you did there."

"No need to go to all the trouble of fetching a dog," Baldwin shot back. "The screeches of a cat would serve just as well, and *you* could provide those."

Anne had gotten up quietly and gone over to the piano-forte. She was sorting through the music stacked on top of the instrument when she found Captain Wentworth by her side.

"Do you need assistance?" he asked. "I can assure you I am a master at turning pages for a musician. My sister trained me well."

"Oh, no, you must not," said Anne, a little flustered. "I am certain the other ladies expect you to dance, for Captain Benwick will not."

"No, poor fellow. It is a pity, too, because there was nothing he liked so well as a dance."

"He is young," said Anne. "I mean..." She suddenly felt like it would be heartless to say that he would recover from his grief before long.

Wentworth smiled to show he understood. "I agree, Miss Elliot. One cannot say such a thing to *him*, of course, but he will no doubt dance again." He picked up one of the sheets of music Anne had discarded and looked it over. "Do you invariably play while others dance?"

"No, not *invariably*. To be truthful, there are not many occasions for dancing hereabouts. However, my father is giving a ball for you in a fortnight, and at that event I will not be asked to play."

"You relieve my mind. It would be too painful if I were unable to dance with you a second time."

Anne blushed and could not think of a reply to make. She kept sorting through the music.

Wentworth took the blush as encouragement. "Will you do me the honor, Miss Elliot, of dancing with me at the ball?"

Anne looked up at him then, shyly. "Yes," she said simply and was rewarded with a delighted smile. An impish impulse made her add, "I think I ought to tell you that the ball is to be a masquerade. You may not be able to find me."

"I am sure that I will," Wentworth said with conviction. "If I can see your eyes, I am quite sure I would never mistake them for someone else's."

Anne had never fainted, and had always thought that the females novels described as swooning at the slightest provocation were beneath contempt, but this pronouncement made her breathless and dizzy, and she might really have been in some danger of showing her emotion in such an obvious way if Mary had not interrupted them,

"Anne, have you quite finished choosing music? Captain

Benwick says he will turn pages for you, if you like, so that Captain Wentworth can dance."

"I suppose I shall have to ask one of the young ladies to dance," Wentworth murmured. "Can you tell me which is the least likely to be a flirt?"

Anne smiled at the question. "I think Henrietta. She is very nearly promised to her cousin, the curate." He smiled, bowed briefly, and made his way toward the eldest Miss Musgrove.

Admiral Croft, who rarely danced, was pressed into service, and Mrs. Clay, who would have liked the opportunity to show off her dancing, most obligingly declared that she was not inclined to dance that evening. She hoped the Elliots had noticed her adaptability. There were four couples, then, and although they traded partners every few dances, the only flirting that could be said to have been done was the occasional glances Anne and Wentworth gave each other over the top of the sheets of music.

A few days later, Elizabeth mentioned at breakfast that she would like to go for a walk, and Penelope entered enthusiastically into the plan, saying that she desired a walk above all things, and it was such a beautiful day that she could hardly wait to exercise in the fresh air. She had been planning to go for a walk herself, and to have Elizabeth's companionship would be perfect.

However, after breakfast the housekeeper approached Elizabeth with a request for an interview so that she could make urgent decisions about the menu for the ball.

"Oh, dear. Yes, I'll come, Mrs. Maberley. You had better go for the walk without me, Penelope." Penelope felt that she could hardly say that she no longer wanted a walk. If only Sir Walter could have been convinced to join her, she might turn the walk to good account. But he never went out into the sun if he could help it, for fear of ruining his complexion. Penelope resigned herself, fetched her parasol, and set forth into the gardens. She wondered how long she would need to walk to keep people from guessing that her eagerness for fresh air was feigned.

She had been strolling for about ten minutes when she saw something moving in the distance out of the corner of her eye. It was William Elliot, walking across the terrace toward the house. He must have been out for a walk, too, she thought. Even from that distance she could see how gracefully he moved and what a fine figure he had. He had danced very well last night—not that she had spent much time watching the dancers: she had spent most of the time conversing with Sir Walter. She would not be at all surprised if William Elliot had come to Kellynch with the hope of marrying either Elizabeth or Anne. He might take Elizabeth with her good will: if he married Elizabeth, her own chances of wedding Sir Walter increased. And if *that* happened ... she sighed wistfully and looked around her at the estate. She would be mistress of all this. A baronet's wife: Lady Elliot. And she would make sure Sir Walter did not keep exceeding his income.

Mr. Elliot had vanished into the house and Penelope resumed her course. She had left the formal gardens now and entered the Park. She knew the path well; it was for the sake of a companion on her walks that Elizabeth had begun to notice her. Eventually the invitations to walk had expanded to spending the afternoon at Kellynch and then to staying there as a guest for a week or two a few times a year. In the beginning, Penelope had thought Elizabeth might become a friend. That thought now made her smile derisively at her own ignorance. Elizabeth wanted a companion, not a friend. She wanted more than a servant: a servant would be able to fetch and carry for her, but would not be the proper recipient of such confidences as Elizabeth might wish to relate. Not that these confidences were very personal; it could not be said that Elizabeth ever bared her heart to another person. Elizabeth's heart was locked away safely and might have crumbled to dust from disuse for all Penelope could tell. But Elizabeth did occasionally share her opinions of how Mary's constant complaining had infused a permanent whine into her tone of voice, or how the rector, Mr. Francis, made his sermons much too long, and it pleased her to have a companion that she might make these comments to. It was too bad, thought Penelope, because although Elizabeth would always be opinionated and probably somewhat abrasive, she was clever and witty, and perhaps the fierce loyalty she had to her family could also be loyalty to a friend.

"Have you found it yet, sir?" said a voice behind the rhododendron bush she was passing just then. A man came around the side of the bush dressed in the clothing of an upper servant. He started on seeing her, and bowed deeply.

"I beg your pardon, madam," he said. "I thought you were Mr. Elliot."

"It is nothing," said Penelope. "I saw Mr. Elliot a few moments ago—going toward the house."

"Ah," said the man. "He did not say anything to you about finding his watch, did he?"

"No, we did not speak—he was too far away for that. Are you his valet?" The man's accent was that of an educated man, unusual in a valet.

"Yes, madam. My name is Borlock. Mr. Elliot has lost his pocket-watch, and thinks he might have dropped it as he was walking somewhere about the grounds. I don't suppose you have seen it?"

"I fear not. However, I will let you know if I do."

"Thank you, madam. The loss is troubling him greatly. It was a gift from his late wife, you see."

"Oh! How very sad." A sudden memory made her catch her breath. "I once lost a locket my husband gave me before he died." Why she said it, she had no idea. It was not her habit to refer to her widowed status, or, indeed, her children to anyone, much less a servant. It was said, however, and could not be taken back.

"I am sorry for your loss, madam." The valet's eyes seemed to hold understanding and sympathy.

"Yes, well, I will look out for it as I walk."

"I would appreciate it, madam. My eyes are not as sharp as

they once were. I would hate to miss it—the thought that it might be found by, say, an under-gardener who would keep it and perhaps sell it, makes me tremble."

"Mr. Elliot cannot look for it himself?"

"He did search. He suggested that we separate so that we could cover more ground. I can only imagine that his feelings overcame him at the thought that it might be lost forever."

"Indeed!" This seemed most unlikely. She could well believe that Captain Benwick might do such a thing, but William Elliot did not seem to be grieving. He had taken part in the dancing last night with no hesitation.

"Yes, madam. He was utterly bereft by the loss of his wife. I daresay you may not have noticed, as he hides it well. And he is much better than he was many months ago. He finds himself compelled to act the part of the cheerful guest. I expect you might understand how that might be. I beg your pardon," he added humbly, as Mrs. Clay began to look a little haughty. "I must not forget my station. You seemed such a kind-hearted lady that I forgot myself."

Penelope softened. She was, in her own view, very kind-hearted, but no one had really noticed it before. And although she never thought of herself anymore as a grieving widow, she had no objection to anyone else thinking her bravely hiding a broken heart beneath a serene and cheerful façade. She inclined her head as if to forgive the indiscretion.

"You should tell the head gardener," she said, "and I can tell the other guests to look out for it if they are walking this way."

"I beg you would not, madam. Mr. Elliot would not wish others to know." He took out his own pocket watch and looked at the time. "I must cease searching now, but I will return in a few hours to look." He sighed. "I wish my eyes were stronger. I can see things close by, but farther away is much more difficult."

"Perhaps I can help you look," said Penelope. "After tea. I am never wanted then."

"Thank you, madam. That is very kind." Borlock bowed and moved off toward the house.

⁓

"I have begun working on Mrs. Clay, sir," said Borlock when he was inside William Elliot's room with the door safely closed. "I encountered her in the park after meeting with the pot-man at The Golden Eagle—the one I was told could get me a supply of French brandy for you."

"And can he?"

"Oh, yes, sir, as long as you pay well and never reveal where you got it. There is a secret cellar there, of course, that the Excisemen would be very happy to discover."

"I don't doubt it. Well, make the arrangements for several bottles, then. And how is it that you are befriending Mrs. Clay?"

"I have enlisted her help in finding your pocket-watch, sir."

"My watch?" William Elliot pulled his watch from his waist-coat pocket and looked at it.

"Precisely, sir. You somehow lost this watch, a gift from your late wife, when you were walking in the park yesterday."

"Nursing my broken heart?"

"Your admirably-concealed broken heart," agreed Borlock. "The lady was very sympathetic. She also had lost something from her deceased husband."

William raised his eyebrows. "In the park?"

Borlock could not repress a smile. "No, sir. Some time past, I believe."

"I am glad she was not such a simpleton as to tell such an obvious lie. The loss of some gift in the past is much more plausible."

Borlock put his head to one side and considered. "I think it may have been the truth."

William shrugged. "Well, if she is feeling even slightly bereft, it will be much easier to talk her into pursuing me. Or you."

"Exactly so, sir." Borlock felt a slight twinge of conscience at the prospect, now that he had actually talked with the lady.

"It would be more enjoyable for you if she were less ill-favored," William went on. "I see that. But there will be some sport in it, nonetheless. Here, you had better take my watch and lose it. Perhaps you can contrive that she will find it in some romantic spot. I feel that I may have walked as far as the folly."

"Very good, sir."

Chapter Five

C aptain Benwick crept as quietly as he could down the stairs that afternoon. Admiral Croft had gently chided him for hiding himself in his bedroom so often and encouraged him to venture out more. If Croft caught him in in his bedroom again he would probably take him out riding or fishing. Benwick thought he would try the library. He preferred solitude, and it seemed to him that the library might be safely empty. Sir Walter, he guessed, would not spend much time reading, nor would Miss Elliot. The younger daughter, Anne, now—she might spend more time with books. However, her time seemed to be monopolized by Wentworth, and they were unlikely to spend their time in the library. His fellow officers would not be there, either; they were more inclined to be out of doors.

The library was a beautiful room. Benwick paused on the threshold to admire it. The library in his father's house was a fairly small room with the bookcases lining the walls. Here, the size of the room was difficult to estimate, as the bookcases stood in rows, like ranks of sailors in formation, and he could not see very far into the room. There were spaces here and there between the bookcases, with comfortable chairs placed for reading—or dozing, if the occupant found the cozy atmosphere soporific.

He passed the first two rows of bookcases and was surprised to see that someone was already occupying one of the chairs: Lady Russell. She looked up from the book she was reading with a start.

"I beg your pardon, ma'am," said Benwick. "I had no idea anyone was here."

Lady Russell waved aside his apology.

"It is a public room, after all—at least, it is at Kellynch Hall. Sir Walter conducts his business affairs in another room. I came to talk with Anne, but she is in the garden, I believe, with Captain Wentworth and Admiral Croft. I thought I would read a little while I waited. Please, be seated." She gestured toward a nearby chair.

Benwick was a little disappointed not to have the isolation he had desired, but he had known Lady Russell a little in London, and he had enjoyed meeting her again at dinner a few days ago. She was kind-hearted and sensible, and he would not mind conversing with her for a little while. He sat down in the chair with a simple, "I thank you."

"I was happy to renew my acquaintance with all of you gentlemen of the Navy a few evenings ago," Lady Russell went on. "Only I seem to remember that there used to be another captain that frequently dined with the Elliots—was not his name Captain Harville?"

"Indeed it was, ma'am. You have a very good memory."

"Only for the things I want to remember. But I remember Captain Harville because we conversed at length one time about his family. You were to have been connected to his family, were you not?" She put the question to him kindly, but matter-of-factly.

"Yes."

"I was sorry to hear of your bereavement—and Captain Harville's as well. How does he do now? Have you heard from him lately?"

"I have. A letter from him reached me yesterday. He is recovering from a leg wound, which he got in service. He is tolerable, I think—better than he was when I left him a month ago."

"Oh, you went to see him when you were released from your duties? I am glad."

"Oh, yes, I stayed with them for a month. They have just moved to Lyme, he says in his letter. He wanted to let me know that he still has my books—not that there are many of them, but they are like old friends to me. I rather wish I had some of them with me here."

"Well, Lyme is not far—seventeen miles or so. You could ride there and back in a day."

"So near? That is an idea." He pondered the possibility for a moment. "I think a long ride might be pleasant."

"Yes, I think it would," said Lady Russell. "You have been too long inactive, if I may say so without offense. Grief has a way of paralyzing one, but if the inactivity is prolonged, it becomes harder and harder to move. You do not want to wither away into the kind of man your betrothed would have been ashamed of."

"No, indeed, ma'am," said Benwick, much struck. "And Admiral Croft often tells me I ought to be in society more. I will make preparations to go tomorrow."

After tea, Mrs. Clay went out to help look for the watch. It had looked like rain before she set off, but the clouds retained their moisture and contented themselves with making the air humid. She met Borlock just beyond the formal garden, and together they walked the path toward the wilderness, Borlock walking respectfully behind her.

"It is a great kindness in you, madam, to have come all this way to help me search. I fear I have been presumptuous—indeed, I beg you would not think that I regularly ask fine ladies to do any such thing."

"You did not ask, Borlock; I offered." It did not bother Penelope in the slightest to be referred to as a fine lady. No doubt, from the position of a servant, she appeared so.

"Very true, madam. It was most kind."

They walked in silence for a while, Penelope examining the ground around her, and Borlock pretending to.

"It's the long grass that is the problem, madam," said Borlock. "If boxwood shrubs had been planted along the path like they are in the gardens at Cheetleworth Park, it would be easier to search."

"Yes. Miss Elliot said last year that she would like to have some shrubs planted along this path. Sir Walter, however, declared that he did not want to ape a new fashion, and he wanted the path to be kept the way it was." Penelope was certain that the motivation for the refusal was because of a lack of funds, not a feeling of nostalgia, but she kept this information to herself.

"Yes," said Borlock. "I suppose we cannot expect the elderly to change their preferences easily."

"Elderly?" The word was out of Penelope's mouth before she realized it.

"Not *very* elderly, I suppose, madam. Perhaps I only think of Sir Walter in that way because my master is so much younger than he."

"Perhaps," agreed Penelope. The thought that others might also deem Sir Walter elderly brought up a long-held apprehension. She could hear the gossip now: "Old enough to be her father!" She had tried to ignore this attribute, focusing instead on his position and his fine estate, but now and then the facts *would* intrude into her plans. She cast about for another topic of discussion.

"Has Mr. Elliot visited often at Kellynch?"

Borlock pretended to see something on the ground and bent to examine it more closely while he decided how to answer this. He wondered how much Mrs. Clay knew of his master's misdeeds. A little rapid reflection convinced him that the Elliots would not publicize a relative's criminal activities and had therefore not spoken of him to people like Mrs. Clay.

"No, that's nothing—only a mushroom. You were saying, madam?"

"Oh, I merely asked if Mr. Elliot had visited often at Kellynch."

"No, not very frequently. As he is to inherit the estate, he has not wanted to seem to be looking over the property with a proprietary air, as you might say. He is a very respectful gentleman—very noble-minded. The late Mrs. Elliot always said so. She considered herself very fortunate to have him for a husband. She was not high-born, as they say, but Mr. Elliot married her regardless."

He had come up beside Penelope and watched the information settling into her mind. He could almost see her weighing her options. On the one hand, she might be able to entice Sir Walter into matrimony. Her youth might attract him, as she might be able to give him the son and heir he had always wanted. That would cut Mr. Elliot out of the entail and keep her and her son in the property. On the other hand, Sir Walter might not want to marry her. Even if he did, she might bear him only daughters, like his first wife. Sir Walter would not live forever, and when he died, she and her daughters would lose the estate to the younger Mr. Elliot.

But William Elliot, now. He was a much more enjoyable person to be around. He was clever and polite, and not nearly as vain. Moreover, he had already once married beneath him and evidently not regretted it. Might he be persuaded into another such marriage?

"I see we are getting near the folly," said Borlock. "It occurs to me that it is just such a place as Mr. Elliot might visit when wishing to be alone with his memories."

They hastened toward the mock-Grecian temple and Penelope searched through the overgrown grass with zeal. She was rewarded. The watch was just beside the marble steps that led to the columned portico.

"Oh, well done, madam!" said Borlock. "I am most grateful

for your help. May I have your permission to inform Mr. Elliot that you were the one who discovered it? I am loathe to take the credit for its recovery."

"Do you think Mr. Elliot would be annoyed that you told me about its loss? You said he would not want it known."

"He would not want it generally known, of course, but Mr. Elliot knows that you are suffering a bereavement yourself and can understand his grief in a way the others would not. I think he would be very grateful to you for your help."

Penelope smiled graciously. "Very well. But tell him I need no thanks, Borlock. I was only too glad to be of service."

The weather continued warm and close, and everyone gathered on the terrace to wait to be called in to dinner. Charles and Mary had driven over from Uppercross for dinner, and Charles was standing with the officers when Benwick brought up the idea of going to Lyme.

"I thought you might like to go along with me to see Harville," he said to Baldwin. "I'm sure it would do him good."

"Of course. I would like to see him, and he must not be made to feel forgotten by his old friends. He has moved, you say? Well then, he probably knows very few people there in Lyme, and if he is not able to get about much he is probably suffering from boredom. We mustn't let him languish there alone—such a good man."

"The best of fellows," agreed Croft. "I would like to see him again myself. Sir Walter would probably welcome him with open arms if he came here. Shall we beg an invitation for him?"

"Unfortunately, I think his wound would prevent him traveling," said Benwick. "And I doubt his wife would like him leaving again now that she has him back."

"No, they are a very devoted pair. We might all go to Lyme," said Wentworth. "A few hours' ride would do us all good." He did not look at Benwick when he said this, but they all knew that was who he was thinking of.

"Was that the fellow you were telling me about the other day?" asked Charles. "The one who sank two ships in a single day during the war?"

"The very man," said Wentworth. "You ought to come with us and meet him. You would enjoy each other's company."

"Yes, you would like Harville," said Baldwin. "And I suppose you would not mind listening to us reminisce about battles fought and won."

"Listening to tall tales, more like," said Croft. "But do come, if you will."

"Thank you, I think I shall."

They were summoned to dinner just then, and obediently went in and took their places at the table.

Mary was seated across from her husband, and no sooner had the first course been served than she said, "Charles, I have a notion to invite the officers here to a picnic at Uppercross tomorrow. The weather will be fine—at least the head gardener thinks so—and the gardens at Uppercross are at their best now. What say you?"

"I should like to, very much," said Charles, "but not tomorrow. The officers and I are going down to Lyme for the day, to see a friend of theirs—a Captain Harville."

"Oh, Lyme! I have long wanted to see it!" said Mary. "I shall go with you. I daresay the fresh air will be ever so good for me."

"We are going on horseback," countered her husband. "If we took the carriage we would spend seven hours just in travel, going and coming back. There would be very little time for talking with Harville."

Mary sulked silently while the pork loin was carved, and ate her Soup à la Flamond with a languor meant to show how dispirited she was at being denied the chance of partaking in the outing to Lyme. With the first remove, however, she came back to life. "I have it!" she exclaimed. The murmured conversations around the table ceased as the diners turned to look at her. "We shall take the carriage for the ladies and make a sight-seeing party. We can travel in the morning and see the sights and visit with Captain Harville. We must spend the night at an inn and return home the next day! We shall all go. Elizabeth and Anne, Mrs. Clay, Henrietta and Louisa. You would enjoy that, would you not, Anne?"

Anne glanced at Captain Wentworth, afraid he might be annoyed with Mary for turning their quick trip into a colossal expedition. He did not look annoyed, however. He even gave a slight nod as if to prompt her to respond positively. The nod was noticed by Charles.

"It sounds delightful," said Anne truthfully.

"And you, Mr. Elliot?" Mary was careful to observe the proprieties. "Will you come as well?"

Mr. Elliot inclined his head. "Yes, I thank you." The more time he spent in Wentworth's company, he reasoned, the more likely he was to be able to find some way to do him harm.

Mary knew better than to ask her father, but Admiral Croft thought it was incumbent upon him to make sure he was formally invited. "Sir Walter, would you do us the honor of joining us?"

Sir Walter shook his head regretfully. "I thank you, no. I have some business that keeps me here." If the Navy still had ships in the harbor at Lyme, he might have been tempted. But the war was over and the only ships there would be merchant vessels. More than that, the sun at the seaside was reputed to be particularly bad for the complexion, and the thought of staying in a common inn repulsed him.

Elizabeth spoke for the first time. "Mary, we cannot possibly make preparations in time to set off on this journey tomorrow. Henrietta and Louisa are not even aware that a journey is contemplated. The coachmen will want a day to prepare the horses and the carriages. The inn, too—might it not be full of summer visitors? And the Harvilles ought to have a little warning before we descend on them like so many locusts."

"Very true," said Charles before Mary could utter objections to this good sense. "We shall go the day after tomorrow instead, if that is agreeable to Captain Benwick. I'll send a servant to make arrangements for us at an inn, and if Benwick will write a note for the Harvilles, he can deliver that, as well."

This was generally agreed to be a good plan, and Mary had all the pride of knowing that it had been her idea.

Charles rode over to Kellynch again the next day to inform the Elliots of the Musgrove girls' eagerness to join the party. Mr. Musgrove was going to allow them, and Mary, to travel in his carriage, leaving the Elliot vehicle to transport Elizabeth, Anne, and Mrs. Clay. They would take only a few servants with them, and there would be plenty of room for two of them to ride on the bench on the hind part of each carriage.

Charles dismounted in the courtyard of the stables, for he considered himself so much part of the family that he would not have dreamed of making a footman hold his horse while a groom was sent for to take the animal in charge. He was hailed by Admiral Croft coming out of the horse barn.

"Good day, Musgrove!" said the admiral. "I was just talking to my groom. I thought my horse showed a slight lameness in his leg the other day when we were riding. Wanted to make certain he was all right before we make this long journey tomorrow."

"And is he?"

"Fit as he ever was," said Croft, "which is not saying a great deal, I grant you. I'll not be the envy of any young bucks on account of my horse! However, he's a reliable old thing and gets me where I want to go. Wentworth, now—his horse is newly-purchased, and well worth looking at."

"I look forward to seeing him in action, then," said Charles, as a groom came out to take his horse. The two men started up the path that led to the house. "So, is Wentworth a good fellow?" continued Charles in a conversational tone.

Croft looked at him in surprise. "Yes, indeed. Why do you ask?"

"He seems to admire Anne. I understand that he is your wife's brother and you must know him well. I daresay you wouldn't wish to speak ill of him, but I feel something of a responsibility for her happiness. I beg you would take no offence."

"None at all," said the admiral genially. "But surely it is more her father's duty than yours to assess any possible suitors?"

"Her father—ah." Charles cleared his throat. "Sir Walter is— Well. No doubt he will make his own enquiries. In time."

Croft suppressed a chuckle. "I understand. You are doing a little informal evaluation, are you not?"

"Exactly. Anne is my wife's sister, you know. We only want to be sure that Wentworth is not the kind of man who trifles with women's feelings. Anne is not the sort to flirt. If he has no serious intentions, he would do better to leave her be. I would not like to see her hurt."

Croft clapped a hand on his shoulder. "Good man, to be taking care. You have no cause for worry, however: Wentworth is not a flirting gentleman. I would not be at all surprised if he spoke to her father soon."

"Good," said Charles. "Very good. And how is he in other respects? Honest? Reliable?"

"Oh yes. A little cocky, and a bit stubborn, but we all have our faults, haven't we?" He chuckled. "I remember Sophie told me that when they were young, he once gave their brother Edward his share of the sugar-plums doled out to them by their mother at Christmas because he found him crying over a lost ball. Fredrick is a kind-hearted fellow, you know. Sophie—she's the oldest—was overcome by greed and stole them all away from Edward when he left them unattended, and hid them among her own things. Fredrick was incensed, I think more because he had lost his own sugarplums to no purpose than because Edward was now mourning the loss of two treasures. At any rate, he found the sweets among Sophie's things and threw them in the fire."

Charles laughed. "A little drastic, was it not? I thought he would eat them all himself."

"Aye, that's what he ought to have done, he said, but he felt himself so ill-used that he did not think of it until they were all burnt up. Then again, he was only about six years old."

"That is some excuse for him, I suppose."

"Yes. And that sort of recklessness—mixed with intelligence, which Fredrick has—is what made him such a good officer. Those timid fellows who hang back and deliberate over the possibilities miss their chance to get the advantage over an enemy."

They found Elizabeth and Baldwin in the morning room, steadfastly ignoring each other. Baldwin was sitting in a chair with a newspaper and Elizabeth was writing at the desk near the window. Elizabeth greeted her brother-in-law and the admiral with such warmth that it was impossible for them not to suspect that she did so to show Baldwin that she liked them far better than him.

"What news, Charles?" said Elizabeth. "Are your sisters to join us tomorrow?"

"They are, and they are most grateful for the invitation. And I have been asked by my cousin Hayter if he can be included in the party."

A quick frown crossed Elizabeth's face.

"I'm sorry to request it of you, but he was there when I brought the invitation, and I think he was a little nervous about letting Henrietta go to Lyme with so many exciting Naval officers. I think he is afraid he will show up poorly by comparison—a curate, you know, cannot cut a dash in the same way an Admiral can!"

Elizabeth heard Baldwin mutter "Women—always at the root of every trouble," and for that reason alone she brushed aside all offense and difficulty.

"Of course he may join us," she said sweetly, "only the servant has already left to arrange for our lodging."

"Hayter said to tell you that he will happily sleep on the floor of someone's bedroom if need be."

Elizabeth stood and moved toward the door. "Very well, then, all appears to be settled. I wonder," she said as she paused at the threshold before going out, "which woman was at the root of the *trouble* which has plagued the armies of twenty or so nations for the past twelve years?"

Chapter Six

When the whole entourage left Kellynch the next morning for Lyme, Captain Benwick could not help contrasting it with his original conception. He had first thought of riding alone to Lyme, or perhaps making the journey with one or two other men. Instead there were two carriages transporting the two Miss Elliots, the two Miss Musgroves, Mrs. Mary Musgrove and Mrs. Clay; the coachmen and grooms and female servants; and the men on horseback: the four naval officers, William Elliot, Charles Musgrove, and Mr. Hayter. And all for a one-day excursion!

Mary had insisted on riding in the Elliot carriage with Elizabeth and Anne, as the Elliot crest was on the panel. Penelope Clay went with Henrietta and Louisa in the Musgrove coach. Elizabeth had made some small attempt to keep her in the Elliot carriage, but Mary's argument that there would be more room if there were three ladies in each carriage won the day. Penelope made no demure; it was always to her advantage to be seen as the most adaptable of ladies.

Henrietta and Louisa could not be said to like Mrs. Clay; she was so much older than they were, and she was not amusing or lively. They did not positively dislike her, either—they merely neglected to take pains to include her in their conversation as they talked about whether the newest fashion for padded petticoats was becoming or not, and what the chances were that there would be any fashionable people staying at the same inn as themselves.

"Of course," said Louisa with a sigh, "It would be far more exciting if there were more officers there. Do you suppose this Captain Harville will have other naval friends who have settled in Lyme?"

"For my part, I hope there are not," said Henrietta. "You have already bored me to distraction with your talk of the Navy and the heroes of the war."

"It is well enough for you," huffed Louisa. "You have our cousin on a string and are only waiting for him to take orders before you marry. But I would be very happy to find another man so handsome and dashing as Captain Wentworth."

"I do *not* have him on a string," said Henrietta with dignity. "He is his own man, and it appears that he has *chosen* me. And he is quite as handsome as I could desire. However," she conceded, "Captain Wentworth is very handsome. And so is Admiral Baldwin."

"Yes, but he is so very ungallant. And *old*—near forty, I think. I wish he had the manners of Mr. Elliot. Now *he* is quite the gentleman. Not as exciting as a captain—and only in trade, of course—Mary turned up her nose at him just for that reason— but I hear he is very well off. No doubt Elizabeth means to have him—she would be able to stay at Kellynch, then, whatever happens."

"I think she ought to be more congenial, then. If she is always so haughty in his presence, it is no wonder Mr. Elliot has not pursued her in spite of her beauty."

Louisa nodded. "She will never get a husband if she does not mend her manner." She glanced out the window and through the dust stirred up by so many horses caught sight of the gentlemen riding ahead of them. "And there is Captain Benwick, of course. He has a broodingly handsome face, does he not? It makes him so melancholy, like Mr. Arnott in *Cecilia*. Would it not be romantic if he found love again to soothe his aching heart?"

Penelope almost smiled at the girls' innocence. An aching heart? They could know nothing about it if they thought mending it would be so easy.

"Shall we let down the window, Louisa?" said Henrietta. "It is so very warm."

"The dust will be quite intolerable," said Penelope, speaking for the first time. The girls started, as if they had forgotten her presence.

"If ours was the lead carriage," said Louisa, "the dust would not be flying around us as it is. But Mary *would* insist on the Elliot carriage being the first!"

"It is the fault of the weather," said Penelope. "If it had not been dry for so long there would be no dust to speak of."

"True," said Henrietta. "But I do think a little dust would be preferable to roasting inside this carriage."

Penelope, mindful of her role as amiable companion, said, "Perhaps you are right," and assisted the girls in letting down a window half-way. Henrietta proved to be correct, as the inconvenience of slightly dusty air was outweighed by the breeze that the open window provided.

They stopped at a coaching inn for a cold nuncheon a little after noon, and arrived in Lyme at about two o'clock. The servant sent on ahead the day before had obtained rooms for them at The Royal Lion, and after they had approved the rooms and washed the dust of the road off their faces, they all set forth on foot to see Lyme.

It is impossible to keep a party of thirteen people walking together. They invariably branch off into smaller groups: some forging ahead to see a particular view, some pausing to investigate some trivial thing they pass by, others so lost in conversation that they forget not only the other people but the point of the whole expedition.

Benwick and Croft went almost immediately to find the

Harvilles' house to tell them the Kellynch party had arrived in Lyme and to invite them to join the travelers for dinner at the inn. Charles and Mary walked together with Louisa, Henrietta, and Mr. Hayter, the women intent on seeing what the shops contained and the men following in their wake. Wentworth and Baldwin were walking and talking together, but after a time, Baldwin perceived that they were drifting ever closer to Anne, Elizabeth, and Mrs. Clay. It was not long before they made a cluster of five.

The footpath was not wide enough for more than two people to walk abreast, and Penelope followed along unhappily behind the others as they walked on the marine parade, following the shoreline. She had not been to the seaside for many years, and her children had never seen the sea. She thought of them now, wishing she could show them the waves and the ships and let them wash their feet in the surf.

"Is that what they call the Cobb?" said Anne, looking out at the massive stone wall that extended a couple hundred yards into the bay.

"Yes," said Wentworth. "It forms a breakwater and protects the town from the worst of storms. There are two levels, you see? The upper Cobb is where you see people walking now, and there are steps to get down to the lower level on the landward side, where there is a more protected walk, and where the boats are tied."

"I should like to walk there," said Elizabeth. "Can we?"

"Indeed, yes," said Wentworth and led the way.

Elizabeth was surprised at how much she enjoyed the walk on the Cobb. There was a stiff breeze, and the waves of the sea crashed into the walls, but they did not come up high enough to wash over the top of the upper Cobb. She found the spray of the salt water invigorating. They walked the length of the Cobb and stood at the end, looking out over the sea.

Elizabeth turned to look back toward the land and, being able to see Admiral Baldwin out of the corner of her eye, was struck by the expression on his face as he looked out to sea. It was a look of familiarity and almost friendship. The admiral was one who knew the secrets of the deep, who had weathered storms and battled seas and tamed winds for his own use. His mien was not that of a conqueror, for the sea was not a vanquished foe, but more like that of someone who regularly had sparring matches with a friend; there was a kind of truce between them. A large wave crashed into the Cobb, sending spray high into the air. "Look at that," he murmured, apparently to himself. He loved the sea, Elizabeth thought, not because it was calm and pleasant, but because it was powerful and majestic.

He turned suddenly to Elizabeth.

"What is it?" he asked in exasperation. "Why do you keep staring at me? Does my hair offend you? Or is my cravat tied poorly? Are you brewing, even now, some witty set-down in your mind?"

Elizabeth felt her face suffuse with color at being discovered staring at him. She had not even realized what she was doing, but there was no denying that she had been looking at him for some minutes. She ignored her own blushes, however, and kept her countenance unconcerned.

"I beg your pardon," she said. "I was looking at your hat—wondering where you could have gotten it."

"Gray's, in London," he said coldly.

"To be sure," she said. "That explains it."

It galled Baldwin that he was left without anything to say. To ask her *what* it explained was to invite insult—no doubt she would say something about the dreadful style of his hat and insinuate that Gray's was hardly the place to go for hats. He had little wish to defend himself to her, particularly in the matter of fashion. He wished for a moment that he could argue with her about battle tactics, for on that subject he could not be beaten. Why did she always contrive to get the last word? Waspish, infuriating woman! If only she had been ugly he could have easily disregarded her.

As they had been walking on the Cobb, Penelope had hung back a little from the other four. She remained close enough that she could be seen as part of the group, but not so close that she would intrude on them. Anne and Wentworth were discussing how the Cobb might have been built and the depth of the port, and Elizabeth and Admiral Baldwin seemed lost in their contemplation of the sea around them.

"Mrs. Clay," said someone at her side, and she looked up to see Mr. Elliot there, tipping his hat to her.

"Oh, hello, Mr. Elliot," she said, nodding in return and smiling as if his presence alone had brightened her day considerably.

"Mrs. Clay, would you do me the great kindness of walking with me? I was delayed in leaving the inn, and have been walking about by myself, trying to find someone I know. Nothing is worse than being left to your own devices when everyone else is enjoying the camaraderie of their friends, I think."

Penelope thought this was more true than he could possibly know, but she only said, "I would be very happy to walk with you."

"Thank you," he said. They had only walked a few yards further when he spoke again. "Mrs. Clay, I have been wishing to thank you for your part in finding my pocket-watch. Borlock was very grateful for your help."

"It was nothing," she said, feeling gratified in spite of her words. "I told Borlock that I did not require thanks."

"Yes, he informed me so, but I could not let it rest without expressing my thanks once, at least. Now I have done." He fell silent then, and they walked on together, Penelope's skirts billowing in the gusts of wind.

"Borlock seems a very faithful servant," said Penelope, feeling that she ought to make an effort at conversation.

"Indeed he is. I could not ask for a more devoted—well, I had almost said friend, but it is hardly respectable to make friends of servants, is it? However, I knew him before he went into service.

You would not think it, perhaps, but he comes of a good family. I need not disclose the circumstances which prompted him to take a position with me, poor fellow, but you may have noticed that his speech and learning are out of the common way for a valet."

"Yes, I had noticed it," said Penelope.

"I hope you will not think the less of me for being on familiar terms with him. I know there are those who see such things as dangerous French Republicanism, leading to a bloody revolution."

"No, indeed. How can I? It is not Republicanism to recognize the humanity in one's fellow-man. I myself had a maid that I considered a friend." Anna, the maid of all work when she was a new bride, had been a most comfortable companion. She had confided all manner of things to her, and they had spent many a happy hour working alongside each other in the kitchen.

They reached the end of the Cobb then, and the presence of others halted their conversation. After a few minutes spent looking out to sea, they all turned back together toward the shore.

Elizabeth, wanting to give Admiral Baldwin no opportunity to walk beside her, took Penelope by the arm and strolled by her side. Baldwin engaged Wentworth in a discussion about the distance from Lyme to France, which left Mr. Elliot to walk beside his cousin Anne. They did not talk much, confining their remarks to commonplaces about the beauty of the place or the number of boats they could see, and Mr. Elliot thought that he would have been bored if he had not believed that he could make his friendship with her useful. When the ladies decided to walk on the lower Cobb instead, it pleased Mr. Elliot to be the one to guide Anne's steps and hold her hand as she stepped down onto the stone paving. He caught a glimpse of Wentworth's face when he did so, and saw the jealousy there.

So it has got that far, has it? he mused. Wentworth was not merely admiring the fair Anne, but already regarded her as his own. How amusing it would be to make Anne fall in love with him and exact some revenge on Wentworth in the process. In fact, if he could marry Anne, he could keep a good watch over Sir Walter and keep him from marrying anyone at all. The idea was worth pondering.

They got off the Cobb and walked on the marine parade until they saw Benwick, Croft, and both Captain and Mrs. Harville coming toward them. The Captain walked with a crutch. It was not long before the two groups met, and Admiral Croft performed the introductions. Captain Harville's greeting of Baldwin and Wentworth was all that was affectionate and brotherly.

"But where is Musgrove?" said Benwick. "I was telling Harville about him."

"I do not know, exactly," said Wentworth. "The Uppercross party separated from us some time ago. They are probably somewhere on the marine parade or the high street. No, there they are, on the Cobb."

"The waves are higher than they were, I think," said Anne. "Is it safe?"

It was a question Charles Musgrove had been asking himself for the past fifteen minutes. Louisa had been determined to go out onto the Cobb, though Charles and his cousin Hayter were both unsure about the prudence of such a venture. The waves appeared to be getting higher and higher as they crashed against the wall of the Cobb, occasionally even washing over the top of it. But Louisa longed to be sprayed with the seawater, declaring that she was too hot to do anything else, and Charles Musgrove thought that his sister had never resembled his wife so much in her life.

He gave in eventually, and they walked out onto the Upper Cobb. Louisa stood much too close to the edge for his comfort. But Louisa had this in common with Mary, and indeed, Elizabeth: opposition made them stubborn, and Charles, though good-hearted, had not the talent for persuading such a temperament. They were coming back now, Louisa triumphant and damp and Henrietta clasping the arm of Hayter, who was pleased to be the sturdy, dependable gentleman she could cling to. Mary was looking petulant: she did not wish to seem less intrepid than Louisa and yet she was not brave enough to venture so near the waves. This made her cross. Charles merely looked harassed. The final introductions were made and the Harvilles promised to join them for dinner at the inn.

That dinner was, for Anne, almost a re-creation of the weeks in London when the officers used to dine with them. The men were in excellent humor, and between their outrageous stories and their banter and teasing, laughter continually spilled out into the corridor of the inn and made the landlord's wife a little nervous lest the hilarity be caused by drink, and the laughter turn to fighting.

"Nay," said the landlord, "there's a party of ladies with them, some of them mighty high in the instep, and you can't think *they* will be drinking themselves under the table! It's the same thing with sailors as it is with soldiers—gather them together after they've finished a war and you can't keep their spirits down."

The food was mediocre, at best, but the diners hardly noticed.

"And what do you think of Lyme?" said Mrs. Harville to Louisa and Henrietta, who were seated near her, when the merriment had died down a little and the men were earnestly discussing the Americans' zest for building larger ships.

"Oh, it is such a beautiful place!" said Henrietta. "We were at Weymouth, once, but this is more charming, I think."

"Oh, yes," added Louisa, "I think it is delightful! Of course, it is more enjoyable seeing someplace with a party of friends."

"Indeed," said Mrs. Harville. She lowered her voice a little. "And I think it is most fortunate that Captain Benwick is surrounded by young people now. Grief makes one feel old before one's time, and it is good for Captain Benwick to be reminded that he is not yet middle-aged."

"Poor Captain Benwick," said Henrietta. "I am sure it must be very difficult for him to recover from such a tragedy. And for your family, too," she added, as she suddenly remembered that the deceased fiancée had been the sister of Captain Harville.

"Yes. I don't know that one *recovers* so much as one endures, but Captain Harville has been grateful to be with his family during this time of grief. I wish Captain Benwick had that comfort, or at the very least, someone to take care of. He is the kind of man who flourishes when he is responsible for another. Do you know, he was famous in the Navy for the midshipmen his command produced. My husband says he was almost a father to those lads. If there was only a lame child or even a sick cat he could devote himself to now, I think his spirits would improve much more quickly."

It was late when the Harvilles excused themselves and said that they really must go home, "for our youngest son sometimes wakes in the night with a nightmare, and Sally—the girl—will not know what to do with him." They said their goodbyes, and the gathering broke up generally then, as the departure of the Harvilles made everyone realize that it was eleven o'clock and that the exertions of the day had wearied them.

"I will bespeak breakfast for us at nine o'clock," said Croft.

"That is much too early, " said Elizabeth firmly. "I intend to sleep until nearly noon, whatever the rest of you do. Anne, of course, will still get up at daybreak; she always does."

"Do you?" said Wentworth murmured to Anne while the rest of the group were debating what time breakfast should be eaten.

"Not at *dawn*," said Anne. "Not in summer when the sun rises at five o'clock!"

"I only thought," said Wentworth, "that here is nothing like the sea in the early morning. If you have never seen it, you ought to."

"I should enjoy that," said Anne. "I think I may go for a stroll along the marine parade before breakfast."

"You ought not to go alone, of course," said Wentworth. "I had better come with you—for your safety, of course." There was a twinkle in his eye as he said it.

Chapter Seven

There was a mist over the water in the morning, as there so often is, but Anne, determined to be delighted by the sea at any hour, gave it as her opinion that there was a definite difference in the way the water looked—it was a different shade of blue and the waves were much calmer.

She and Wentworth walked along the marine parade for a time as the captain described to her the color of the waters in various parts of the world. He had seen it as blue as a turquoise and as green as an olive and every shade in between.

"Shall we look for shells on the beach?" suggested Wentworth. "The summer visitors will no doubt pick up all they find later in the day, but we are the first ones here, except for the local fishermen. We can inspect what the sea brought to shore overnight."

The beach they had wandered to, beyond the Cobb, was mostly pebbles with little sand, and as they searched for shells, Wentworth told Anne of the beaches made up of pure white sand he had seen in the far parts of the globe. "Much easier to walk on than these rocks," he said, although truth be told, neither of them minded the fact that he had to hold her hand to help her keep her footing as she tried to preserve her balance on the uneven stones.

They found one shell, and then another—small ones, but

exquisite to Anne, who had not been accustomed to seeing seashells. She was looking at one of them—a limpet shell, the captain said—and admiring the neat stripes on the inside of it, when Wentworth said, "What is that?" He plucked the item from between two stones and held it out to Anne. It had four long metal prongs with a filigree design at the other end.

"It's a comb," said Anne. "It must have fallen out of a lady's hair. I wonder how we could find the owner? Should we ask at the various inns in Lyme to see if any lady staying there has mentioned losing one?"

Wentworth took the comb back into his hand and examined it. "No. This must have lain here for some time. See how the brass has begun to tarnish? And it is not an expensive item that someone would think valuable enough to search for."

"But it might be valuable for sentimental reasons."

"It has sentimental value to me already." Wentworth gently poked the comb into the hair arranged on the back of Anne's head. "I think we may safely deem this 'found treasure,' and keep it as a memento of our morning walk."

Wentworth thought that of all the beauties of nature he had seen in his travels, nothing equaled the sweet loveliness of Anne's smile at that moment.

"I wonder if we will all walk out to the Cobb again today," Anne said when they began walking over the rocks again, this time back toward the inn. "Do you think the Harvilles would join us if we did? I should like to meet their children."

"I think it very likely," said Wentworth. "But if we do walk, I refuse to be in the same party as Baldwin and your sister Elizabeth. I prefer a storm at sea to the quarrels of those two, witty though their banter might be."

"I wonder what makes them so hostile to one another?"

Wentworth shrugged. "You know your sister best."

"She has said nothing to me about it. I did think they liked each other very well when we were all in London. Perhaps she thought Admiral Baldwin intended more than he did."

"Perhaps. We none of us—officers, at least—were thinking much about the far future at that time." He smiled apologetically as he accounted for his own lack of interest in Anne during those weeks—something he could not imagine now. "Baldwin may have liked your sister more than he wanted to and showed more attention than was seemly. He has always shied away from matrimony. He is fearless in battle, but a coward in love."

"But why?" Anne's curiosity overcame the awkwardness she felt in speaking of love with Captain Wentworth, even if it was someone else's heart they were discussing. They had reached the steps going up from the beach, and Wentworth took a moment to consider her question as they ascended.

"I think there are two reasons," he said when they had reached the top and were once more walking side by side. "One is that he is a cautious fellow by nature. Even in war, he was prepared for any eventuality and he made his decisions and tactics with confidence based on things he had already thought through. In the matter of a wife, I think he has not decided what it is precisely that he wants, and hesitates to make a move until he is sure."

"I see."

"But there is another—and I think more important—reason: I believe he is afraid of loving someone and then losing them, like Benwick."

"That is a danger, of course," admitted Anne. "But it is a risk one takes when loving anything in this world. Nothing earthly lasts forever."

"Exactly," Wentworth said. "And for all his grief now, Benwick was a better man for loving Fanny, even if he lost her. He does not regret his attachment to her."

Elizabeth had risen earlier than noon, of course. She had not meant it when she had said she would be in bed that long—only she had wished to impress upon Admiral Baldwin that she was a lady of leisure who regularly slept as late as she would. He need not think that he could have had her even if he had wanted her.

She dressed in a leisurely fashion, contemplating the day ahead. After breakfast they would probably all walk about the town again, and perhaps out on the Cobb. If they did, she must be very careful not to be anywhere near Admiral Baldwin. She would either get into a quarrel with him, which was really beneath her dignity, or worse, she might forget herself and stare at him again. He had appeared in her dream last night, proud, cold and aloof, but unquestionably handsome. There was no telling what she might do if she let her guard down.

Then they would all journey back to Kellynch. This time, she thought, Mary ought to travel with the Musgroves instead of the Elliot carriage. She would protest, of course, but Elizabeth really could not bear another long journey with Mary's constant inconsequential chatter and complaining. She would speak to Anne about it as soon as possible. Anne, though useless in so many things, often seemed to manage Mary better than others could. Anne might think of a way to get Mary into the Musgrove carriage with a minimum of fuss.

She requested the maid to fetch her sister, but the girl reported that Anne had gone out for a walk, very early.

"Is it not vexatious?" said Elizabeth to Penelope as she came by her room to see if she was ready for breakfast. "I had something particular to speak to Anne about and she is not here. I must see her without loss of time."

They walked together toward the staircase, passing Mr. Elliot as he was about to come out of his room. He stepped aside politely to let them go first, and he heard Mrs. Clay say, "I will go and find her, Miss Elliot. I am sure she cannot be far—she must be on her way back for breakfast by now. I will just get my bonnet and gloves."

"It is very good of you, Penelope," Elizabeth said as Mrs. Clay turned back toward her own room.

Instead of following Elizabeth, Mr. Elliot stayed where he

was, thinking. After a moment he went back into his room, where Borlock was folding night clothes in preparation for packing.

"Borlock," he said. "If you were thinking of engaging Mrs. Clay in conversation, you have just been given the opportunity. Mrs. Clay is even now preparing to go in search of Miss Anne on the streets of Lyme to fetch her in, probably for breakfast. I think you might be of some assistance to her."

The valet bowed briefly and left the room. After passing through the inn's kitchen and surreptitiously appropriating several glass bottles of preserved fruit, he made his way out onto the street and found Mrs. Clay not far from the inn. That is to say, he contrived to jostle her slightly as he brushed by her with his arms full of bottles.

"Excuse me." He bowed slightly, and then pretended to suddenly recognize her.

"Oh! A thousand pardons, madam. So clumsy of me—I was not careful about where I was going." He had purposely snatched more bottles than one man could easily carry, and he had arranged them in his arms so that one was balanced precariously on the others. He managed to dislodge it from its perch with a twitch of his finger, and as it began to slide toward the ground, Penelope caught it.

"Here, you had better let me carry this," she said. "What is it?"

"A bottle of preserved fruit, madam, such as they have in France."

"How quaint," she said and looked more closely at it. The bottle of peaches had a much wider mouth than was usual for bottles that held liquids, and there was a large cork stuck into it. Sealing wax seemed to cover the top, and wire was twisted around that to make it difficult to get the cork off.

"My master remarked these at the inn," explained Borlock. "He has seen them in France, you know, and thought it would be just the thing for an ailing former servant of his that he is going to visit before long. He bought them from the landlord, and I am going to look out a basket that will fit them to travel in." Borlock was rather proud of this story, conceived the moment he had seen the bottles of fruit, lined up decoratively in their shiny glass splendor on a kitchen shelf as he passed through on his way to intercept Mrs. Clay.

"Well, you must give me one or two of them to carry—how many do you have? Five? That is far too many to carry safely."

"I beg you would not trouble yourself, madam. I can manage."

"Nonsense. You would not want to lose any, would you?"

"Well, no, madam, but I could fetch a boy from the inn to help."

"Not at all. I am here now and there is no reason to delay your journey. Why did you not leave the bottles at the inn until you had the basket?"

"There you have me, madam," Borlock said, abashed. "That would have been the wise thing to do. Only I was not confident I would be able to estimate the right size of basket from my memory."

Penelope smiled and shook her head at him. "Men may have great energy, but they often lack the forethought that would keep them out of difficulties."

Borlock knew a moment of triumph. Already she was seeing him as a man, and not merely a valet. "Very true, madam. My nursery-governess used to say the same thing to me. 'Boys are always so heedless' is the way she put it."

It was on the tip of Penelope's tongue to say, "You had a nursery-governess?"—highly unusual for someone in the servant class —but Mr. Elliot's words about Borlock's good birth came back to her. It was a shame, she thought, that such a handsome and well-spoken man should have suffered such reverses of fortune. Why, he very well might be better born than she was.

She smiled. "I cannot say that *all* males are heedless—far from it. However, my late husband often said that he could not survive without a wife to help manage his affairs."

"I have no doubt you were a true helpmeet to him, madam, as my master's late wife was to him. And I am certain that I myself would—" He broke off suddenly, but Penelope was sure he was about to say that he would be helped by a wife as well. She felt a surge of compassion for him: he had probably given up the notion of getting married when he had become a valet. It must have been difficult to go into service when he had been accustomed to having servants himself.

"Never mind, madam," continued Borlock, clearing his throat. "You had better give me those bottles and finish your errand."

"I was only going to look for Miss Anne," said Penelope, "and I can do that very well as I am walking with you to the basket shop. Do, please, lead the way—there is no need for you to walk behind me. I do not know where I am going."

"Very well, madam, if you are determined." Borlock was not at all sure where a shop might be that would sell baskets, but ten to one he would pass something of the kind on the high street. He moved off in the direction of the beach, Penelope beside him.

It was a pleasant walk for Penelope. The morning air was crisp but not cold, and she had the pleasant sensation of being helpful without any ulterior motive. It seemed a long time since she had walked beside a man without needing to be vigilant about everything she did or said, lest she give an unfortunate impression. As they walked, Borlock told her of Mr. Elliot's amiable temper and his wish to do good things for the Kellynch estate, should he ever succeed to the baronetcy.

At last they reached a shop which seemed to sell all manner of things for travelers—boxes, baskets, trunks, and travelling-cases. In the window of the shop was a small toy ship, complete as to details, with rigging and sails arranged in a very life-like way. Penelope paused to gaze at it.

"Look at that," she cried in delight. "It is just such a thing as Francis would love!"

"Francis?" repeated Borlock, obediently looking at the ship.

"My-my son." She never mentioned her children to anyone outside her family. Sir Walter, in fact, had probably forgotten the existence of these progeny. But she had been too relaxed, too carefree, and she had spoken without thinking.

"He must be a very handsome lad, madam," was all Borlock said, but there was something besides mere politeness in his tone as he looked admiringly at her, and the implication was not lost on Penelope. Her eyes widened.

The valet became flustered. "I beg your pardon, madam—I only thought for a moment that my master might—That is, he is so much more suitable than Sir Walter—" He seemed to be struggling to find words. At last he sighed and shook his head. "I have no excuse, madam. I have not learned to keep my thoughts to myself—not with any success, that is. I must beg you to forget I said anything. I shall not speak to you again."

He looked so humbled and embarrassed that Penelope's heart went out to him. She noticed for the first time how very blue his eyes were.

"Mrs. Clay?" said Anne's voice behind them.

The two of them turned and saw Captain Wentworth and Anne Elliot standing there. Borlock took a step backward, as any good valet would do, to let his social superiors converse unconstrained.

"Good morning, Miss Anne," said Penelope. "Your sister sent me to find you, and then Mr. Elliot's man, Borlock, needed assistance ..."

The look on both Wentworth and Anne's faces was a blend of doubt and disapproval. To be seen in friendly conversation with a manservant on the streets of Lyme! It could well be seen as a clandestine assignation. Penelope colored.

Borlock saw her discomfiture and spoke. "Mrs. Clay was very kindly assisting me, madam, to carry these bottles of preserved fruit to this shop so that I might buy a proper basket or box in which to transport them. Mr. Elliot was very desirous that something be arranged before we leave today."

"I see," said Wentworth. His frown relaxed a little.

"Now, madam," Borlock said to Penelope in the distant, respectful voice of an upper servant talking to a gently-bred lady, "I thank you again for your kindness in saving me the embarrassment of smashing some of these on the pavement, which is no doubt what would have happened if I had carried them all this way by myself." There were a few baskets set out in front of the shop to advertise the wares within, and Borlock gingerly set his bottles into one of them. Penelope added the one she carried and nodded a farewell to Borlock. She resisted the unexpected urge to look back at him as she followed Wentworth and Anne back to the inn.

After breakfast, the Harvilles appeared with their three young children, and they all walked along the marine parade and out to the Cobb together. The walk was leisurely, both because Captain Harville's injury kept him at a slow pace and because they were all aware of the impending departure and they wanted to enjoy the sea, and their new friends, while they could.

Louisa's high spirits made her an immediate favorite with the children, and they attached themselves to her and to Captain Benwick, who had been beloved by them for the past two years. Asked by Louisa what her favorite animal was, three-year-old Jane said a chicken, and began to cluck and flap her arms in the manner of hens. Inspired by this performance, five-year-old Arthur said he liked rabbits, and happily hopped along the Cobb until he came to the steep, uneven steps formed by stones jutting out of the wall, leading to the lower level. Seeing that Arthur was proposing to hop like a rabbit down them, Benwick intervened.

"Hold, there, Arthur. I must go down the steps first to prepare the way for the rabbit. These steps lead to the rabbit burrow, you see, and I am the old grandfather rabbit who goes first to make sure there is not a snare at the bottom! You creep behind me—no hopping, mind!—until I get to the bottom and can hold your hand while you jump down the lower steps."

This plan was carried out safely, and Louisa applauded little Arthur's hops.

"Now you come down!" shouted Arthur up to Louisa. "Hop!"

Amused, Louisa started slowly down the steps.

"No, hop!" insisted Arthur.

Louisa had no intention of jumping down all the steps; she meant to satisfy Arthur by hopping down only to the next step, but the surface of the stone was less level than it seemed, and she lost her balance as she landed on it. She wobbled there for an instant, and then with a cry, fell.

Benwick, who had been standing as closely beneath her as he could, with some vague notion of ensuring her safety, had his arms out to catch her before she even shrieked. It was over in a moment. Louisa dropped into Captain Benwick's arms as neatly as if it had been rehearsed a dozen times, and was set down uninjured on a nearby bench. Arthur immediately clamored for the pair to "do it again!" and that noise, added to Louisa's cry as she fell, brought the rest of the party to the edge of the upper Cobb to look down on the scene.

"It might have been a very nasty accident!" said Charles, when the near-calamity had been explained by a still-shaken Benwick. He descended the steps as he talked. "What were you thinking, Louisa? If you had hit your head on the stones, you might be lying lifeless on the ground at this moment!"

This remark, true as it may have been, was unfortunately heard by Mary, who began to scream in an excess of sensibility. "Louisa! Oh, Louisa! Are you still alive? Oh, my nerves! Why does she not stand? She must be injured!" She started down the steps, and Charles was forced to give attention to his wife, lest she, too, lose her balance and fall. He came back part-way up the steps to give her his hand, and thus escorted her safely down. She clung to her husband, burst into tears at the sight of the pale Louisa, and seemed in great danger of falling into a swoon.

Charles patted her a little helplessly and murmured whatever comforting things he could think of. Henrietta came speedily but carefully down the steps and sat next to her sister, who had been calm, but was now beginning to tremble.

"I am sorry," Louisa managed to say before starting to cry.

Admiral Baldwin, increasingly uncomfortable at the sight of two weeping women—and in his experience, it would soon be three, for Henrietta would no doubt soon be in tears as well—began to look for a way of escape. At least Elizabeth, he thought, would not be in any danger of becoming lachrymose, cold-hearted as she was. Anne did look concerned, but not enough to fall into hysterics. He was unsure about Mrs. Clay, who, to do him justice, had not decided herself whether to cry and be seen as warm-hearted and sympathetic, or to remain calm and be seen as capable and sensible.

Wentworth, after asking Anne if she was all right, moved to give his assistance on the lower Cobb.

"Nay, nay," said Croft quietly. "Let Benwick help her. It will do him good."

Wentworth nodded his understanding. "Perhaps Mr. Hayter should stay with them—he can help Miss Henrietta if she needs it —and the rest of us can wait for them at the inn. We might as well oversee the loading of the trunks on the carriages and have the horses harnessed, ready to leave as soon as all arrive back at the inn."

This idea was approved by the Harvilles, who felt unreasonably guilty for the incident, both because it was their move to Lyme which was responsible for Louisa's presence on the Cobb, and because their son's demand for hopping had precipitated the accident. Benwick assisted Arthur up the steps to his parents and siblings, and Mr. Hayter came down them.

The party on the upper Cobb made their way back to the inn much more quickly than the others. It was a few minutes before

Louisa felt that her legs would carry her, and another few until Mary was calm enough not to be making a spectacle of herself. She was supported by Charles, and Henrietta by Mr. Hayter, and it fell to Benwick, of course, to let Louisa lean upon his arm. Louisa, with her youthful and impulsive disposition, had never struck him as a weak, clinging, and needy girl who wanted a protector, but it came to him now that she ought to have someone to rescue her from herself. He was thankful to have been of service to her.

Chapter Eight

S ir Walter was happy to see his guests back at Kellynch. Mr.
Shepherd had been to visit him again while they were gone,
and there had been another painful scene—painful to Sir Walter,
that is. Shepherd had asked for another jewel to sell, and it was
only because of the picture he painted—guests to the masquerade
ball dancing in complete darkness because the chandler had
refused to send candles until the bill of payment was settled—that
Sir Walter consented to release an emerald necklace. Sir Walter's
spirits had remained low until the sight of the officers on their
horses riding back to Kellynch to enjoy his hospitality restored his
tranquility. After all, he was Sir Walter Elliot, baronet, of Kellynch
Hall, entertaining the heroes of the Navy in lavish style. What was
one emerald necklace more or less to that?

The ball was but four days hence, and preparations for the
grand event were now underway. The time was all too short for
Elizabeth, who discovered that the butcher had not yet delivered
the veal knuckles, a laundry-maid had given notice, and they did
not have nearly enough packs of cards for those who would spend
the evening playing whist in the morning room. Sir Walter refused
to be perturbed by these trifles, and spoke constantly of the
coming revelry.

"Where does he imagine we will obtain costumes for this masquerade?" Baldwin asked Wentworth after breakfast two mornings after their return. Sir Walter had spent the meal apologizing for the absence of any dukes or earls on the list of guests, and afterwards the two men had escaped to the terrace. "I refuse to travel to London to hire a fancy-dress for this occasion," Baldwin added.

"Never fear." said Wentworth. "There will be no elaborate disguises, Miss Anne says, just masks and dominoes. No need to re-create the clothing of a historical person or try to disguise yourself as a bishop or a harlequin. Those domino cloaks will cover whatever you wear. Miss Anne says they have ordered a number of them, for our use."

"Miss Anne says so, does she?" Baldwin looked amused. "And what else does she say?"

"She says that the dinner will be good and the musicians will be skillful." He smiled reminiscently. "And also that she will dance with me."

Baldwin looked at him with narrowed eyes. "You have been spending an inordinate amount of time with that young lady, you know. You ought to be careful or you will find yourself in danger of a breach of promise suit."

"No danger of that. I intend to marry her."

This surprised a cry of pain out of Baldwin. "What? Not another one!"

"Another what?"

"Husband! All my friends turn husband! Shall I never see a bachelor of three score again? Must I be the *only* one who does not succumb?"

Wentworth smirked. "I will see you, before I die, look pale with love."

"With love?" Baldwin scoffed. "No. Pale with anger, with sickness, or with hunger, my friend, but not with love. However, it is not my marriage we are discussing, but yours. A bit hasty in this business, are you not?"

"I know what I want."

Baldwin shook his head. "You always were an impulsive fellow. Remember that horse you bought three years ago? Looked decent from a distance, but before long you discovered it was forever throwing out a splint."

Wentworth drew himself up. "You are not, I hope, comparing Miss Anne to a horse."

"No, indeed. I mean no disparagement to Miss Anne—only your rush into matrimony. Miss Anne is a treasure, from what I can see. Unlike her sisters," he added darkly. "However, I meant only that it is a habit with you to make instant decisions."

"With good result," Wentworth shot back. "I am always right."

"Usually," corrected Baldwin. "*Usually* right. Remember the horse."

"One occasion!"

Baldwin could have furnished more examples, but there was no point in making Wentworth angry. "Well, then," he said in what he hoped was a conciliating tone, "if you are determined, I wish you joy."

"Admirably said!"

"So long as you do not spend your time mooning about and composing sonnets to her eyes."

"I wonder if Anne would enjoy such a thing?" mused Wentworth. "No doubt she would. A very good notion: I thank you for the thought!"

"And will you try your hand at writing songs, as well?" asked Baldwin sarcastically.

"Oh, I think so," said Wentworth with a straight face. "I shall learn to play the lute, too, in case Anne might enjoy being serenaded."

"There will be no enduring your company. I shall have to start hiding in the library, like Benwick does."

"Is *that* where he keeps disappearing to?"

"Well, it was. I have not seen him going in there since we returned."

"Yes, he has seemed in better spirits since the trip to Lyme. I think we may call the trip a success."

Wentworth, remembering his morning walk with Anne, smiled. "Oh, yes. I think we may certainly call the trip to Lyme a success."

At almost the same moment, Borlock was helping to ease Mr. Elliot's exquisitely fitted coat over his shoulders.

"I spoke with Captain Wentworth's man this morning, sir," said Borlock. "He says he has been making enquiries about purchasing a small estate, no doubt with a view to settling down."

"Well, well. It is heartening to see that my assessment of the situation was correct. It would give me inexpressible pleasure to extinguish his nuptial plans. The only question is how it can best be managed."

"I am certain you will find a way, sir."

"Yes, no doubt I will." He studied his image in the mirror and adjusted his cravat slightly. "How are you getting on with Mrs. Clay?"

"Pretty well, sir. I think she has now abandoned hope of Sir Walter and has decided that you would make the better husband."

"Excellent." He took the snuff box out of his waistcoat pocket, opened it to see if there was enough snuff in it, and put it back in its place. "The only question is what to do with her now? I could, perhaps, persuade her to come away with me when I leave Kellynch, and ... er ... live under my protection. She would then be ineligible to marry Sir Walter, even if she changed her mind. And she will be extremely anxious to please me as long as she thinks there is a chance I might marry her. And she is not *so* ill-favored that I could not endure her company for a while."

For once Borlock felt a twinge of repugnance at the thought

of Mr. Elliot seducing Mrs. Clay. She was not a guileless innocent, but neither was she a rapacious social climber who deserved to be tricked. Borlock's conversations with her had revealed a softer and more vulnerable side, and he could not quite forget her face when she had mentioned her son, Francis. However mixed her motives had been in trying to help him, he was certain that not everything she did was self-seeking.

He felt an impulse to object to his master's plan, but immediately suppressed it. Any appeal to morality would bring his master's scorn down upon him. Instead, he said evenly, "I think, sir, you will not win any praise from the Elliots if you abscond with Miss Elliot's companion. You know not what situations might arise in the future; it might be impolitic to have them as your enemies."

"True." William considered that point for a moment. "You have done admirably in your endeavor to woo her for me. I could remain aloof but always on the verge of noticing her, whilst you become her friend and ally until you totally eclipse me. It would be so very amusing to see her languishing after my valet!"

Borlock smirked, as was expected of him.

"And she is not so beautiful that I will regret neglecting the opportunity of keeping her in some establishment for a time. Very well, Borlock. I leave it to you to cultivate Mrs. Clay."

That afternoon, Baldwin, wondering if Croft or Wentworth would like a game of billiards, was just coming down the stairs in search of them when he heard Wentworth say, "Yes, we could very well walk into Kellynch village—I am certain the shop there will sell what I need." The voice came from around a corner, and Baldwin paused on the bottom step to see who Wentworth was talking to. The idea of walking into the village was not wholly unattractive to Baldwin, but it depended on the company.

Then he heard Anne's voice saying, "I will invite a few people to come with us. Mrs. Clay, I think, said she needed something for the ball."

"You do not mean to invite *everyone*, do you? The good people of the village will think us a mob come to attack them."

"Not at all. A small party. Only Elizabeth and Mrs. Clay and perhaps Admiral Croft or Admiral Baldwin."

Baldwin shuddered at the thought of being included in this venture. He would certainly get no conversation with Anne or Wentworth, who would be wrapped up in each other, and he would either end up walking by himself or trying to be civil to Elizabeth and Mrs. Clay. Neither prospect was at all enticing. He had reached the bottom of the stairs now, and it was of first importance that he not be found. *The library*, he thought, and ducked into it. He could not fault Benwick for spending time here: it was an admirable spot for hiding, and he prowled about the room until he found a comfortable chair near a window, not visible to a casual visitor. He spied *The Vicar of Wakefield* on one of the shelves, pulled it out, sat down, and began to read.

There had not been a ball at Kellynch for many years. When Elizabeth had taken out pen and paper three weeks before to make a list of those to be invited to this affair, it was borne in on her just how few there were. Lady Russell had once called it a "scanty neighborhood," and it was no less than the truth. However, circumstances favored the Elliots: two neighboring estates had large parties of guests visiting, and naturally they were included in the invitation. Elizabeth also invited families on the fringes of the region and hoped they would be intrigued enough to join them. As it turned out, she had no reason to fear a small attendance. The novelty of naval officers being there meant that the men were eager to make their acquaintance and hear thrilling tales of battles won, and the ladies were eager to dance with them: two of the officers single, one of them (though married) personable, and another in a romantically tragic state to view. And for those invited who cared little for the Navy, the rare circumstance of a ball being given at Kellynch brought those who were merely curious. And the novelty of a *masked* ball served to lift the event even further above the ordinary.

Elizabeth—over Mary's objections—even invited Charles Musgrove's cousins, the Hayters—"for with everyone in masks and dominoes, no one will be able to tell whether they are shabby-genteel or fabulously wealthy," she explained. "As long as they can dance, they will lend us more credit than if they stay home and we have a very thin company for the ball."

"They might not even *have* dominoes," Mary said gloomily. "Or they may have some that are impossibly worn and ragged."

"It is no matter," said Elizabeth. "We have ordered masks and dominoes from Crewkerne—for it is most unlikely that our own guests have any with them—and you may distribute some of these to the Hayters if there is need of it."

The domines and masks arrived the day before the ball. The suppliers had sent two dozen of them, as there was not much call for them in summer, masquerade balls usually being held in the winter. Along with the usual black, the trunk that arrived also contained dominoes in blue, white, red and yellow.

On the morning of the ball, the sun rose in a cloudless sky—beautiful weather, only rather too hot for comfort. The house was full of activity that day with extra servants, hired temporarily for the purpose, polishing, scrubbing, and decorating. The kitchen maids, under the direction of the cook, were kept busy, and the fire roared. The flowers in the ballroom began to wilt sooner than they were expected to. Baldwin hid himself in the library more than once. He found it restful and cool, and he wanted to finish the book. Meals that day were simple and cold, which no one minded.

Benwick would not be dancing, of course, and Sir Walter assured him that he need not put on a mask for the card-room. As the hour drew near for the start of the ball, he was the first to emerge from his bedroom and come downstairs. He was drawn outdoors as the heat of the day had finally dissipated and there was a cool breeze to enjoy. The other officers appeared one by one on the terrace as they waited for their hosts to appear. Their masks hung by their strings from the men's hands.

"Eight o'clock," said Croft, looking at his watch and then snapping it shut and putting it back in his pocket. "I wish Sophia was here. She would enjoy a masquerade ball."

"Any news of her brother's wife? Is she improving?" said Benwick.

"Some, according to her latest letter. I hope it will not to be too long now before Sophie feels able to leave her."

"Here," said Baldwin, coming over to them. "Am I sufficiently disguised? This domino is insufferably hot. How is one supposed to dance in this heat?"

"It will be cooler soon," soothed Wentworth.

"Not indoors, with the masses of candles illuminating the ballroom."

"Let us hope the windows stay open," said Benwick.

Directly above the terrace, Penelope could hear indistinct voices through her open window, but she paid no attention to them. She smoothed out the note she was holding and read it for the fourth time since she had found it in her bedroom an hour before. "One who Admires you hopes to have the Pleasure of Dancing with you this Evening. If you will stand beside the Palm at Eleven of the Clock, the Gentleman will Approach you." There was no signature.

A gentleman who admired her ... who? Could it be Mr. Elliot? Sir Walter was not the sort of man who would send an anonymous letter, nor could she imagine one of the naval officers doing such a thing. And it could not be anyone unconnected with Kellynch—how would they know about the palm that had been newly placed along the west wall of the entrance hall?

She folded the note again and tucked it into her reticule—it would not do to leave it lying around where servants would see it.

Although she had her doubts that any of the maids at Kellynch could read. Then again, if a valet like Borlock could be well-educated and even well-born, there was no telling what a servant might be able to do. Poor Borlock, who might have at one time attended a ball like this and was now reduced to arranging the clothing of his master, and perhaps being pressed into service giving out glasses of punch to the dancers!

At that moment, Borlock was also pondering his fall from affluence as he descended the servant's stairs to the kitchen. His true history was not so very different from what Mr. Elliot had confided to Mrs. Clay. He was the fourth son of a clergyman with an easy competence. On his mother's side, he was the grandson of an impoverished knight, and he had grown up on the very fringes of the fashionable world. He had gone to school in the usual way, and become a steward for a landowner in the north of England. There he had succumbed to temptation and stolen some of the money with which he was entrusted. It was sheer bad luck that his theft had been found out immediately, and he was dismissed. He had changed his name and moved to the south of the country, but the only work he could find was as a butler. He had a natural talent for this, and his educated speech and understanding of the polite world made him a success, until he had once again stolen— a ruby ring, this time—and was dismissed. His employer had the greatest dislike of scandal or notoriety and it was only this that kept Borlock from being delivered up to the law.

Mr. Elliot had been a friend of this employer, and offered Borlock a position as his valet, with the tacit understanding that there was to be no more thieving, and that he would do whatever Mr. Elliot asked and keep his mouth shut. In return, Mr. Elliot would keep him employed, pay him well, and forget his former indiscretions. It had been a useful arrangement for them both, until now.

"Be sure your sin will find you out." Odd how his father's voice, reading from the Bible, came to him at various times. His father had been a perfunctory clergyman, known more for his

genial mien than his piety and scholarship. He had been against the Evangelical movement, giving it as his opinion that there was no need to be fanatical about religion—Methodists and other overly-zealous sects were prone to hysteria, in his view. Nevertheless, throughout the years of his childhood Borlock had listened to innumerable texts of Scripture being read out in church and in school, and the repetition had had its effect. The words were indelibly etched into his memory.

"Be sure your sin will find you out." Well, his sin certainly had found him out in former days, and he was used to shrug his shoulders at the aptness of the quotation. He had transgressed the law and taken the consequences. Now, for the first time, he wondered if his current misdeeds would also bring about a judgement. *"For God shall bring every work into judgment,"* said his father's voice promptly. Was he, perhaps, digging deeper into vice and storing up more wrath for himself? He shook his head to clear it. What a moment to be having odd religious fancies! He had work to do tonight.

Chapter Nine

The musicians had been instructed to begin playing as soon as the first guests arrived, and so it was into a world of color, music, and light that the revelers entered. The Elliot family greeted the guests unmasked and undisguised, and Elizabeth and Anne, and indeed, Sir Walter, were in their best looks.

Baldwin skulked at the corners of the room, furtively watching Elizabeth. There was no refuting her beauty. Anne, as sweetly elegant as she looked, was nothing to her sister. Elizabeth's bearing, her smile as she greeted her guests, and her cultured voice marked her out as a woman of quality. He had determined to ignore her, but for some reason his eyes kept traveling back to where she stood. There was something of the old Elizabeth there, the one he remembered from London. There had been one particular ball there, he remembered, at Endicott House, when he had danced with her. He had enjoyed it—too much. It had awakened him to the danger of falling in love with her. He had been more cautious after that and made a cutting remark to her, and shortly thereafter he had gone back to sea. But he had never danced since without wishing he could have a partner he liked as well again.

Suddenly, he realized that here was the opportunity to dance with her without her knowledge—in fact, without anyone's knowledge. No one could tease him for weakening in his aversion to her, least of all her! He determined to be the one to lead her to the floor when the dancing started. Tactics! That was what was needed. He sauntered out of the hall and into the billiard room. There was a door leading outside from there, and in a moment he was through it and in the garden. He could have wished it was dark already, but the summer evening promised at least two more hours of light. Never mind, he thought. He had managed once to board an enemy ship in broad daylight; surely he could get around to the front of the house undetected.

He moved stealthily from covering shrub to tree to another shrub as carriages drove up the drive to discharge their occupants. When he neared the front of the house, he waited until a carriage decanted its party of four and then he moved into position behind them. He looked again at the carriage and recognized it as the Musgroves'.

"For pity's sake," came Mary's voice. "You have trodden on my gown, Louisa! Charles, *where* is my fan? I shall need it on an evening such as this."

He followed in their wake as they approached the front doors.

"Why are the Elliots not in dominoes?" Henrietta's voice came floating back to him.

"You can't expect them to receive their guests in disguise!" said Charles. "I'm sure Elizabeth and Anne will put on masks before the dancing starts."

Baldwin joined the queue of guests behind the Musgroves and was received in due course by the Elliots. When he came up to Elizabeth, he took her hand and bowed low over it. Imparting a slight Scotch accent to his speech, he asked, "Will you do me the honor of dancing the first two dances with me, Miss Elliot?"

Elizabeth almost laughed. To think that Admiral Baldwin considered himself disguised by a domino, a mask, and a Scotch accent! Anyone could recognize his tall figure and that slight dimple in his chin. And such an elaborate ruse—to enter the house with the other guests! But she could not help being flat-

tered; he had wanted to dance with her. She had secretly wished
to dance with him, as well—she had not forgotten those long-
ago dances in London, either. Well, she would indulge him. As
the hostess, she would lead off the dancing, and it was agreeable
to have a partner who would not disgrace her—and he
would not.

"I thank you, sir, yes," she said, and curtseyed. He bowed his
thanks and moved on, more elated than he would have cared to
admit. When the bulk of the guests had arrived, Elizabeth and
Anne withdrew to put on masks and dominoes. Baldwin had
been on the watch for them, and he came up to Elizabeth as she
reappeared.

"Shall we?" he said, holding out his hand. She took it and he
led her to the ballroom.

It was up to Elizabeth to call the dance, and she chose "Upon
a Summer's Day." The musicians struck up the lively tune and she
and the admiral began the dance. It was one they had danced long
ago, and she knew it would show them both to best advantage.
They danced remarkably well together, and more than one young
lady, in watching them, wished she had devoted more time to
practicing her contratems and rigadon. They danced their way
down the set and then stood in their new positions while the
other couples took their turns.

"Upon my word, ma'am, you are light on your feet." Baldwin
could not help saying it. Her eyes sparkled behind the mask and
the smile on her face was full of genuine delight, far removed from
the haughty looks of scorn she had bestowed on him ever since he
had come to Kellynch Hall. "I thank you, sir. You are an excellent
dancer yourself."

He was gratified for a moment, but then had a moment of
panic. What was he doing? To flatter her like this would only
make her more insufferable—she was already vain enough! She
might dance well, but he could not forget the caustic things she
had said to him, and if he fed her conceit, she would likely say
even worse. She ought to be chastened a little bit. He smiled

mendaciously and added, "I cannot believe you are as shrewish as you have been painted."

The smile faded a little. "Have I been painted so, indeed?"

"Oh, yes. I believe 'disdainful' was the word used, and there was mentioned something about wit."

"Perhaps it was said that my conversation contained much of it?"

"No, no, not that ... let me think what it was. Oh! I have it. It was that your clever remarks were all got out of books."

"Out of books?" said Elizabeth. "Come now, I must know: who said such things?"

"I beg your pardon, but I will not tell."

She smiled coyly. "And will you tell me who you are?"

"Not at present."

Elizabeth kept her features in an expression of tolerable amusement, but she was fuming inside. She had thought he wanted to dance with her because of some latent admiration for her, but evidently he had only craved an opportunity to insult her. *Well, there's two can play at that game.*

"Never mind," she said sweetly. "You need not tell me, mysterious stranger, who spoke of me thus. It must have been Admiral Baldwin."

"Baldwin? Which one is he?"

"I am quite certain you know him well enough," Elizabeth said drily.

"No, no, I have assuredly never met him."

"I daresay you are right, for you would never forget him if you had. We call him 'the court jester' among ourselves. A very dull fool, really—his only gift is in devising impossible slanders. He is popular, I believe, with libertines and rakes; they like him for his villainy, not his wit, of course. He might well be called a laughingstock."

What could be seen of her partner's face had taken on a reddish hue, but he said lightly, "When I meet the gentleman, I might just tell him what you say."

"Oh, yes, do! He will say something similar about me, I expect, but when no one takes notice of his comments or laughs at them, he will become melancholy and refuse to eat his supper —which will save a partridge wing or two."

They were near the top of the set now, and there was no more time for talking before they were called upon to show again how well-matched they were.

With twenty-five couple forming the set, it was more than half an hour before the dance was completed. Elizabeth parted courteously from her ostensibly unknown partner, and went outside to cool her cheeks and her temper. She found that she was not the only one on the terrace. Many of the dancers, and even some of those who had watched them, had come out into the twilight of the evening. There was a most beautiful sunset. She thought she could catch a better glimpse of it from the west end of the garden, and she went down the terrace steps and along the path toward the low stone wall that marked the garden boundary. She felt a tear of frustration well up in her eye, and put up her hand to wipe it away; her mask was in the way. She untied it and took it off, letting it dangle from her fingers as she walked. She reached the wall and stood there looking at the sunset.

A crunch of feet on gravel caused her to turn around to see who approached. It was Admiral Croft. He had already taken off his mask.

"Splendid sunset," he said. "Rare to see one like this on land —in England, at any rate. Well, now, this is a restful spot. I think I have had enough of dancing for the evening—not used to long sets like that. I don't think I acquitted myself particularly well— not like you. The trouble with being hostess is that everyone knows who you are—no way for you to hide your identity when everyone saw you lead off the dancing."

Elizabeth smiled. "There was nothing the matter with your dancing—I saw you."

"What, is a mask not enough to make me anonymous?"

"Your domino has no hood," she pointed out. "Your hair gave you away."

"No doubt. My graying locks look out of place in the ball-room. 'Tis a young man's sport; I am getting too old for such exercise. Baldwin is a full ten years my junior, and I have frequently known him to dance every dance at a ball. I remember, you and Baldwin danced together years ago, in London; you were well matched. I hope to see you dance again this evening."

Elizabeth cast a glance at him to see if he was teasing; did he know that she had already danced with Admiral Baldwin? Could it be he had not recognized her partner? There was no reading his face. She elected to pretend complete ignorance of her partner.

"I fear not, Admiral. I have little wish to dance with a gentleman who disparages me to others."

"Disparages you to others?" repeated Croft. "For shame! He ought not to do such a thing. He can be the most unaccountable fellow. I do not blame you for wanting to distance yourself from him."

Wentworth had not tried to engage Anne for the first two dances. It was not because he could not find her: no, he could have pointed her out at any moment. Her domino did not have a hood, and Wentworth could see the comb they had picked up on the beach in Lyme like a crown in her hair. She had promised to dance with him, and he was confident she would. His plan was to ask her for the dance before supper: she would then be his partner for the meal as well. For this first dance, he had asked some unknown woman if she would care to stand up with him, and spent most of his time looking on Anne's partner with a critical eye.

This man, unbeknownst to Wentworth, and indeed to Anne, was Mr. Elliot. He made desultory conversation with her as if he had no idea who she was, asking her how she liked the house and the grounds, and if she had travelled far to be there. He spoke softly, trusting that sound of the musicians and the conversations and dancing around them would make his voice unrecognizable.

"No, I have come from quite nearby," Anne said, doing her best to suppress a smile.

"And have you encountered the naval gentlemen as yet?"

"They must be among us," she said, "though I have not seen beneath any masks to know which men might be they."

"What are their names?" asked Mr. Elliot. "I have heard them, but cannot remember."

"Captain Wentworth, Captain Benwick, Admiral Croft and Admiral Baldwin."

"Ah, yes. I think I have heard of Captain Wentworth. Is he not the one—no, a lady such as yourself would not have heard about it."

"What was it?" asked Anne curiously. "Some act of bravery? I can well believe he did something of note."

"No, it was not that," said her companion. "Far from it, in fact. During a skirmish ... well, it is not a story for the ballroom—sordid and ugly in the extreme. He was very nearly court martialed, but I think they had not enough proof of treachery to prosecute him."

"No, indeed! You must be mistaken," Anne protested. "Captain Wentworth is all that is honorable!"

Mr. Elliot frowned as if in thought. "I was certain that was the name. Wentworth, Fredrick Wentworth. I remembered it particularly."

"Then it there must be another captain with the same name," Anne said stoutly.

"You must know the captain very well, to be so confident."

"I only know him well enough to be certain that he could not take an action that would disgrace his profession." Her mouth was set in obstinate lines, and Mr. Elliot know that she would not be persuaded without absolute proof.

"Forgive me," he said. "I perceive you have a high regard for the gentleman. I must doubt the soundness of my information. I would not wish to slander one who ought to command my respect."

The severe look on Anne's face softened. "No, indeed," she said earnestly, "for I can answer for it that he is the best of men."

Her heart is already given to him, thought Mr. Elliot, and would have cursed aloud if he had been alone. There would be no wooing her away from Wentworth. He would have to find another way of ruining Wentworth's matrimonial hopes.

After Elizabeth left the ballroom for the terrace, Baldwin immediately asked another lady to dance. He had no idea who she was and he did not much care. He asked of her a few polite questions, but she seemed little inclined to talk. And all the time he was standing up with her, the words Elizabeth had said went round and round his brain. *Court jester—Ha! I was never called anything like it! And if I was called so, it would only be because I have a cheerful disposition. My friends would attest that I tell clever jokes; that does not make me a fool. I have wit enough—I have been called amusing a score of times. But 'court jester'? Never. And as for laughing at me behind my back, no one does any such thing! It is all from the imagination of Miss Elliot! And —mark this!—it is all of a piece with own character. I have heard it said that liars often accuse others of lying. I daresay it is the same for slanders like this! Her jibes say much more about her own character than mine. And if this is how she speaks of me to others—for she knew not who I was—then she ought to be publicly denounced!*

So busy was he defending himself that the music ended without his noticing, and he alone started a chassé step toward his partner when the other dancers did their courtesies. He wandered into the morning room and saw Benwick there, playing whist at one of the tables.

"Thinking of playing cards?" asked Croft, who had appeared

at his elbow. "Tired of dancing so soon? Not an hour ago I was telling Miss Elliot that you could dance all night."

"Miss Elliot! Was she her customary sarcastic and bitter self?"

"No. I must say, I thought her a little downcast. A gentleman she danced with told her that you belittle her to others."

"Ha!" Baldwin said a little louder than he had meant to. Several nearby card-players looked over at him. He cleared his throat and lowered his voice. "She danced with *me*, unknowingly, and I made but one comment—one exceedingly mild comment! —to keep her from being too puffed up about her superior dancing. She could not have known who I was, but she began disparaging me, calling me a court jester!"

"Stings a bit, does it?" said Croft. "Perhaps she knew it was you, and wanted to punish you a little."

"She could not have known my identity. I took on the part of a Scotsman—you know I can do it well."

"Indeed you can. What puzzles me is why you asked her to dance. Ah, look, there she is, coming this way." Elizabeth had put on her mask again, but she was wearing a distinctive green domino, and neither man could mistake her regal bearing.

"Good heavens! Shall I never get away from her? Quick, give me a task to do. Can I deliver some message to Benwick? Or to Sir Walter? Perhaps you could send me to London, to Whitehall. Is there no midshipman you could recommend to the Admiralty? Come, have you no commands at all?"

"Why, no," said Croft, chuckling. "Except to stay in my company."

"I beg your pardon, that I cannot do. I will not endure any more of her tongue." He moved off toward the door, giving a brief, perfunctory bow to her as he passed.

Elizabeth came near to Croft. "I see Admiral Baldwin has run off. Where has he gone? The library? He thinks no one knows that he hides there—forgetting that there is a perfect view of that library window from the corner of the terrace."

"I am afraid, dear lady, that you have lost the heart of Admiral Baldwin."

"Yes," she said, a little forlornly. "I am quite sure I have. He lent it to me once. and I paid him back with interest: a double heart for his single one. But it appears he plays with loaded dice— so you may very well say that I have lost it." It was hardly modest to be discussing the affairs of her heart with Admiral Croft, and it is very likely she would never have confided such a thing to him if she were not wearing a mask. The disguise, slight as it was, emboldened her tongue. She summoned a rather wan smile. "However, as the poet says that the rules of fair play do not apply in love and war, I suppose I cannot blame him. Admiral Baldwin is, at all events, accustomed to being at war. Pardon me, sir, I must speak to the butler." She curtseyed and disappeared back through the door she had entered by.

William Elliot had taken pains to identify the officers in spite of their disguises. He had obtained intelligence from Borlock as to which colors of dominoes the men were wearing, and he had made certain that Wentworth's mask was distinct from the others —a little row of stitches in dark blue along the top of mask made it unique. Borlock considered that the slight of hand he had used to substitute the altered mask for the ordinary one was worthy of any pickpocket.

He saw Wentworth leave the ballroom after the dance and followed him out onto the terrace.

"Admiral Baldwin, isn't it?" he said. He pitched his voice higher than his natural tone, and made himself a little unsteady on his feet, as if he had been imbibing the punch a little too freely.

Wentworth turned and looked him over. He could not imagine who this fellow was, but he might easily be a man who decided, in his intoxicated state, that he ought to fight a duel with the Admiral or some such nonsense. He had known it happen before. Wentworth decided to play along.

"Yes, I am Admiral Baldwin. And who might I have the pleasure of speaking with?"

"Ah!" said Mr. Elliot with a tipsy giggle. "I shall not tell you. What have you to say to that?"

"Very little," said Wentworth. "I shall leave you to enjoy your anonymity."

The man giggled again. "For once we are all masked, not just the Elliots of Kellynch Hall!"

Wentworth began to be amused. "The Elliots always wear masks, do they?"

"But of course they do! Consider Sir Walter. He is giving this ball just as if he had plenty of money, but all the county knows he is very nearly ruined."

Wentworth smiled a little at the accuracy of this.

"And Miss Elliot—she seems so very elegant and polite, but she hides a heart full of disdain for men. And the youngest Elliot daughter, now Mrs. Musgrove—so very full of the Elliot pride! With her pretensions to noble birth and the best society—it is easy to see through her. Miss Anne is not so transparent, but then of course she is much cleverer than Mary."

Wentworth was startled, though he did not show it. "What about Miss Anne?"

"Oh, surely you've heard her reputation." The tone in the man's voice was unmistakably salacious.

Wentworth was a hair's breadth away from challenging the man to a duel, but remembered in time that he was supposed to be Baldwin. If he kept up the charade, he might hear more.

"No, as it happens. I have not heard. Pray, tell me."

"Oh, if you have not heard, I'm not one to tell tales." The man tried to put a finger to his lips, but in his apparently intoxicated state he missed his mark and ended up pointing at his chin.

"But I must know! My friend Wentworth is much attached to her. I ought to warn him there is sufficient reason."

"No doubt she appears to return his affection. Her languishing looks appear very artless, do they not? But she was born to act upon a stage! She has smiled in that way at more men than ... but enough. Perhaps she has done with that way of life. Lady Worsley settled down with some poor fellow in the end, did she not?" The man looked around the terrace and gave a little start. "By Jove, there she is! Remember, not a word!" He gave a bow that nearly unbalanced him, and tottered off toward the house. There was no sign of Anne at all on the terrace.

Wentworth felt a hatred for the man burning within him. Anne, a flirt, or worse? Ridiculous! Anyone could see that she was honest and loyal. A thousand little incidents proved it. The man had an overactive imagination. There couldn't possibly be any gossip about Anne—it was the fevered imagination of a drunk. His mind's eye conjured up picture after picture from his memory: Anne looking up at him when he had put the comb into her hair at the seashore, Anne taking pains to draw Benwick into conversation, and Anne playing the piano so the others could dance. One only had to look at her to know she was kind and good. She was not a flirt—he had met enough of those to identify them easily.

She was born for the stage, the man had said. Perhaps she was feigning virtue and doing it very well. No, impossible. She was too transparently good. The fellow was drunk and imagining things, that was all there was to it. He sighed and made a conscious attempt to think of it no more. He might laugh at this conversation someday, but it would be a long time. And he was very sure he would never tell Anne. If this was the sort of society she was subjected to, he could do nothing better than marry her and take her away from it.

≈

At eleven o'clock, Borlock, in a mask and domino, approached Mrs. Clay, dutifully standing beside the palm in the hall. She smiled, nervously, he thought, and he bowed and kissed her hand.

"I was not certain you would meet me," he said, retaining her hand as he led her toward the ballroom.

"But how could I not?" she answered. "A mysterious and unknown admirer is too intriguing!" She tittered in a way that was meant to be flirtatious. Borlock thought how much more attractive she was when she was not trying to behave like a girl just out of the schoolroom.

"That was my hope," he confessed. "I was afraid you would not dance with me if you knew who I was—I am not anyone of note."

She cast a sideways glance at him, trying to determine if he was indeed Mr. Elliot. She thought not, but she could not be sure. The domino he was wearing had no hood, and she thought Mr. Elliot's brown hair was a shade darker than this man's.

"I am sure that I could not bear to refuse someone with such an ardent attachment to me."

Borlock sighed. "I wish that might be so, madam."

They took their places in the long set, and waited for their turn to begin. There was something familiar about the man—Penelope was sure of it. Something in the way he moved or the way he spoke ... she could not place it.

"The flowers in the ballroom are lovely, are they not?" she said. If the man would talk more, she might be able to recognize his voice.

"I confess I had not noticed them," he said.

"You must have been very preoccupied."

"By the hope of dancing with one I have long admired? Of course."

She blushed. "But now you do see them, what do you think of them?"

He shook his head. "I have not leisure to look at them now. I will view them when I have finished dancing with you."

The words might have sounded fulsome to her at another time, but in these romantic circumstances they conveyed nothing but sincere admiration. There was no more time for banter. The music for the dance began, and she must pay attention to the steps—she would not want to spoil this dance for the man she had unknowingly captivated.

~

While Borlock was leading Penelope to the ballroom, Wentworth, who had been keeping an eye on Anne all evening, approached her. It was the last dance before the supper, and he was determined to claim her for the next hour or more.

"May I have the honor of the next, Miss Elliot?" he said.

"How do you know I am Miss Elliot?"

"Come now," he said with an mischievous grin. "You cannot possibly think I would forget that comb in your hair, do you?"

"No," she said with an answering smile, "no more than I would."

She gave him her hand and he led her to the set. Her dancing, though not spectacular, was unexceptional, and even elegant. Neither of them attracted the admiring gaze of fellow dancers or those who watched from the sides of the room, but Anne and Wentworth were perfectly satisfied with their dance. Neither could imagine a more blissful state of existence than to be dancing together.

When the last strains of "Ramsgate Assembly" had died away and the couples began to drift toward the supper room, Wentworth took Anne's hand.

"Come with me," he said impulsively, and led her toward the French door leading out to the terrace. There were few guests there, and those that remained were moving toward the house in anticipation of the supper. The moon had risen, and the stone balustrades were still faintly warm from the heat of the day. Anne leaned against one of them, looking out toward the lake. The fragrance of the roses in the formal garden perfumed the air. Wentworth took in the scene and found it hard to imagine a more perfect setting for a declaration of love. He had not planned to speak tonight, but there would not be another moment like this one, and he could not waste it.

"Anne."

He had never called her that before. His use of her Christian name, as well as the tone in which he said it, compelled her to turn toward him. He was taking off his mask, and smiling at her in a way that set her heart beating wildly.

"Let me see your face," he said.

Anne untied the strings of her mask with trembling fingers, and the silk slipped from her hand and fell to the ground.

Wentworth knelt down to pick it up. He looked up at her, and instead of standing again, remained where he was.

"My dearest Anne, you cannot be in any doubt of my attachment to you. I cannot live any longer without declaring my love. Will you do me the honor of becoming my wife?"

"I will." Anne's voice was only a whisper, but it was enough. The terrace was completely deserted and only the moon saw Wentworth rise and embrace his beloved and bestow on her a tender kiss. They stood there for a few minutes, enraptured by the thoughts of each other's love.

"The supper," Anne murmured eventually. "We ought to go in. My father will wonder where I am."

"I suppose you are right. I will speak to him when the ball is finished."

While Wentworth and Anne had been exchanging words of love, Penelope Clay was going into the supper room alone. She had assumed her masked admirer would take her in to supper, and she was hoping that in closer proximity she would obtain a better view of his face. She might have a better chance of identifying him if it were so. But when the dance was finished, her partner said, "Forgive me, I must leave you now."

"Must you?" Penelope asked. The man was an accomplished dancer, and although they had not spoken much, his appreciative gaze had been fixed on her face for much of the dance. She thought there was something familiar about him, but she could not determine what it was. After the supper there was to be an unmasking, and Penelope was eager to see what he looked like beyond the brown hair and blue eyes she could already see. She was almost certain that the man was not Mr. Elliot.

"Alas, I must. It would be most agreeable to join you for supper, but there are reasons I may not. I must thank you, madam, for giving me my heart's desire: a dance with you. I shall always remember it. Farewell!" He raised her hand to his lips, kissed it, and disappeared into the crowd.

She stood there looking and feeling bereft for a moment. Well, she would not be the only one who was not escorted to dinner by a partner. She joined the throng heading in to the feast.

Chapter Ten

The last of the ball-goers did not leave until four o'clock in the morning, and although some of the party had slipped off to bed much earlier (including Admiral Croft and Captain Benwick), Captain Wentworth needed to wait until the last carriage departed before asking Sir Walter if he could speak to him privately in the library.

Sir Walter was not quite as enthusiastic over the proposed engagement as Wentworth expected him to be. As much as Sir Walter privately admired the Navy, he was well aware that some of his fellow members of the peerage, like Sir Basil Morley, would think it a poor match. Wentworth might have made a fortune in the war, but he did not come from a distinguished family. Sir Walter spoke at great length to the suitor, trying to impress upon him the great honor it would be to wed an Elliot of Kellynch Hall. Wentworth let him talk, occasionally putting in a compliment about the estate and the dignity of the family. In the end, Sir Walter gave his blessing to the union, and Wentworth was free to tell Anne, waiting in the morning room, that there were no impediments to their marriage.

"We must sleep now," said Wentworth when he had given Anne the news and stolen another kiss. "Your father made me promise to urge you to retire immediately—something about lines forming around the eyes from lack of sleep."

They left the room together and met Elizabeth in the hall.

"Wish us joy, Sister," he said, pausing to shake her hand enthusiastically, and leaving her standing there looking after them as they ascended the stairs to their bedrooms.

Anne did not wake up until nearly noon. It took her a moment to remember why her heart was so light. Then it came to her: Captain Wentworth had declared his love and asked for her hand. That such a man—brave, honorable, and handsome—had become attached to her was still astonishing. To love Anne Elliot, when he might have had any of the other young ladies! Louisa, for example, would have been eager to accept an offer from him.

Louisa—surely it would not be difficult to find a husband for Louisa. Any officer of the navy would probably be acceptable to her. And Henrietta—well, no worry about her. She should marry Mr. Hayter as soon as possible. Anne smiled as she realized that she was matchmaking. Well, why not? She wished everyone to be as happy as she was. Who else needed a husband?

There was Mrs. Clay. If only there were a nice, prosperous farmer who would take an interest in her, somewhere far from Kellynch! That would be very suitable. And then Elizabeth. She had seen the stricken and somewhat jealous look in Elizabeth's eyes last night for just a moment before she had hidden it behind a mask of smiles. Another mask.

Poor Elizabeth. Anne had seen her transformed from a hopeful girl into a disappointed young lady and then to a rather bitter spinster. It was pride, Anne thought, that had turned her disappointment to anger, and it was pride that kept her bitter. Elizabeth had resolved not to be the poor young lady whose love was unrequited—better to be the witty, beautiful, and unattainable Miss Elliot of Kellynch Hall. If a baronet had appeared and was willing to marry her, Anne was quite sure Elizabeth would say yes, but she would not be tempted by anything less.

~

Lady Russell came in the afternoon to talk over the ball with Anne. She was curious to hear all the details, for although she had been invited, she had not attended the event. She did not dance and had felt little desire to don a mask herself or to try to discover any of her acquaintance among the other masked and cloaked guests.

She discovered most of the house's inmates finishing a cold nuncheon in the dining room. Sir Walter was not there, but the naval officers were, along with Elizabeth and Anne, and all joined in inviting her to sit with them. Captain Wentworth immediately apprised Lady Russell of his great happiness in Anne's acceptance of his proposals, and Lady Russell said everything that was proper.

"And for the rest," Lady Russell said, "how did it all go off? Were the musicians as good as they were reported to be?"

"They were very good," said Elizabeth. "Many people remarked on it."

"Yes, the dancing was very good," said Wentworth. "Although I must say there was one dance I particularly enjoyed." He smiled at Anne, who blushed very prettily.

"Aye," said Baldwin, who felt that he could not endure any more mawkish sentimentality. "I enjoyed the dancing too." He glanced up to see Elizabeth looking at him, and he hastened to add, "except for one dance."

"How strange," Elizabeth said. "I, too, had only one dance that I did not enjoy. Skill in dancing alone does not make an enjoyable partner." She rose. "I must speak to the housekeeper. I beg you will excuse me." She left the room with as much self-possession as any queen.

"I wish I might have seen her dance," said Lady Russell. "She is so very graceful; she always reminds me of a swan."

"A swan with claws," muttered Baldwin.

"I wonder that you detect claws in women that everyone else sees as very mild mannered," said Wentworth. He had glimpsed a troubled look on Anne's face, and was annoyed with Baldwin for causing it. "Is it only the ladies you cannot charm who vex you? Perhaps it is a case of sour grapes."

Baldwin became rather red in the face, but said calmly enough, "Ah, well, that's a matter of opinion isn't it? I shall leave you to your speculations, gentlemen. Ladies." He bowed briefly and left the room.

Anne looked at Wentworth. "Is he angry?"

"Cross, more like. He cannot bear to look foolish. I would like to see him in love; it would humble him."

"So it would," said Benwick, "but only if she was the right kind of woman—someone who could match him in temperament and wit. A forceful personality, but not vulgar."

"Someone like Elizabeth, you mean," said Anne.

"Aye, she would do," said Croft. 'Tis a pity they antagonize one another so, because he is exactly the kind of man *she* needs—intelligent and strong enough not to let her run roughshod over him or anyone else. But not a tyrant; she needs someone with a heart. I think her compassion may have gone a little dormant, and a man who can be kind would awaken it."

"For my part, I think his need of a spouse is more urgent," said Wentworth. "Miss Elliot is exactly what he needs—someone to challenge him when he is ridiculous, someone witty to keep him from being bored, and someone who isn't cowed by him."

"They both need those things," said Lady Russell. "I daresay her antagonism to him is only because she thinks he despises her. If she thought he loved her, she would soon abandon the armor that is covering her heart."

"I'll warrant the case is the same with him," said Benwick. "I think if he had come to Kellynch and found a civil, cheerful lady, he probably would have fallen in love with her without much delay. He liked her well enough before we went back to sea two years ago; it was only that he had persuaded himself that he must be undistracted in his duty to the crown."

"And he did render good service to the Crown," said Croft. "Now, however, it is time for him to marry."

"I agree," said Lady Russell. "And it is past time for Elizabeth. They are too stubborn, too proud, to back down of their own accord. They will have to be tricked into it."

If Lady Russell had wanted to shock the room, she could not have said anything better. Those around the table froze in astonishment.

"Tricked?" repeated Anne faintly.

"I have, in my time, orchestrated any number of matches," Lady Russell said. "I have never yet encountered a couple so determined to hate each other, but I do not think it will prove impossible to match them."

"Well," said Croft, smiling. "I cannot say that I have ever played matchmaker, but I have studied battle tactics for some years, and even dabbled in espionage. I daresay that experience might stand me in good stead for such a mission as this. I have reason to think," he added, thinking of her words to him the evening before, "that Miss Elliot was not at all indifferent to him at one time."

"It is settled, then," said Lady Russell majestically. "I think if we work together, we may have a wedding before long. If you, gentlemen, will undertake to convince Admiral Baldwin of Miss Elliot's affection, then Anne and I will convince Miss Elliot of his."

Penelope Clay had remained in the ballroom until the very end of the dancing, hoping—without much conviction—for the return of her anonymous admirer. He had never reappeared. She now did her best to be indifferent to the whole episode. It had been a charming little interlude, but there was no future in it. If the gentleman had meant to woo her, he would have stayed to be unmasked, for certainly she had been as encouraging as she could without behaving like a forward woman. Undoubtedly he had no real intentions. He might even be already married—that was a lowering thought!

What was really disturbing was that Sir Walter had paid her no attention that evening. In fact, he had hardly noticed her since the officers had arrived weeks ago. Moreover, the closest she had gotten to attention from Mr. Elliot since his arrival had been the compliments of his valet.

With these discouraging contemplations running through her head, she prepared for bed, noticing, to her chagrin, that her bracelet had gone missing. To be sure, the clasp had long needed mending, but she had thought it secure for at least one evening of dancing. No doubt a servant had found it and kept it.

She slept poorly, and when she awoke she did not feel equal to meeting anyone in the house. She stayed in her room until the afternoon and rang for a tray of food to be brought up to her.

"This letter came with the post for you, madam," said the maid when she brought the tray, nodding at a neatly folded and sealed missive with "Mrs. Clay" written on it sitting on the tray beside the plate. Penelope waited until the tray had been set down and the maid dismissed before she opened it and read.

"The One who had the Pleasure of Dancing with you last night Begs Leave to tell you he has much Joy in the remembrance of it. He wishes to say also that he spied a Bracelet on the floor which he thinks may belong to you. It is made of Amber Beads, and is small, such as would fit a delicate Wrist like yours. It is now in the Possession of the writer. If the Bracelet is your property, you may leave a Missive for the writer at the folly. There is a Loose Stone in the steps at the front of it, and a Note inserted into the crack there will be Safely Hidden. If it is not your Bracelet, he is sorry to have troubled you. He is only happy to have had to opportunity to thank you again for the Dance."

This note was also unsigned.

In spite of the good sense she had possessed last night which had instructed her not to be elated at the attentions of this man, she was cheered. There was no reason to believe that this admirer could provide what she needed for the future; that is, a wealthy husband. However, she could not fail to be moved by the man's gratitude for the dance. How long had it been since anyone was grateful to her? The Elliots made use of her all the time, and she sacrificed her own desires and wishes to make sure they were happy, but she was rarely thanked beyond a cursory polite acknowledgement. The gratitude this man expressed was like water to her parched spirit. And no woman could be less than flattered that he thought her wrist delicate. She *did* have delicate wrists, in her opinion, but she had not expected him to notice.

Who could he be? This was the most puzzling thing. She had thought that he must be an inmate of the house, for otherwise he would not have known about the palm. And, too, the previous note had been put into her bedroom. Now, however, a note had come with the mail, and the place of meeting, or at least communication, he referred to was outside the house. Perhaps the man did not reside in the house after all, but had used an acquaintance who did to deliver the first note. It was all very puzzling.

She looked again at the note for any more indications of the man's identity. Whoever the gentleman was, he had education and breeding, of that she was certain. She was half-tempted to ask her father if he knew of anyone around Kellynch who might fit that description. If Sir Walter's man of business had not been her father, she might have suspected him! But there might be another man, unknown to her, in a similar position. It would not answer, however; a man like that would have no wealth to speak of, and could not rise in society.

At all events, the letter needed a response. She obtained a piece of paper from her writing desk and composed a note. There should be no personal information, she knew. The note was unlikely to be found by anyone else, but if it were, it must not be traced to her.

"Sir, the Item you have found is indeed mine, and I must Thank You for informing me. May I not know to whom I am Beholden? I will look into the place you mentioned every Afternoon for further information." Penelope hesitated and then wrote, "The Event to which you Allude also gave much Pleasure to the writer, and you are Thanked most heartily for the Occasion."

Penelope read it over and was satisfied. There was nothing written there that would give her away, even if the note was found by another. She glanced at the clock. It was nearly two; She would walk to the folly now.

A note arrived from Charles Musgrove that evening, inviting the Kellynch party to join them for a picnic in two day's time.

"Mary is very low, you see," Charles wrote. "After all, the excitement of the ball is over. Louisa and Henrietta are also eager to see the inmates of Kellynch again. Please do come. The boys are clamoring to meet the admirals and captains, and I will answer for it that they will be kept in check."

There is always a little dullness when the excitement of a ball is over—unless one has had the good fortune to get engaged during it—and the invitation fell on willing ears. Lady Russell, who had stayed to dine, declared her intention of coming to the picnic, too. "I have not been to Uppercross yet this summer," she said to Captain Benwick, "and the gardens are lovely. And," she said, lowering her voice, "if I mistake not, we may use this picnic to advance our plans."

After dinner, when the gentlemen rejoined the ladies in the drawing room, Admiral Baldwin found himself watching Elizabeth talk to Mrs. Clay from across the room. The memory of last night's dance came back to him—the smile on her face, the flush of pleasure on her cheeks, the sparkle in her eyes. Before he knew it, he was wishing that someone would suggest that they dance now, and that he could find a way to dance with her again. He remembered, with a twinge of discomfort, the way her smile had faded when he had told her she had a reputation for shrewishness, and wished he might unsay the words.

Fool! he said to himself, alarmed by the turn his thoughts had taken. *Look at her sitting there so haughtily—thinks herself above everyone else! No doubt she believes that just because a man tells her she is light on her feet, he is ready to fall down and worship the ground she walks on. I was quite right to give her a set-down.*

His gaze shifted to Wentworth, sitting beside Anne. They were speaking in low voices to each other, but Baldwin caught the look Anne gave her betrothed and for one moment he wished Miss Elliot would look like that at him.

Good heavens! he told himself. *What madness has seized me? I desire nothing less than to be like Wentworth, who has gone from being a fighting man to being a dreamy idiot.* His eyes travelled back to Miss Elliot, determined to find more flaws in her, but he was distracted by the way one little curl had escaped its fellows and was resting on her cheek.

He got up from his chair and moved to sit beside Croft, who looked like he was beginning to nod off, and spoke to him relentlessly about the new laws restricting the importation of food until he could excuse himself and go to bed.

Chapter Eleven

All the next morning, Penelope found it hard to settle to anything. She sat with Elizabeth and worked at her embroidery, but her eyes kept drifting over to the clock. Never had a morning seemed to last so long. She had written in her note to the unknown admirer that she would come to the folly every afternoon, and she was impatient to see if there was any reply. She chided herself repeatedly for making so much of it all, but she could not stop herself from wondering. She forced herself to wait until two o'clock, and then she slipped out of the house while Elizabeth was writing a letter.

Penelope tried not to hurry as she walked up to the folly; if she was seen by anyone it must appear that she was merely taking the air a little. She was thankful that the intense heat earlier in the week had subsided. The day was, in fact, cloudy, and she wondered if there would be rain tomorrow. She hoped not: a picnic at Uppercross sounded delightful. Furthermore, she really must do something to get closer to Mr. Elliot. She had neglected cultivating him—in fact, the only progress she felt she had made was in gaining the goodwill of Borlock. To be sure, that was worth something. An intelligent and cultured valet who had the ear of his employer and was very nearly a friend to him was a powerful ally. From the little conversation she had had with him, it seemed that Borlock might be in favor of her wedding Mr. Elliot. He had certainly been most complimentary to her.

Poor Borlock, she thought again. *He might have made such a worthy gentleman.* She reached the folly at this point in her musings, and after a pause to survey the land around her and make sure there was no one nearby, she bent down to the crack next to the loose stone in the folly steps. There was something there! Her hands trembled a little as she took the folded paper out of its hiding place and unfolded it.

"I will be Most Pleased to restore your Property to you," it read. "I dare not trust any Messengers. Meet me tomorrow at the folly at Two o'clock."

Two o'clock? But we will all be at the picnic! thought Penelope. Here was further proof that the man was not an inmate of Kellynch: anyone living in the house would know about the picnic.

"Meet me tomorrow..." It seemed that he would come in person, but she would not be there. Well, she could leave a note explaining her absence. She imagined the man—the man who admired her so intensely—standing at the folly, looking in vain for her to come, and then finding only her note. It made quite a depressing picture.

Borlock had also slipped out of the house, with only his master aware of his mission. His destination was the Golden Eagle, where another bottle of French brandy waited for him to collect it. It was rather a long walk; the place was near the village of Winthrop. He cut across fields instead of going by the road, the better to keep his journey a secret, but when he neared Winthrop, his path joined with the road. It was not a busy thoroughfare; in fact, there was but one man on it, holding a horse and looking at the ground. The man called out to him when he saw him approach.

"I am sorry to trouble you, but can you help me for a moment?"

"What is it?" Borlock asked as he drew near.

"My horse threw a shoe and I cannot find it." He straightened up and Borlock recognized him: the cousin of the Musgroves, Mr. Hayter.

He, in turn, looked curiously at Borlock. "But surely I know you, do I not?"

Borlock bowed. "I am Mr. William Elliot's valet, sir."

"Of course. I remember you from our trip to Lyme. Borlock, isn't it?"

"Yes, sir. And certainly I will help you look."

The two men scanned the ground around them for the missing shoe; it was Borlock who found it lying in the tall grass at the side of the road.

"Thank you," said Hayter, taking it from him. "The black-smith will be pleased not to have to forge another." Instead of re-mounting his horse, he led him down the road toward the village.

"He doesn't go well with one hoof unshod," he explained, and then continued conversationally, "You are a long way from Kellynch. You have business in Winthrop?"

"I have a commission from my master," said Borlock, bowing slightly.

"I see," said Hayter. A good valet would not disclose his master's affairs, and Hayter felt no surprise that there was not more explanation. They walked on in silence for a little while. There was a long stone wall along one side of the road in a state of some disrepair, and before long they came to a gate through which could be seen the ruins of a once-fine house.

"What place is that?" asked Borlock. It reminded him a little of the Squire's house when he was young.

"That is the old manor house. There was a fire a century or so ago, and it was left to go to ruin. It was called Fortuna House, which I have always thought a little ironic."

"*Stet Fortuna Domus*, eh?" Borlock, chuckled a little as he thought of his old school's motto, which meant 'Let the fortune of the house stand."

"Yes," said Hayter, looking again at his companion. "Harrow man, are you?"

"As you say."

There was silence for another long moment as Hayter wondered how to politely ask why the man was a valet when he had gone to one of the finest public schools in England.

Borlock could see the young man struggling. "Reversals of fortune, as you might say, have brought me to my present employment."

"Ah. I am sorry to hear it. The fortune of a house—or of a man—does not always stand, in spite of school mottos."

"*Faber est quisque fortunae suae,*, as my Latin master used to say," said Borlock, and then grimaced. Why did these things keep coming into his head?

"Each man is the maker of his own fortune," translated Hayter. "I suppose that is true, in some respects, but it is not always so. In your case, I daresay, there was some other cause for your difficulties."

Hayter spoke as to an equal, which both surprised and gratified Borlock. At least, that was the reason, he told himself later, that he responded as he did to Hayter's words. He sighed and said, "I thank you for your kindly thoughts, but I fear the proverb is apt in my case."

"Then I am even more sorry to hear it. Regret is a loathsome burden to carry."

Regret. It was a notion that had not often presented itself to Borlock. He had been slightly rueful when he was found out, but he could not remember feeling much real remorse. That was odd, now that he thought of it.

"Would there have been more regret at the time of transgression," he said. "There is a time when regret comes too late."

Hayter looked at him keenly. "It is interesting you should say so—I was just speaking to a parishioner about that an hour ago."

Borlock looked at him in surprise. "You are a parson?"

"A curate—at present in Aldgate, not far from here, but hoping to be taken on in Uppercross very soon."

"There are no distinctions in dress for clergy anymore," said Borlock, to excuse his ignorance. "And your profession was never mentioned in my presence."

Hayter waved away any offence. "The more surprising thing would have been if you were aware of my being in orders. But you were speaking of regret coming too late."

Borlock shook his head. "I beg your pardon—I ought not to have burdened you with my problems. Those of your own flock are no doubt enough to fill your time."

Hayter smiled. "Well, not exactly. Only now and then some find relief in explaining their misdeeds to me—as if I could grant them forgiveness instead of counsel. Still, there is something to be said for a man confessing his wrongdoing instead of continuing to cover his sin."

His father's voice once again sounded in Borlock's mind: *He that covereth his sins shall not prosper: but whoso confesseth and forsaketh them shall have mercy.* He could not explain why, but it terrified him. Suddenly he saw his life now for what it was: nothing but dishonesty and covering up sin—both his own and his master's. His actions that day passed under review: the duplicitous note he had left for Mrs. Clay, the conversation with Wentworth's servant which had been full of spurious friendship and goodwill, and even this journey now which Hayter presumed to be innocent but was actually in pursuit of something illegal.

The thought darted through his brain that he ought to forsake it all and somehow find mercy—leave Mr. Elliot's employ and begin a new life somewhere else. Even as he pondered this, he recognized the impossibility of it. What honest work could he do? Mr. Elliot would not give him a reference, and of course, no previous employer would, either. He would not be able to find work in anything but the most menial of positions.

"I think we part ways here," said Hayter, and Borlock became aware that they had entered the village of Winthrop and were, in fact, in front of the blacksmith's. "Thank you again for your help. And for your conversation."

"Not at all, sir. I bid you good day," Borlock said, and thrusting all disturbing thoughts from his mind, went on to the Golden Eagle to get the brandy.

That afternoon, Baldwin played a game of billiards with Wentworth. He found it very tedious, as Wentworth continually talked of his plans for buying an estate, his determination to order a new carriage without delay, and even possible names for his first-born son. Baldwin had little trouble emerging from the contest victorious over his starry-eyed friend. He excused himself from playing another game and crept into the library for a little peace. He took his book off the shelf and sat down in his usual chair. He had just gotten absorbed in the story when he heard the library door open.

"Yes, it's empty," said Croft's voice.

Baldwin was just about to let his presence be known when he heard Benwick's voice say, "I suppose it is the one place in the house where we are safe from either Miss Elliot or Baldwin over-hearing us." That stayed his mouth. It was so unlike his friends to be secretive, and to mention both Elizabeth and himself! He stayed quietly where he was, irresolute.

"All right, now, Wentworth," said Croft. "What was it you were saying about Miss Elliot? It *sounded* like you said that she is in love with Baldwin, but that could not be right."

"Yes, that is exactly what I said. Miss Elliot has lost her heart to our friend."

Baldwin became immobile.

"It seems impossible," said Benwick. "She appears to hate him."

Impossible! echoed Baldwin in his own mind.

"But it is true. She is hopelessly in love with him."

"How can you possibly know that?" said Benwick. "She does not behave like any woman in love I have ever seen."

"Ah," said Wentworth, "but she acts differently when she is alone with Anne. Just yesterday, Anne found her writing what she thought was a letter, but when she came nearer, she found that it said nothing but 'Admiral and Mrs. Baldwin,' 'Mrs. Elizabeth Baldwin,' and even 'my dear Thomas.'"

Baldwin almost dropped his book at that. *Ridiculous. She would do no such thing! They must be joking!* But even as the words floated through his mind, he was aware that Benwick was not the sort of man to make jests like that. Since Benwick's bereavement, he was such a sober fellow. And Croft, too! He had never been known for pranks or hoaxes. Moreover, they were talking in such serious tones!

"Someone should tell him," said Benwick. "Baldwin should be informed. For if he cannot love her, at least he could stop tormenting her with cruel words."

Cruel words? Baldwin winced a little.

"Very true," said Wentworth. "But do you think he *would* stop? For my part, I doubt it. He would probably think it all very comical and torment the poor lady all the more. He is not a brutal man, but he does pride himself a little too much on his wit. He might keep on, not thinking how much he was hurting her. Certainly he has little sensibility himself, and cannot understand it in others."

"That would be a very bad," said Croft gravely. "The lady is not only beautiful, but refined and intelligent ... not that falling in love with Baldwin was the brightest thing she ever did."

"Yes," said Wentworth. "Anne is worried for her state of mind. She is well-nigh distracted—wanting to be near him and also trying to hide her affection for him from everyone."

"Poor woman," said Croft, "to be charmed by him before he went to sea and then to have him come back and despise her! For there is no doubt they were taken with each other in London."

There were murmurs of agreement from the other men.

"But why has he changed?" asked Wentworth. "Anne and I have wondered about it together."

"I know what it is." Croft lowered his voice so that Baldwin had to strain to hear. "He was afraid to ask her before he went to sea and is now too proud to admit that he likes her after all."

"That's it," said Benwick. "What else could it be? He has made such a noise about never marrying that he will not climb down and admit his affection for her. A pity—she is exactly the sort of lady to make him a wife."

"And he is a good man, whatever his faults," said Wentworth. "I would welcome him as a brother-in-law. He might be unworthy of Miss Elliot, but then, I am not worthy of her sister, either."

"Well, gentlemen," said Croft with a sigh. "I fear there is nothing we can do. The poor woman will likely pine away with unrequited love. We must be as kind to her as we can—I would dread her to think that because one man scorns her, she is seen as defective by us all."

"Agreed," said Benwick. "And I suppose we ought to leave the library before someone comes in search of us. I should loathe trying to explain what we are all doing in here!"

"Very true," said Wentworth. "We ought to go and dress for dinner, anyway."

There was a sound of footsteps, then, and a door opening and closing. Baldwin was once more alone, his thoughts in a whirl.

Ridiculous! he thought. *There must be a mistake. Anne must have been teasing Wentworth.* He paused to consider that possibility. It seemed most unlikely; he had never seen much humor or foolery in her. Elizabeth was far more likely to make up a story like that to cause mischief. They had used to laugh quite a lot.

He began to pace back and forth between the rows of books. If any of the sailors who had been under his command could have seen him at that moment, they would have recognized this behavior: he was thinking hard. Alas, there was more room for pacing on the quarter deck of a ship than there was between the bookshelves of Sir Walther's library. He needed more space. He left the library and went through the house and onto the terrace.

Miss Elliot—in love with me? He resumed his pacing. *Bah! It cannot be! And yet ... why would they say such a thing if it were not so? They might be teasing me ... but that would only be if they knew I could hear them. They could not have known! And why would Wentworth drag Anne into the story if it was not true?*

He shook his head. It was unbelievable, and yet it must be! He reviewed their words again. *She writes our names together, does she? Admiral and Mrs. Baldwin ... Elizabeth Baldwin... No one could deny that the names sound well together! And they blame me for her melancholy! But they have not considered! I could not have engaged myself to her when we were in London—I had my duty! A distracted Admiral is a bad Admiral. Yes, I would have been distracted on the high seas, missing her company. And if anything had happened to her—well, that would have been more distracting still. Heaven only knows what would have happened to Benwick's command if he had known that Fanny had died while he was still commanding the ship! Fortunately, he did not find out until after he had come back to England. It was the biggest imprudence to have given his heart while he was at sea! And, as it happens, he lost her. I was quite right not to give my heart to Elizabeth: I could have lost her.*

Quick on the heals of this satisfying conclusion came another thought: *You have already lost her.* The words came to his mind with a conviction that stopped him in his tracks. *Do you think Benwick wishes he had not loved Fanny?* The question came, insistently, from somewhere deep inside him. He knew the answer immediately: Benwick could have no such wish. He had become a better man through loving Fanny and being loved by her.

And I would have been a better man, too, if I had let myself love, Baldwin admitted. His character had faults; there was no denying it. His friends had discussed his pride, for example, and they were right. He could not assert that his behavior at Kellynch had been that of a humble man.

What they said of her is true, too, he thought as he resumed his pacing. *She is beautiful—I have always acknowledged it to myself. And she is intelligent. I daresay she is the cleverest of her family. Anne is intelligent, to be sure, but she is too meek for me. Elizabeth is more spirited. But not a hoyden—no, she is unquestionably a lady in everything she does. A gentlewoman who is not cowed by anything. Except, of course, my wretched tongue!* He sighed again at the difficulties his selfishness had made for the both of them.

I must not be proud any longer, he resolved. *Happy are the men that hear their detractions and can put them to mending. And for her to love me—and love me so much, too! And rather die than give any sign of affection. Poor thing! I have been cruel indeed to her, not knowing that she thought her love was unrequited! And it is not unrequited!*

Again, he stopped pacing. *I love her, I think.* It was the first time he had ever admitted such a thing to himself, and he found that the thought did not seem strange at all. Indeed, it seemed the most natural thing in the world. *I may have loved her all the time, and yet beaten down my affection and muffled it.*

His feet began moving again. *The devil of it is that I did keep saying I would never marry. I shall be teased mercilessly, I suppose, about changing my mind. I will never hear the end of it! Dreadful thought! But I have always been renowned for my courage. If I can face a barrage of enemy cannon fire, I can endure teasing in the path of duty. For it is my duty! What would happen if all men refused to marry? The world's population would all come to an end in one generation. It is my duty to the world, and not only to Elizabeth.*

This logic was highly satisfactory to Baldwin, for it seemed completely reasonable. *Furthermore, I can always say that when I vowed that I would die a bachelor, what I meant was that, being in the Navy, I did not think I would live long enough to get married!*

It was at this moment that footsteps behind him made him turn around to see Elizabeth coming out onto the terrace. Her beauty, now that he really let himself look at her, took his breath away.

"I am sent to bid you come in to dinner," she said shortly, and turned to go.

He assumed his most appreciative expression, and bowed slightly. "I am grateful, Miss Elliot, for the trouble you took to do so."

She turned back. His tone of voice was different than it usually was. She rather expected him to make a joke out of it, but he said nothing more.

"I took no more trouble to earn those thanks than you took trouble to thank me. I would not have come if it were a trouble to me."

"So you were glad to come and get me, were you?" Again, he had a strange sort of smile on his face, almost as if he knew a secret. She wondered if he was somehow mocking her.

"Oh, yes," she said sarcastically. "I was as delighted as you are when you stub your toe."

His reaction to this sally was unusual—he only chuckled, as if she had made a witty remark. It crossed her mind that he might have been in the sun too long. At any rate, she wasn't going to stand here having this ridiculous conversation any longer.

"I see you have no appetite for dinner, sir," she said. "I will leave you to yourself, then." And with the briefest of curtsies, she went back into the house.

So it is true! thought Baldwin. *Now that I know what is in her heart, I can see the marks of love in her. Even her words just now— they have a double meaning. When she said, "I took no more trouble to earn those thanks than you took trouble to thank me. I would not have come if it were a trouble to me' that's as much as to say, "Any thing I do for you is as easy as saying 'thank you.'" She may have determined never to let me know of her love, but she will not be to hide it forever!*

Chapter Twelve

Penelope had spent half the night wondering what she ought to do. Should she go to the picnic and work on Mr. Elliot? Or should she stay at Kellynch and meet the mysterious man at the folly?

The folly! she said to herself, as she turned her pillow again, as if a lumpy pillow was responsible for her failure to sleep. *Aptly named: it is folly for me to meet this man. Impossible that he should be an appropriate suitor, else why would he need to disguise himself? If he cannot woo me openly, he must not be eligible, and there is certainly no reason for me to be wasting my time with him. Mr. Elliot, on the other hand, is very eligible, and I had much better spend my time talking with him.* The decision made, she nestled into her pillow and closed her eyes.

Ah, but does Mr. Elliot think you are eligible? Her mind refused to consider her decision final, and her eyes opened again. *What are the chances he will marry you? They say one in the hand is worth two in the bush—a very vulgar saying, but an admirer is an admirer, even if he is a—a highwayman, or something!*

A highwayman! That gave her thoughts a new turn. She imagined a nobleman, accused of a crime he had not committed, who had taken to highway robbery in order to survive. He would be an honorable highwayman, she decided, one who never killed anyone but only robbed those who could well spare it. She shook her head at the fancy, but she could not quite dislodge it—it would explain so much.

By morning she knew that she would meet the man at the folly. She pleaded a headache when the carriage was brought around for the ladies and the men were mounting their horses. It was not lost on her that Elizabeth did not seem to care much that she was unwell, or that her company would be missed. From her bedroom window she could see the party going down the long drive toward Uppercross.

Uppercross was a manor in the old fashion, but they did provide a good table. The senior Musgroves—having been talked into it by their offspring—had put tables out under the trees and loaded them with cold meats, salads, and pigeon pies, and after that there was a solid whipt syllabub and queen currant cakes The guests ate their fill and then wandered about the gardens in pairs or groups.

The gardens were as old as the house, and they were extensive. Elizabeth joined Admiral Croft, Lady Russell, Anne, Wentworth and Benwick in exploring the low-walled garden. Wentworth was deep in a discussion with Croft about someone in Gibraltar, and Anne talked to Lady Russell about wedding clothes. For some time Elizabeth and Benwick walked side by side in silence, and then Benwick spoke.

"Look, Miss Elliot, there is a merlin." He pointed across the garden toward a field that could be seen over the garden wall.

"I beg your pardon?" Elizabeth had no idea what he was pointing at.

"A bird, Miss Elliot, a merlin. I have not seen one in some time."

"I see," said Elizabeth civilly. "You are fond of birds?"

Benwick chuckled. "I don't know that I could say that I am

fond of them, but I do find them interesting. I used to hunt for birds' nests when I was a little lad. That was in Norfolk."

"And how do you like the birds in Somerset? Do they compare favorably?"

"Oh, yes. There are some here that I have never seen elsewhere. And Charles told me there is a pair of kingfishers that he frequently sees here at Uppercross. Have you ever seen them, by chance?"

Elizabeth shook her head. "I don't know. I'm afraid I have never paid much attention to birds. Perhaps you will see one today."

"I think not," said Benwick. "They stay near water, and I can see no water near the garden."

"Oh, but there is a stream nearby," said Elizabeth. "It is not far from the bottom of the garden—just on the other side of the garden wall." She turned to point out the spot. "Where the trees are. Do you see?"

"Yes, I do. Thank you, Miss Elliot. Ah, look, here comes Baldwin. No doubt he intends to join our party."

Elizabeth looked up and saw Admiral Baldwin sauntering toward them. She thought he had been looking at her more than usual that day, and she had little doubt he was brewing up some further insults to provoke her.

"Oh, heavens!" she muttered.

"Yes, Miss Elliot?" said Benwick.

"I wonder," she said, seized by a sudden inspiration, "would you escort me to the stream? I should very much like to see a kingfisher."

"Now, Miss Elliot?"

"Of course! If we delay, we might miss it!" She had no very clear idea of what she meant. She only wanted to get away before Admiral Baldwin joined them.

"As you wish," said Benwick politely, and the two of them walked down the garden toward the gate that led to an open field. They passed through the gate and onto the less cultivated grounds. The soil was a little marshy, and Elizabeth grimaced at her shoes.

"The ground is very soft," said Benwick. "Shall we not go back?"

"No, no," said Elizabeth. She was determined not to expose herself to more insults from Admiral Baldwin if she could help it.

"Look," said Benwick, "here is a bench close by the wall. We are not far from the river now. We might see a kingfisher if we sit quietly there."

"That is a very good idea." Elizabeth would not have cared if she never saw a kingfisher in the whole course of her life, but jumped at the opportunity to save her shoes and avoid Admiral Baldwin.

They sat there in silence for some minutes, and in spite of herself, Elizabeth enjoyed the shade of the wall and the sound of running water. They could not see the water from where they were—the trees blocked the view—but they could hear the babble of the water. The sound mingled with the murmur of voices in the distance.

"Oh, look, there it is!" said Benwick suddenly.

"Where, exactly?" said Elizabeth.

"Oh, he has gone into the trees." Benwick stood up and craned his neck to find the bird again. "I think he has gone into that tree right there."

"Would you not like to go closer and look? I am perfectly content here," said Elizabeth.

"Are you certain? I would not wish to leave you alone."

Elizabeth waved him off. "Go, please. I am entirely happy here, and I would not want you to neglect this opportunity."

"Thank you, Miss Elliot," he said, and quickly moved toward the trees. In a moment he was no longer visible.

Elizabeth sat peacefully there for five minutes, wondering how long Benwick would be chasing the bird. She was in no hurry for him to get back. The clouds of the early morning had cleared, and the sun was shining; it made the shade she was sitting in very welcome.

The voices were closer now, female voices. She was thankful she was unseen on the other side of the wall, and she sat, careful to make no noise, until they should pass. The wall was not high, and if she stood, she would certainly be seen. Gradually the words that the women's voices were saying could be understand as the footsteps drew nearer.

"No, truly, Lady Russell, she would never consent."

"But are you sure, Anne, that Admiral Baldwin loves Elizabeth so entirely?"

"That is what Captain Wentworth and Admiral Croft say."

"And they asked you to tell her so?"

"Oh, yes, for they were certain that if I but spoke to her, all would be well. But I advised them that if they loved their friend, they should tell him to conquer his affection and never speak of it to her."

"But why?" Lady Russell sounded puzzled. "Is he underserving of a woman like Elizabeth?"

"Oh, no! He deserves anything that can be given to a man. The things Captain Wentworth has told me about him assure me that he is well worthy of any good woman. But nature never framed a woman's heart of prouder stuff than that of Elizabeth. You know as well as I do, Lady Russell, she thinks of herself so highly that she cannot love another."

"I think perhaps you are right," said Lady Russell. "Self-endeared is, I think, the term I would use. Truly, she is a byword for pride and arrogance in the neighborhood. Upholding family dignity is one thing, but she has made a kind of religion out of it. And that being the case, if she knew he loved her, she might well tease him and make sport of him."

"Very true," said Anne. "Her pride turns all his good points to bad. But who dare tell her so? I cannot. She would not take any heed of any advice of mine."

"No," said Lady Russell, with a pensive sigh. "Nor mine. I

suppose it is better for Admiral Baldwin to be like a fire that is covered for the night—burn up inwardly with no outward show. It would be so humiliating to be openly scorned and mocked for his love."

"I have once or twice been tempted to speak ill of her to Captain Baldwin, to help him overcome his passion for her. Was there not a poet who said, 'an ill word may empoison liking'?"

"Oh, no, Anne," protested Lady Russell. "You must not do her such a wrong. She does have intelligence, you know, and I have sometimes thought her judgement very sound. I very much wonder if she could outright *refuse* such a man as the admiral, if he asked her. He has made such a name for himself in the Navy!"

"I know it," said Anne. "He is as worthy a man as I have ever known, excepting my own dear Fredrick." Here Elizabeth could tell that Anne smiled as she said her fiancé's Christian name, as if she were savoring the sweetness of being able refer to him thus to another. "And more than that, he is constant. Captain Wentworth tells me he has loved her long, only, fearing that she would not have him on account of her more noble birth, he went away to sea without asking. And now, of course, he pretends to despise her so that he is not tempted to throw caution to the wind and confess his love, and be rejected."

"Well, my dear," said Lady Russell, "I suppose there is no help for it. Poor Admiral Baldwin! I fear he will never master his regard for her. But we had better talk of other things. Come, we have been standing here too long. Mrs. Musgrove will send out a search party for us if we do not get back soon."

Anne agreed and the two of them walked back toward the house. When they were safely away from the place where Elizabeth still sat, rooted to the spot, Lady Russell laughed. "My dear, I have not had such amusement for an age!"

"Nor I. I am glad you saw her and Captain Benwick leave the garden. I wonder if that was his idea?"

"We must ask him. But it is fortunate the wall is low, and we could see where they were—and also when Captain Benwick left her to herself. I wonder how he contrived it?"

"I do feel a little guilty," said Anne. "I am not accustomed to deceiving anyone."

"Very likely not, my dear, and very proper. You are doing Cupid's work, and it is not often that mere mortals can assist in a match."

"Cupid has often seemed a little warlike to me; he shoots his victims with arrows," said Anne.

"Victims! What nonsense! I consider them to be more or less invalids—those who are suffering and need the help of an experienced guide. And Cupid does not always use arrows, you know; sometimes he uses traps."

Elizabeth stayed where she was until she was sure they were well away. She had received a severe shock. That Admiral Baldwin should be in love with her! And from such an early date! She could see it all now: fearing to be rejected, he had spurned her first. He had not wanted to figure as a disappointed swain, like a lovesick youth. She could easily comprehend it. His pride had got in the way.

Pride! That was what Lady Russell and Anne had censured her for—and if they were to be believed, the whole of society condemned her for it as well. *Can it be true? Does my whole acquaintance disparage me for scorn and pride? Am I truly a byword for arrogance?*

Uncomfortable recollections began to come to her mind— dismissive words about those she found vulgar, indifference to those beneath her, and all the set-downs she had given, not least to Admiral Baldwin. Suddenly she saw it all for what it was—ugly, dishonorable, and ignoble. She had been thinking that her lofty attitudes would win her the admiration of those beneath her, but she now saw that she was more likely to earn their contempt. Yes, she was stubborn—she had long known it and counted it a virtue. She now remembered her governess telling her that she was obstinate, and that she could be called pig-headed if she did not mend her ways. What a thing to remember after all these years!

Two paths seemed to lie before her; she could keep on in her old, arrogant ways, or she could change. To continue on, knowing that she was only damaging her own reputation, would be nonsensical. The only course open to her was to alter her behavior. More than that, she would need to alter her very self. The thought was terrifying. How could one change the habits of a lifetime?

"Well, stubbornness can work both ways," she said aloud. "I can be just as stubborn in letting go of my pride as I can in keeping it, can I not?" Unconsciously, she squared her shoulders. "Farewell to pride, then! No more will I make cutting remarks and think myself superior to others. I shall be as sweet and humble as Admiral Baldwin could desire."

The thought of the Admiral turned her thoughts back to his apparent love for her. *He did want to dance with me at the ball. He was complimentary at first, I remember—no doubt he added the insult lest he give away his feelings. If only he had known my heart! Oh, love on, dear sir. I will requite your regard, taming my wild heart to your loving hand. Others say you are deserving of love, and I do believe it—I believe more than they have reported. You shall have your heart's desire, my dear Admiral ... and I shall have mine.*

Penelope reached the folly at exactly two o'clock. There was no one there, and she could not decide if she was disappointed or relieved. It was still against her better judgement that she had come, but her curiosity could not be quelled. She looked at the crack in the steps; there was nothing there. She sat down on the steps to wait a little while.

"Mrs. Clay?" said a voice behind her.

She jumped. She stood and looked around, but could see nothing but the empty portico and pillars of the folly.

"I am here, madam, behind a pillar. I dare not let you see me, but we can converse."

"But why may I not see you?"

"I am not worthy, madam."

"I do not understand," said Penelope. "In what way are you so unworthy? I can think of nothing that would make you unworthy, unless … you do not already have a wife, do you?"

There was a crack of laughter from behind the pillar. Borlock had not anticipated Penelope's thinking *that* was his dark secret.

"No, madam, I have never been married."

"Well, then, I can think of no other reason for you to hide your face. To be sure," she added in a teasing voice, "if you were a highwayman or an outlaw, that would be some excuse, but that is not likely to be the reason!"

There was no response to this. Penelope felt a thrill of apprehension. "*Are* you a brigand of some sort?"

"Not exactly," came the reluctant response. "I would, however, tremble to meet with a constable."

"You are hiding from the Law?"

"Please, madam, ask me no more."

"I cannot believe it," she said. "You have not the speech of a common criminal."

"Have you never heard of gentlemen thieves? Good birth is no guarantee of good character."

There was silence for a moment. "And have you a bad character?" Penelope asked in a small voice.

The sigh that came from behind the pillar was more genuine than anything else that had come out of Borlock's mouth. "I am afraid so, madam."

"You may mend a bad character," she said hopefully.

"I wish I could." He had forgotten he was playing a part now. "Now, madam, you may take your bracelet."

An arm extended out from the pillar, with her bracelet

hanging from the gloved fingers. Penelope drew near and took it. There was not much to be deduced about the man's identity from the sleeve of the coat—it was a perfectly ordinary black coat sleeve, the cloth neither very worn nor very expensive.

"Thank you," she said.

"It was my very great honor to serve you. You had better go now."

Suddenly it was very important to Penelope that she not lose him. "Shall I see you again?"

"You are not afraid of me, madam?"

"No. I cannot tell you why, but I am not afraid."

Borlock paused. That Mrs. Clay was desperate to meet again with an unknown admirer who was on the wrong side of the law told its own story. She was not a silly, thoughtless young girl who might be overly romantic; no, she was so starved of affection that any crumb of it was enough to attract her.

"Very well, then, madam. I will leave you a note here at the folly tomorrow, to tell you how we shall meet. I may have to come at night. Go now. Promise me you will not try to follow me."

"I promise," said Penelope. She curtseyed toward the pillar out of habit, and blushed when she realized how silly it was. "Goodbye," she said, and walked back toward Kellynch Hall without a backward glance.

Chapter Thirteen

Sir Walter had stayed at Kellynch Hall instead of going to Uppercross for the picnic, pleading his dislike of bright sunshine and over-exertion. He sat in the morning room when everyone had gone, reading the newspaper from Crewkerne. In it was an account of the ball at Kellynch which glorified the event almost to the level of an assembly at the Court of St. James. Sir Walter was more than gratified. The expense had been worth it to be host to such a splendid gathering. He wondered why he had never hit on such a plan before—inviting important guests so that there was an excuse for elaborate entertainments.

And the officers would be leaving soon. They had not given him a particular day, but Admiral Croft had mentioned at breakfast that his sister-in-law was definitely on the mend, and he hoped it would not be long before he could be reunited with his wife. What a pity he had not used the men more often as an excuse to entertain! He must remedy that. Perhaps he could invite two families for a dinner—no, three. Three unexceptionable families would be invited to dine, to celebrate his daughter Anne's engagement to Captain Wentworth. Everyone would be pleased: the guests would be happy to meet the officers of the Navy (for it was most unlikely that they had had much opportunity to get to know them at the ball), and the officers, particularly Wentworth, would be pleased to know of the genteel connections that the Elliots had. As soon as Elizabeth arrived home he would tell her to issue the invitations and make arrangements with the cook.

By the late afternoon, the gardens had all been explored and the picnic-goers began to make noises about going back to Kellynch. Baldwin had been watching Elizabeth from afar all afternoon, admiring her beauty and grace and wondering how he had resisted her charms for so long. The one time he had plucked up his courage to join her and those she was walking with, she had gone off with Benwick to the garden gate and left the garden altogether. Whether she had guessed his intention or not he did not know, but if she had been trying to avoid him, chasing after her would hardly endear him to her. He could not blame her for such an action: he had so often made a cutting remark to her—and before others, too!—that it was no wonder the poor lady would not wish to be in his company.

Elizabeth saw Baldwin watching her. He looked hesitant and unsure; had he always looked at her thus? She did not know. She had been trying to avoid looking at him ever since he arrived at Kellynch. She could well imagine that he was hesitant to approach her, lest she fire some stinging remark at him. If only she had guarded her tongue! She tried to listen to the conversations of others, conscientiously trying to put into practice her new humility, but all she heard was Louisa, involved in a spirited debate with her brother and Captain Wentworth about whether she could drive the pony and trap as well as they could.

At length the carriage was called for and the men mounted their horses. Thanks and farewells filled the air as the whole party moved off. Wentworth found himself riding beside Mr. Elliot as they neared Kellynch.

"Have you fixed a day for your wedding?" asked Mr. Elliot.

"Three months hence," said Wentworth. "I would be happier if it were sooner, but I wish to secure a home before I wed. I think it cannot be done earlier."

"Ah, that is a pity," said Mr. Elliot. "You might marry and stay at Kellynch until you find the estate you wish to buy."

Not likely, thought Wentworth. *One of the reasons I am marrying her is to get her away from here!* But he said lightly, "Or I could elope with her. I know which is the window of her bedroom—see there? Two windows from the right, with the trellis of roses rising beside it. I could climb up to her room in the middle of the night—well, no, I suppose then she would have to come down that way, and it would be most difficult in a gown!"

"I think your best plan would be to take her out for a drive, and simply keep driving!"

Wentworth grinned at him. "You may be right. It lacks the romantic touch of a midnight escape, but it would undoubtedly be easier."

When they arrived back at Kellynch, Wentworth went smiling up to his room to change his clothes. The thought of absconding with Anne was undoubtedly attractive, if impractical. If he and Anne were both ten years younger, he would have seriously considered the notion. She would have been seventeen and he would have had no money—they would have had to go to Scotland to be married. As it was, Anne would shrink from such a scandalous start to their marriage, and he himself would not like to do such a disreputable thing.

He opened his bedroom door and found a piece of paper on the floor with "Wentworth" written across it. He set down his hat, took off his gloves, and opened the note.

"My Dear Sir, I have been Informed that you have become Betrothed to Miss Anne Elliot. I beg of you to break the Engagement, as she is not the Pure and Innocent Woman that you suppose. To say it Baldly, she has been Unmaidenly. If you Marry her, she will certainly bring Scandal upon you. I could not Permit you to bind yourself to her without telling you the Truth. From Your True Well-Wisher."

Wentworth crumpled the note and wished there was a fire burning in his room to throw it into. It could not be true, but it was so very odd that he had heard this about Anne for a second time. He wondered if the writer could be the same tipsy man who had accosted him at the ball. He might have been more than drunk—he might have been insane. For no one could believe that Anne—sweet, virtuous Anne—could have ever been 'unmaidenly."

She might have an enemy, he thought. *Someone who desires her not to marry me. But who? A jilted suitor might, if angry enough, put such a dreadful slander about, but Anne has no jilted suitors. Or might it be another woman, jealous of Anne's happiness?* He did not know the inhabitants of the neighborhood well enough to determine if that might be the case.

He might ask someone who did know, but who? He could not tell Anne about the note: it would upset her exceedingly, and he had no desire to cut up her peace. If Sir Walter had been a more sensible man, he might have been tempted to ask his advice, but there was no telling how the erratic baronet might respond. Elizabeth or Mary might know of something, but he had no dependence on Mary keeping quiet about it, and he was not quite sure about Elizabeth. He went down to dinner still pondering what he ought to do.

He strove to act naturally and be no different than usual all through dinner and in the hours that followed. But when he went upstairs to retire for the night, he was stopped by Mr. Elliot.

"You have seemed a little preoccupied tonight, Captain. May I ask if you are well?"

"I am very well, thank you," said Wentworth. It occurred to him that Mr. Elliot might know the neighborhood a little; he was family, after all. "Tell me," he said in a low voice, "Have you ever heard that Anne has any enemies?"

Mr. Elliot looked surprised. "Enemies! Anne? No, indeed. Of

course, I am not a resident of this part of the country, but I have always understood that she was a favorite with those in the village and on the estate. She has often been friendly with even those of the lower orders—perhaps she might be criticized for not preserving enough distinction between landowners and tenants. But certainly I can think of nothing she might have done which would cause her to have an enemy! Why do you ask?"

But Wentworth was not prepared to tell Elliot about the note. He made a vague answer and bid Elliot goodnight.

The following morning, Benwick set out on foot for the village of Kellynch. He could have ridden, but he wanted time to think, and fancied that a leisurely stroll on the little-travelled road between the Hall and the village might be a good setting.

He needed to think about the future. This time he had spent in Somerset had been good for him. He had arrived with a mind distracted by grief, unable to plan for anything beyond the next week or two. The friendship of his fellow-officers and the kindness of the Elliots and the Musgroves, not to mention the society of young people, had done much for him. He could not say that his broken heart had healed, but he felt a renewed interest in life. There might still be a future for him, one that was not as bleak and agonizing as he had imagined.

Croft would leave Kellynch soon, that was certain. Wentworth would be busy buying an estate and making preparations for his marriage. Baldwin ... he chuckled as he thought of Baldwin. The poor fellow kept looking at Elizabeth from afar, and it seemed to Benwick that for the first time in his life, he was unsure of himself. Elizabeth, Benwick had noticed, was quieter and less opinionated. The words of Lady Russell and Anne must have had an effect. At any rate, it was plain to see that Baldwin would soon be making plans of his own.

That left himself. Where ought he to go? He had money now,

thanks to his exploits in the war. For the first time, he could think of buying himself a small estate and gathering friends around him. In his mind's eye he could picture such a thing—only it was the residents of Uppercross and Kellynch that he saw there.

He reached the village and went into the bookshop. It was not every village that had one, but he was thankful that this one did. He had been talking yesterday at the picnic with Louisa, and found that she had never read *Waverley*. He had told her briefly about the tale, and privately thought that she would benefit from reading about the characters of Flora and Rose—she would naturally be more like Flora, and he thought she ought to learn to be more like Rose, who had a happier end. Louisa had said the story sounded exciting and promised to read it whenever it came in her way. At that moment Benwick had determined to buy it. He thought it would seem a little odd to present it as a *gift* to Louisa, but he thought he might, with all propriety, lend it to her. Perhaps that ought to be his new aim in life—benevolent encouragement to a better character.

Not that Louisa's character needed much improvement, he thought, as he left the shop with the newly-purchased *Waverley* in three volumes wrapped in paper and tied with string under his arm. She might be impulsive, but she was sweet. Vulnerable, needing someone to take care of her. Her father loved her, of course, but she did not pay enough heed to him. A husband, that was what she needed. He would like to have the choosing of that young man. He would need to be someone who was appreciative of her lively spirits and would not crush the exuberance out of her. On the other hand, he needed to be a steady fellow—to marry her to an equally impulsive man would be a disaster.

The noise of a horse-drawn equipage behind him made him move to the side of the road and turn to see it. It was a gig driven by a lady—a close bonnet made it difficult to see if she were young or old. It was an unusual sight, but not completely unprecedented. She drew near to him and now he saw that it was Miss Louisa Musgrove.

"Oh, Captain Benwick!" she said as she passed by him. "I am on my way to Kellynch!"

He waved in acknowledgement.

Suddenly, she looked back at him to say, "Oh, Captain Benwick, I forgot to tell you—"

At that moment, the gig struck a rock at the side of the road. A slower pace would have merely jarred its occupant, but Louisa had been going fast enough that the gig went up into the air on one side and came down with a thud. The highly-sprung seat bounced her neatly out of the gig and onto the bank at the side of the road.

Benwick ran to her side as the horse, with the empty gig rattling behind it, slackened its speed. "Miss Musgrove! Are you injured?" he cried as he knelt beside her.

"My arm," Louisa moaned, and Benwick quickly surveyed her form to see if there were any other injuries.

"Can you move your head? Your feet?" Benwick asked anxiously.

"Yes, yes, I believe so," said Louisa, beginning to move her head and her limbs.

"Good, good. Can you move your arm?"

Louisa tried, but gasped in pain.

"We will have to get you to Uppercross," he said. "Or, perhaps, to Kellynch," he added as he saw her face growing pale with pain. "I think your arm may be broken."

Louisa looked at her arm. "I think it is sound," she said. "It is not bent in an odd way. It only hurts."

"The bone might have a crack in it. I have seen it happen more than once. However, your arm may just be bruised. There must be a physician that can be fetched to Kellynch."

"Oh, Captain Benwick, I do not think I can drive." Tears were coming down her face, but Benwick was heartened to note that she had not fainted or gone into hysterics.

"No, no, of course you cannot. I will drive. Thank God the horse has not bolted."

Indeed, the horse was a sturdy cob, probably much more often used on the home farm than as a carriage horse. He had come to a stop not far from them and was placidly tearing mouthfuls of grass by the side of the road. Benwick fetched the horse and brought it back to where Louisa lay. He helped her to sit up but she was in so much pain he had little doubt her arm was broken somewhere between her shoulder and her elbow. A sailor on his ship had once had the same affliction.

She was holding her injured arm with her other hand and would need a sling to travel in any kind of comfort. His cravat was the only thing to hand. Without any fuss, he took it off his neck and fashioned a sling out of it. Gently he put it around the afflicted limb and then around her neck.

"There now," he said. "I hope you will be easier. I must get you into the gig somehow. Do you think you can stand?"

With her arm in a sling, she was able to use her other hand to grasp his as he helped her up. She stood beside the gig, still gasping with pain, and tried to put her foot on the hub of the wheel in order to climb in, grasping the side of the gig with her good hand for balance.

"No, no," said Benwick. "You might easily slip, and if you fall, your arm will be much worse. I'm afraid I must lift you up."

Louisa nodded. "Thank you. I did not think I could get in by myself."

With as little fanfare as he had taken off his cravat, he picked her up gently and set her feet on the floor of the gig. From there she could grasp the front apron of the gig and get onto the seat.

Benwick picked up his volumes, which he had put down on the grass when he had come to Louis's aid, gathered the reigns and got up into the gig. "Now then," he said. "Have courage, Miss Musgrove! I think we are about half a mile from Kellynch. I fear it will not be a comfortable ride, but it will not last long."

He drove slowly, for every bump in the road resulted in a cry or a gasp of pain out of Louisa. He apologized for every jostle, and eventually Louisa said, "you must apologize no more—you are not to blame for any of this. I was heedless—too confident in my driving." She cried out as a slight dip in the road caused the gig to jolt. When she could speak again, she said, "You seem fated to be always rescuing me from the consequences of my folly."

"Not folly, Miss Musgrove," said Benwick kindly, "only lack of experience."

The journey was agonizingly slow for both of them, but at last they did reach Kellynch. Louisa was settled into one of the bedrooms, and the surgeon was called for. He ascertained that the bone was indeed broken, but not badly. He gave her laudanum to help with the pain, told her not to jar her arm, and said the pain would decrease in a few days. But she must be careful to keep her arm in a sling and refrain from using it for at least a month. He recommended that she stay at Kellynch for a few days, at least, to let the bone mend without any chance of jarring. A servant was sent to Uppercross with the news, and to bring back Louisa's clothes and a maid to wait on her.

Borlock thought hard before he wrote a note to Mrs. Clay. It was ridiculous to have scruples, he knew. She was well and truly caught by him. He had, in the moments he had glimpsed the group all together, noticed that Mrs. Clay was no longer paying much attention to Sir Walter, nor she particularly attached herself to Mr. Elliot. Her thoughts seemed to be centered on the one man who had showed some admiration for her—himself. She seemed so pathetic—easily manipulated by anyone. He was glad she would not be tricked by Mr. Elliot, ruined beyond all hope of recovery. For a moment he wondered if it would not be better for her to wed Sir Walter after all—she would be secure, then, at least until Sir Walter's death. He paused a moment to consider it. He was not at all sure that Sir

Walter would marry a woman of lower birth, no matter how flattering she was.

He did not know why he felt responsible for her, except that she was in his power now. He could not forget her question, "And have you a bad character?" He did, and he should not make it worse. He had some idea of nudging her gently toward another man, like a barrister or a gentleman-farmer. He had no idea how this might be accomplished, but at the very least, he ought to make himself less attractive to her. Of course, he could have disclosed that he was Borlock, and she might have shied away from him on that fact alone. But she would despise him for his trickery and for raising her hopes, and for some reason, her good opinion mattered. Then she might turn her attention back to Sir Walter, which was the whole reason he had begun this charade to begin with.

No, he would play along for a little while longer, only he must be careful not to raise hopes that she would have any future with him. He left a note at the folly, telling Mrs. Clay to meet him in the rose garden at midnight.

She was punctual. The butler had locked up the house by that time, of course, but Penelope managed to get out of one of the ball-room windows, leaving it slightly open so that she could raise it again to get back in. She went down the steps of the terrace to the formal garden, and then off to the side and under the arched trellis to the small rose garden. There was very little moonlight, and she crept slowly between the bushes. The gravel under her feet made only a faint noise, but it seemed to be enough for the man who waited there, for he called softly, "I am here, by the wall."

She came up to him and stood there, shivering a little in the dark.

"You are cold," he said, and took off the dark cloak he was wearing and put it around her shoulders.

"I ought to have brought a shawl," she said. "Thank you."

"It is nothing." She thought he spoke very formally.

"I have been thinking," she said. "about what you said when we last met."

"What was it that I said?"

"You said you wished you could reform."

"So I did. But it is not possible, madam."

"I think it is," she said earnestly. "If you were a truly bad man, you would not wish to change your character. All you need to do is stop doing the wrong things. As I tell my children—" she stopped.

"Yes?" he said. "What do you tell your children?"

There was real interest in his voice, as if he were not at all surprised to hear that she had children. How could he have known that? But his question remained unanswered. She found her voice.

"I tell them that all it takes to stop being a liar is to tell no more lies. All it takes to stop being a thief is to steal no longer."

"That is a profound truth, madam. And yet ... one may stop wrongdoing, but the consequences of one's actions may follow one—may entrap one into circumstances that are hard to escape."

"Is that where you find yourself?" she asked with sympathy.

Borlock suddenly felt that this was the strangest tryst he had ever kept. He had imagined that there might be a great deal of romantic talk between them, and perhaps a kiss in the dark. He had not imagined a moral discussion with Mrs. Clay in the role of preceptress!

"It is true, madam," he said. "My misdeeds in the past have put me where I am." He leaned back against the wall.

"And you cannot start afresh somewhere else?"

"I do not know, madam. My—" he had almost said 'my master," and stopped himself just in time. "My friends—my disreputable friends—are depending on me, and would make leaving very difficult."

"I see." Penelope mulled this over in her mind. "You are, I think, useful to them?"

"Yes. A tool, as you might say."

"I can see why they would not want to lose you. Are they using you even now?"

Borlock shifted his feet. "Yes. Even now. They—they wish to injure those at Kellynch Hall. I myself wish the Elliots no harm," he added quickly. "I had no quarrel with them before, and now that I am bound by affection to a member of the household, I have even less wish to cause mischief."

He heard her catch her breath. "Bound by affection," she whispered.

He knew an impulse to pull her to himself and kiss her. She liked him, and not because she thought there was anything to be got out of him. She had genuine sympathy for him, and she believed him to be a better man than he was. To say the truth, she was probably the only person on earth who cared for him at all now. He resisted the inclination and said, "I will do what I can to see that no harm comes to Kellynch."

"And you will do what you can to escape, yourself?" she said.

He looked down at her; he could faintly see her expression by the dim moonlight, standing there, trusting him when she had no reason to. "I will consider it. You must go now."

"And will I—"

"Yes." He answered her question before she finished it. "We will meet again."

She took his cloak from around her shoulders and gave it back to him. He grasped her hand and kissed it.

"Go carefully, my dear," he said.

"I will," she said softly, and walked away.

Chapter Fourteen

Borlock had not been in church for so many weeks in a row since he had come to work for Mr. Elliot. Mr. Elliot rarely went to church and never required his servants to go. However, as guests at Kellynch, they fulfilled decorum and took their places at Kellynch Church with everyone else. Borlock sat in the balcony with the other servants. He had been thinking about Hayter's words on that walk into Winthrop: all about covering up sin, and the verse that mentioned finding mercy. He could not understand why he should care so much about it—thoughts of repentance had never troubled him before—but he could not banish them from his mind, try as he might. For the first time he could remember since he was a small child, he paid attention during a church service.

There were two other people in the congregation who were also truly listening despite years of habitual indifference. Elizabeth had been in church almost every week of her life, but she had rarely had any interest in the homily. She would have been more able to report what every woman in the congregation had worn rather than which texts had been read out. This Sunday, however, she was still full of her new ambition to eradicate her pride, and it occurred to her for the first time that the divinity that was said to rule the world might have something helpful to say about it.

Baldwin, likewise, had not been used to pay much attention to sermons, but he had never before been so unsure about what to do. His own selfishness and pride, he thought, had driven poor Elizabeth into a position where she would rather die than admit her love, and he needed to woo her carefully. A forthright declaration of love on his part would probably be met with—well, incredulity—but after that there would be a stout rejection. And the laws of polite society dictated that he could not ask again. He did not really think that the rector would tell him, in his sermon, how he ought to win Elizabeth, but he was dimly aware that he had not the wisdom to figure it out on his own.

"A Lesson from the Psalms," said the rector, and began to read from the thirty-eighth Psalm. Borlock listened with conviction weighing his heart down with every word. The phrases, still familiar from his youth, battered into his brain like hail on an open field.

"Thine arrows stick fast in me, and thy hand presseth me sore ... For mine iniquities are gone over mine head: as an heavy burden they are too heavy for me ... My wounds stink and are corrupt because of my foolishness ... I am troubled; I am bowed down greatly; I go mourning all the day long ... For I am ready to halt, and my sorrow is continually before me ... For I will declare mine iniquity; I will be sorry for my sin ..." And then the words Borlock knew were coming; he even whispered them along with the rector: "Make haste to help me, O Lord my salvation."

The rector removed his spectacles and said, "Here endeth the lesson." The service flowed on, but Borlock remained stuck on the final words of the Psalm: "O Lord, my salvation." Here was the difficulty, then. The Almighty would not come to his aid because he was not his salvation. Borlock might be sorry for his wrongs, but he had no claim on forgiveness. The thought of bearing this guilt for some long, indeterminate time made him feel like a cloak of doom had settled over him, never to be lifted.

Louisa, of course, had not been able to go to church. Her arm was bandaged and the laudanum that the physician had left for her had enabled her to sleep the night before. She passed a rather dreary Sunday in bed, neither sleeping much nor able to do anything else. Her mother had visited her the night of the accident, but the house was too full to allow her to stay, and assured that Louisa would have the best of care, she had gone back to Uppercross. Louisa hoped that on Monday, Henrietta would come to visit her, but Henrietta sent word that she had caught a violent cold and had better stay at home until she was better.

By Monday afternoon, Louisa was weary of being in bed and insisted on being dressed and coming downstairs. Most of the house's inmates were out of doors, and she sat discontentedly in the morning room, wishing someone would come and talk to her.

She was fortunate: Captain Benwick passed by the room and saw her there.

"Miss Musgrove, you are out of bed!" he said, coming in to sit beside her. "It is good to see you so well."

"I do not *feel* well," said Louisa, pouting a little. "My arm still aches dreadfully, and am so very bored. There is nothing to do. I need not sit in bed, for I am perfectly able to stand. But moving around much is painful, so I do not want to go for a walk. And the laudanum makes me sleepy. I cannot write or draw, and no one wants to sit and talk with me."

"It must be very difficult," said Benwick sympathetically. "But wait! I have an idea." He left the room and came back some minutes later, bearing a book.

"Do you remember that you said you would like to read *Waverly*?" he asked, sitting down beside her again.

"Is that the novel you said was so interesting that day at the picnic?"

"Yes. There are intrigues and battles and brushes with death—very exciting!"

"Well," said Louisa, "I daresay it would amuse me. However, it is hard for me to give attention to things with my arm hurting. Anne gave me a book to read—some volume of poetry. I tried to read it, Captain Benwick, but I found it very hard to understand, and also very dull."

"Ah, but I will read to you," Benwick said. "For who knows? If you try to read it yourself, the laudanum might put you to sleep and then you would blame the book, and you will never be persuaded to try reading it again."

Louisa smiled. "It is very kind of you, Captain. But surely there are other things you would rather be doing."

"Not at all, Miss Musgrove," he said, settling himself comfortably in his chair, and opening the book. "There is nothing I would rather do."

Elizabeth, determined to demonstrate that a lady of rank did not demean herself by being useful, decided to follow Lady Russell's example in working in the garden. She had no desire to pick up a shovel and dig potatoes in the kitchen garden, but snipping the dead heads of flowers was a genteel pastime which would also be useful. She invited Penelope to work with her, and in the afternoon the two of them entered the rose garden with two pairs of strong scissors and a basket for their trimmings. Penelope thought that Elizabeth was more quiet than usual, but she accounted for it by the slight headache she had mentioned at breakfast.

"Is your headache worse, Elizabeth?" said Penelope. "You are so quiet."

"My headache?" said Elizabeth, "Oh, yes, my headache." In truth, she had only said such a thing to make an excuse to get away from the breakfast-table, out of sight of Admiral Baldwin. Now that she knew his feelings for her, she was always catching him looking at her—far more than she had noticed before. It made her self-conscious: she had begun to think twice about anything she said, lest her words might sound arrogant. It was unnerving.

"I have no headache now," she said. "I was merely lost in my thoughts." She had been wondering what a lady might say to a gentleman to encourage him to speak his heart. There was very little, it seemed. But here she was, again, selfishly thinking of only her own concerns instead of Penelope's. She had not inquired about anything in Penelope's life.

"How are you feeling? You seem a little tired."

"I am a little tired," Penelope admitted. She had not been sleeping well since the advent of the mysterious stranger. "I have been ... thinking about a decision I have to make."

Ordinarily, Elizabeth would not have cared what decision it was, but she was determined to be interested. "What sort of decision? May I be of some help?"

Penelope was taken aback. Such interest as this was unprecedented. What should she say? She could not tell her of her mysterious admirer, of course, but perhaps she could ask for her advice in a general way.

"Thank you, Miss Elliot. I wonder—how would you decide whether or not to encourage the attentions of one who is beneath you?"

"Beneath you?" Elizabeth could not imagine who could be beneath Penelope in the circle of their acquaintance. Anne, in fact, had more than once hinted that Penelope was setting her sights very much above her—on her father, in fact. The question, however, applied to Elizabeth more than Penelope could know.

"Well," said Elizabeth. "I know a little of what you mean. I think the character of the person is more important than their social standing."

"Their character." It was Penelope's turn to echo a phrase. Was not that the difficulty in her case? The unknown man might not be beneath her in terms of birth, but he was the one who claimed himself to be unsuitable due to his character.

They worked together in silence for a little while.

"There, that looks much neater," said Elizabeth, surveying the bush she had been trimming. "Very satisfying."

"Do you think a man may change his character?" said Penelope. "Reform himself?"

Elizabeth paused to consider. "It may be. I suppose anyone may change their character if they have a mind to do so. And often it is the love of a good man—I mean, a good woman—which provides the motivation for the change." She found another dead flower to cut off and applied her scissors. "On the other hand," she continued, "I would not marry a man who has not already determined to change his character—indeed, someone who has made a start in reforming. Look at Earl Fotherfield—marriage to Lady Endicott has done *nothing* to alter his character. He is as profligate now as he was ten years ago."

"Yes, yes, I see," said Penelope. The unknown gentleman—how she wished she knew his name!—had yet to make a start, but he did seem determined to do so.

"Whatever you do," said Elizabeth, "do not reject a man simply to keep your pride. Pride is a very empty comfort when you are alone." It was as near to a confession of the heart as she had ever gotten, and Penelope was so surprised that she stopped her work to look at her.

"No, I shall not," she said.

The ladies became aware at the same moment the indistinct sounds in the distance were voices—masculine voices—on the terrace, and they were growing louder. They ceased their talking until, in a few minutes, Admiral Baldwin and Admiral Croft came into view.

"Ah, what a delightful occupation for young ladies," said Croft, entering the garden. "Here you are, surrounded by roses and doing your part to make the garden an even lovelier place."

The ladies smiled at him.

"Mrs. Clay," said Croft, "I have no wish to disturb you, but you were telling me yesterday about your pen knife—the one that had belonged to your husband? You said it was inlaid with ivory and that you would show it to me. I have a notion to have one made for Mrs. Croft, as a gift. I thought I would ask you before I forgot."

"Oh, yes, of course. I can go and get it for you now."

"No need to trouble yourself to bring it all the way out here; I will come with you. Baldwin here will take your place at the rose bush."

Croft could have laughed aloud at the ludicrous expression on Baldwin and Elizabeth's faces. They had studiously avoided speaking to each other for days, and here they would be forced to do so without any third party to mitigate the awkwardness.

Indeed, Baldwin's first instinct was to make an excuse and escape, but he was afraid such an action would be seen as proof that he disdained Elizabeth's company. Penelope gave her scissors to Baldwin and took Admiral Croft's arm. They left the garden together.

Baldwin reacted to his embarrassment by attacking the nearest bush with more zest than precision. A number of perfectly good flowers fell to the ground. Elizabeth bit back the sarcastic words that were hovering on her tongue and said instead, "Have you tended roses before, Admiral?"

He stopped cutting and surveyed the fallen stems. "No. Forgive me, I suppose I am not doing it correctly."

"I have not done it often, myself," said Elizabeth, "but my mother did. She used to tell me to work slowly, to be certain of which stem I am cutting."

He watched her while she cut a few. "I see. Cut them above that cluster of leaves." He tried it and looked to her for approval.

"Yes, like that," she said.

For a while they snipped without speaking. Baldwin wondered what he could say that would move them closer to a rapprochement. *My dear Miss Elliot, I know you love me.* No, no, far too abrupt, and she would probably deny it, and then where would he be? What about *Dearest Miss Elliot, I have long loved you*? That was no good, either. She might faint with the shock, and he could not desire that. No, the best thing would be to start off by praising her. Not something about her beauty, which might seem like mere flattery, but something about her character. *Miss Elliot, you have great strength of mind.* Oh, dear, no; that was what one said to stubborn old ladies when one was required to say something complimentary.

"You are a good friend to Mrs. Clay, I think," he said finally. It was not a brilliant remark, but he could come up with nothing better.

Elizabeth looked at him in surprise. She had not considered Penelope a friend so much as a useful companion. She wondered how the admiral had gotten that idea. A few days ago she would have been affronted that someone considered Mrs. Clay a *friend* of hers, but now she was trying so hard to be humble. At least today their talk had been more like that between friends, with Penelope asking advice and her giving it. She could with honesty say she had been a good friend to her today.

"I am trying to be so," she said. "Mrs. Clay has been a very loyal ... friend ... to me."

"Yes, she seems so."

Elizabeth cast about for something else nice to say about Penelope, to show that character was now more important to her than rank. "She is very amiable, you know; she never complains. And she could: widowed with two young children, living with her parents again ... it is not an easy life, Admiral Baldwin."

"No," he agreed, because he could think of nothing else to say.

"It is my dearest wish that she should marry again," Elizabeth said, even though she had only first had that thought that very minute.

"Oh?" Baldwin could not help but feel that they were getting further and further away from his declaration of love to Elizabeth, and he was not sure how to get the conversation back to it.

"Yes. I think it is her wish, as well. She asked my advice on affairs of the heart just before you and Admiral Croft joined us."

"I suppose there is no man hereabouts to match her with?"

Elizabeth sighed. "I know of none. Of course, there are some eligible men who would not think of her because she is not a woman of rank. For my part, I think there is nothing worse than a man who allows a woman of good character to slip through his fingers just because she is not as well born as he is." *There,* Elizabeth thought. *If that does not show him that I would not reject him because of his birth, then nothing will!*

This speech gave Baldwin pause. There was something in Miss Elliot's manner that seemed to indicated that her sentiments were significant for him. Could it be she wanted *him* to be the second husband of Mrs. Clay? No, for according to Wentworth, she was in love with him herself. Perhaps, though, she had given up all hope of marrying him because of his mocking treatment of her, but she loved him enough to want him to be happy. And no doubt she wanted to see her friend cared for by a good man. This was a daunting prospect, and he snipped a few more roses while he thought. He could not encourage this line of thinking, but he must be courteous.

"I feel sure, Miss Elliot, that there will someday be a man in the neighborhood who would be suitable. You ought not look further afield; I believe Mrs. Clay is the kind of woman who would not like to live far from her family."

Elizabeth agreed to this—at that moment she would have agreed to almost everything he said—and was spared the effort of thinking of anything more to converse about by the return of Mrs. Clay and Admiral Croft.

That night, as Mr. Elliot prepared for bed, he watched his valet out of the corner of his eye. Something had changed in Borlock, and he had not yet determined what it was. The man had always been taciturn, and he was not likely to begin baring his soul. Mr. Elliot got into bed, sat back against his pillows, and said, "So, tell me, Borlock, how are you going on with Mrs. Clay?"

Borlock spoke briefly of his meetings with the woman and added, "She believes me to be a gentleman thief, the tool of unsavory companions. I think she means to reform me." He felt, unreasonably, that he was betraying Mrs. Clay by sharing this information, a feeling that deepened when Mr. Elliot chuckled.

"And what is your plan now? Shall you unveil yourself and see her turn ashen to know that she has given her heart to a valet?" The scorn in his voice was thick.

"I ... I had not yet decided, sir."

Mr. Elliot picked up the glass of brandy which was on the table beside his bed and took a sip. "Well now, I will tell you what to do. You assured me weeks ago that I would think of some way to take revenge on Captain Wentworth, and you were right. Indeed, you have given me the perfect way to do it. We strike tomorrow night. Was it the Bard who said 'revenge is sweet'?"

"I believe so, sir," said Borlock, who nevertheless thought, *"Bread of deceit is sweet to a man; but afterwards his mouth shall be filled with gravel."*

Mr. Elliot frowned. "You do not look particularly pleased."

"Perhaps, sir, I am merely unsure of the plan."

"It is a cunning one, I assure you. Together we will not only break off Wentworth's engagement, but I will marry Anne myself in less than a year." He glanced at his valet and laughed. "You look astonished, Borlock. Do you think I will not succeed? Listen then: you will dose Anne's nightly glass of wine and water with laudanum. Not too much: only a few drops, to make her sleep heavily. She will not taste a small amount, mixed with the wine."

Borlock listened without comment, only inclining his head to show that he understood.

"When she has gone to sleep, you will meet Mrs. Clay in Anne's bedroom. I do not know on what pretext you will get her there—perhaps the evil companions you spoke so eloquently of to her will have drugged Anne and you need Mrs. Clay to help you protect her jewels. I leave it to your imagination. At any rate, you will be seen with Mrs. Clay at the window of the room, and you will then climb down the trellis outside the window and disappear into the night. I will arrange to have Wentworth and Croft see the spectacle, and it will not be difficult, I fancy, to convince Wentworth that his fiancée has been entertaining a man in her bedroom. He will break off the engagement very shortly."

"But have you considered, sir, that Mrs. Clay is very likely to tell the Elliots and Captain Wentworth that Miss Anne is innocent?"

Mr. Elliot raised his eyebrows in mock surprise. "What? Admit that she has been meeting an unknown man clandestinely? I think she will preserve herself and remain silent."

"I am not certain of that," said Borlock, thoughtfully.

Mr. Elliot put down the glass of brandy and looked fixedly at his valet. "Tell me, Borlock, are you inclined to abandon my scheme? To refuse to do your part?"

Borlock said nothing.

"Because if you are, let me remind you that I do not hesitate to bring down my enemies. Nothing would be easier than for me to accuse you of theft. You have a habit, you know, of making off with your masters' property. It would not be difficult to convince a magistrate that you had taken something valuable of mine."

"No indeed, sir," said Borlock respectfully. It would be extremely simple for Mr. Elliot to do such a thing. If found guilty of stealing something worth more than five shillings, he could be sentenced to hang. He might be transported instead, or put into prison, or even branded on the hand—none of them attractive possibilities.

"You have been a useful valet thus far," said Mr. Elliot. "It would inconvenience me to have to find another one. But I will, rather than have my plans upset. I trust you understand me."

"Yes, sir," said Borlock in a tone void of all emotion.

"Very good. When the engagement is dissolved and Wentworth has gone away, I will suddenly discover that all has not been what it seems. Anne's innocence will be established, along with her credit in the neighborhood. And I will marry her. And now," he yawned, "I will go to sleep. Tomorrow may be a taxing day, and I ought to be well-rested."

Chapter Fifteen

B orlock spent the greater part of the night wondering what to do. He had no stomach for this plan of revenge on Captain Wentworth, and to use Mrs. Clay for the plan was particularly evil. He wished to have no part of it. He even thought of absconding immediately, in the middle of the night, but that seemed to be an extreme notion. He assured himself that there was no guarantee that Captain Wentworth would think so little of his fiancée as to immediately assume she was an immoral woman. Bah! One only had to look at her to know she had never thought of doing such a thing! And if Wentworth did not fly into a temper and the whole thing came to nothing, it would not be the fault of Borlock, who had faithfully done his part. Besides, if he ran away now, Mr. Elliot could easily pursue him with the law, just as he had threatened: he was not a man who liked having his will thwarted. Borlock would have to go into hiding somewhere, and just now he had very little money. It seemed a most foolish proposition.

And now and then he suspended his deliberations to wonder: why should he be so squeamish now? Why was he suddenly remembering passages from the Bible? He could not account for it. And if such a thing *had* to happen, why had it not done so years before, when he first began to go wrong? *Go wrong,* indeed! Very likely the atheists were right after all, and it was only the pedantic and pious fools who would condemn him thus. He spent many hours arguing with himself, and at last he talked himself into doing what Mr. Elliot wanted. But the feelings of repugnance and guilt would not recede.

While the ladies and gentlemen were at breakfast, Borlock left a note in Mrs. Clay's room, asking her to meet him at the folly at two o'clock. He had committed himself to the scheme, and he resolved not to think anymore about morals; he felt he would go mad if he considered metaphysical matters any longer. To get the laudanum was an easy matter. Louisa still had a supply which was carefully meted out to her in very small amounts, and as Louisa was often seated in the morning room while Captain Benwick read to her, the supply was usually unguarded. Borlock was able to smuggle a small amount away in the early afternoon, just before he went to meet Mrs. Clay.

Penelope arrived at the folly at two o'clock precisely. There seemed to be no one there when she arrived, but just as she was stooping down to see if there was a note in the crack, she heard his voice.

"Hello, my dear." She looked up; she could just see part of his arm behind the same pillar he had hidden behind before.

"Hello ... sir."

There was silence for a moment.

"Why is it, sir, that you asked to meet me?"

"I wished to tell you that I will take your advice and go away—make a clean start somewhere else." He had not, actually, been sure that he would do so, but as soon as he said it, it was a promise, both to her and to himself. He would take part in this one last plot with Mr. Elliot, pray that it would not have the disastrous effect it was supposed to, and then he would make plans to leave Mr. Elliot as soon as they departed from Kellynch.

"Oh!" There was mingled relief and disappointment in Penelope's voice. "I am glad to hear it. Where will you go?"

"I do not know."

"And when will you leave?"

"Soon."

Penelope felt her heart drop. She had told herself repeatedly that she ought not let herself care for this man—this nameless, faceless man!—but she had not listened to her own wise counsel. Now she would miss him inexpressibly. But it was better that he have a good character—much better, in fact, for he was just as lost to her if he had a bad character as if he lived a hundred miles off.

"Shall you ever come back?" She clung to the smallest bit of hope.

"I do not know." For a moment there was only the sound of birds in the nearby trees, and then he said, "Forgive me for my short answers, so lacking in information. I ... I do not wish to leave you."

"I wish you would not leave, either. I suppose there is no other way."

"No, I think not."

After another moment, Penelope said, "If you must go, may I not know your name? I honor you for your decision. I would dearly love to know who it is I honor."

"You have not guessed, madam?"

"Guess? How should I? I have never seen your face without a mask, or in daylight."

"But you have, madam. On the day you were so helpful to me, down at Lyme."

There was only just time for Penelope realize what he meant before Borlock came out from behind the pillar. She gasped and looked up into his face, into the clear blue eyes she remembered from that morning by the sea.

"You!" Her voice did not show loathing or revulsion, he was thankful to note, just surprise.

"Forgive me, madam, for hiding my identity. I thought that as a servant I would have no chance with you, and at first only ventured to claim a dance. I did not mean for it to go on."

"I did not know," she whispered. She had not really observed him since that day—a gentleman's valet had little reason to be seen by female guests. He had been the object of her pity in the days and weeks that followed, but he was wholly unconnected in her mind with the masked man who had asked her to dance.

"And you are—he? You are the one of good birth who is used by wicked men as a tool? But you are a valet, are you not?"

He came forward and grasped her hands. "I am. I am all those things. I cannot explain it all to you now. Only know that you have helped me. I *will* reform, I swear it."

"Can you not take me with you?" It was foolish, not to mention rash, to say such a thing. Penelope said it impetuously.

He smiled gently at her. "Would that I could! But your children would suffer, madam. As yet I have nowhere to go. And when I have made plans ..." he smiled ruefully. "I guarantee that I will not be in affluent circumstances. I could not support a family."

"In time?" asked Penelope.

Borlock looked down at her tenderly. He was still holding her hands. Even a month ago, he would have promised to return for her, taken her kiss—or more—and abandoned her without a thought. He could not do it now. "I hope," was all he could say.

Penelope could feel tears pricking at the back of her eyes but she would not let them fall. She nodded to show she understood, but to say anything would ruin her self-control.

"Go now," Borlock said softly. "I will speak to you again before I leave—if I can."

Penelope kissed his hands which were still grasping hers, turned, and walked swiftly down toward the house. Borlock stood watching her go. He felt wretched.

There was no time to pander to his feelings, however. As soon as Penelope was out of sight he started toward the house himself, his destination the servants' entrance. He must contrive to have himself pressed into service in setting the table. He knew where Anne always sat: it would not be difficult to add the few drops of laudanum to her empty glass. The dinner table at Kellynch Hall was always set with colored glassware, and there would be no danger of anyone noticing it.

While Borlock and Penelope were meeting at the folly, Benwick was reading to Louisa in the morning room. She had become enthralled in the story, and he was reluctant to stop even to take a sip of water, so eager was she to know what happened next. The love of Edward for Flora and then for Rose, the many difficulties in their paths, and the decisions these women made fascinated her. She listened with rapt attention as Benwick read out what Flora told Edward about Rose: "If her husband is a man of sense and virtue, she will sympathize in his sorrows, divert his fatigue, and share his pleasures."

"Yes," whispered Louisa.

Benwick looked up to see a singular expression in Louisa's eyes—it was a look of affection. No woman had looked at him in that way since he had last parted from Fanny. "She is beginning to care for me," he thought. Later on it struck him as strange that the idea did not worry him, for of course he could not return her love —not yet. At the time, however, he only felt gratitude, and wonder.

That evening, after dinner, Anne began to feel very tired. She stayed with the others in the drawing room, trying to pay atten- tion to the questions Mr. Elliot was asking Captain Wentworth about navigating by the stars, but she found herself nodding off even as she sat. Finally she excused herself and went to bed early. Her maid had hardly finished helping her into her nightclothes than she got into bed and fell asleep, neglecting even to pull up a blanket over herself or put out her candle.

An hour later, Penelope, who had a violent headache caused by two hours of crying after she had left Borlock, decided that she might as well go to bed. She was too distracted by her own thoughts to contribute much to the general conversation. She bade the company goodnight and went up the main staircase. She had almost reached the top when she saw Borlock coming toward her down the hall.

"Oh, madam," he said quietly, "Thank goodness you have come!"

"What is it, Mr. Borlock?" She did not notice that she had called him "Mr," as if he had been a gentleman instead of a servant, but Borlock did.

"I fear something is wrong with Miss Anne," he said. "I thought I smelled laudanum in the glass she drank from tonight. Did she seem just as usual?"

"Why, no," said Penelope. "She was very sleepy and went to bed early." It did not occur to her to wonder how Borlock would have known which glass was Anne's, or indeed, why he was anywhere near the glasses that had been used at dinner.

"As I feared," he said. "Will you, in kindness, go to Miss Anne's bedroom and see that she is well?"

"But surely her maid would know," objected Penelope. "Can you not ask her to look?"

"I cannot find her maid," said Borlock. This was not strictly true; during the hour when the family were at dinner, he had gone to Elizabeth's room and purposely placed one of her flagons of French perfume on a lace shawl carelessly draped on her dressing table, covering the bottle completely. The maid, as he had foreseen, snatched up the shawl from the table, accidentally knocking the perfume bottle off the table and onto the floor, where it broke, spilling the perfume all over the floor. The maid had thus been busy for an hour, sweeping up the broken glass, opening the windows, scrubbing the floor to lessen the powerful scent, and attempting to devise the best possible explanation for why her mistress's favorite perfume was no more.

"More than that," Borlock went on, "I do not wish to get the servants into an uproar. If they begin to suspect that someone was poisoned ...well, you know what servants are, madam. There will be no keeping it quiet."

"But why would someone harm Miss Anne?" Penelope was bewildered by this sudden turn of events.

"I must say that I suspect my— my friends, madam. I cannot tell you all, but I am afraid they mean some mischief to her."

"Good heavens!" said Penelope. "Should we not inform Sir Walter?"

"Not yet, madam," said Borlock. "Please, can you not go into her room and see how she does?"

"Very well," said Penelope. Quietly she went down the hall with Borlock following after, until she came to the family bedrooms. Borlock waited outside while she went in.

"Miss Anne?" whispered Penelope. The candle beside her bed was still burning. Anne was sleeping in an unnatural position, almost as if she had fallen on the bed. She was definitely alive, however; her breathing was even and untroubled; she appeared to be in a deep sleep. "Miss Anne?" said Penelope in a louder voice. Anne did not stir. Penelope gently tapped her shoulder. When that provoked no response, she shook her gently. Anne slept on.

Penelope went back to the door, which she had left slightly ajar. "I think she is sleeping deeply. As you say, she appears to have been given laudanum. What should we do?"

Borlock pretended to think for a moment. "Perhaps we should talk in the room instead of in the hall. If anyone sees us talking here, there will be questions."

"Of course," said Penelope, and stepped away from the door

to let him in. He came in but kept his eyes averted from the figure on the bed.

"I have been thinking," he said. "If there are those who wish to do her harm, it may be that they mean to rob her. No doubt they intend to use the trellis outside her window to get in and out —with the summer night being so warm, of course the windows are open."

"Shall I tell the butler now?" asked Penelope, her brow furrowed with concern. "He could post two footmen outside, under her window."

Borlock looked as if he were considering the idea. "I think not. I have a better plan. I will climb down the trellis now, myself, and hide in that shrubbery, just outside. If anyone comes, I can stop them."

"Stop them?" Penelope's throat constricted. "You might be killed! If a gang of ruffians attempt to burgle the house, you will not be able to prevent them. You are only one man!"

"No, my dear." Borlock spoke soothingly. "I will not stop them by force, but by argument. I will tell them I am in love with a lady in this house. They have a little honor—precious little, but enough—and some small regard for me. They will not come if I tell them this."

"You love me?" The words, the look, and the tone in her voice wrung Borlock's heart.

"I do. God help me, I do," he breathed. "When I am safely out the window, go to your own bedroom, lock the door, and say nothing to anyone. It may be that nothing will come of it. Miss Anne is but sleeping and is not in danger. Promise me?"

She gave her promise and followed him over to the window. She offered her hand and he took it. By the glow of the candle and the moonlight shining through the window he could see her upturned face. Along with the anxiety in her expression there was love and trust. He bent down and kissed her lightly.

He sat down on the window-sill, swung his legs over, and disappeared out of her sight. Mindful of her promise, Penelope put out the candle, left the room, and locked herself in her own bedroom.

~

Across the lawn, where Wentworth and Croft had been attempting to point out the stars they used in navigation to Mr. Elliot, there was a petrified silence. They had seen the man kiss a woman in Anne's bedroom and then escape out the window. They watched as he climbed down the trellis and ran away from them into the trees at the far side of the house.

"So it is true, after all!" said Mr. Elliot, as if to himself.

"What is true?" Wentworth's voice was sharp.

"The rumors. I heard something from a man in the village—spite, I thought, and discounted it. But it seems he was right. Miss Anne is—" he stopped abruptly and looked at Wentworth. "But I forget myself. I must beg your pardon, Wentworth. I am certain there is another explanation."

"Of course there is!" Croft's voice was harsh. "It is unthinkable that Miss Anne do anything dishonorable!"

"I have been warned—twice," said Wentworth hoarsely. "I thought it foolishness, or the work of an enemy, but now everything confirms it."

"Nonsense!" growled Croft.

Wentworth turned to him and said fiercely, "You saw with your own eyes a man leaving her bedroom—and on a night when she left our company early! There must be truth in it."

"I beg you, wait a little," said Mr. Elliot earnestly. "I know another man in the village whom I can trust. He will know if there is any truth to these accusations. I will go to him tomorrow. There is nothing to be done tonight, anyway. Let us return to the house."

~

"You did well," said Mr. Elliot when he and his valet were both back in his bedroom. "The kiss was perfectly timed, and the candlelight—it was at the perfect angle. You are a wonder, Borlock." He flicked a guinea to his valet. "Your part is finished. You may release Mrs. Clay from your association with her—she has served her purpose. I think you ought to ask Anne's maid about why Mrs. Clay was putting some kind of liquid into Miss Anne's glass at dinner... the maid will remember your question later, when Wentworth is discovered to be mistaken, and it will assist us later in putting the blame onto Mrs. Clay. She will soon be known as the wanton who invited a man into the bedroom of her hostess, after dosing her with laudanum, which, I may say, is not altogether implausible. Very well, then, you need not stand there like something carved in marble. Fetch me my night gear."

Chapter Sixteen

For the second night in a row, Borlock failed to sleep much. He had thought he would feel better when his part was finished and he could begin to plan his future away from Mr. Elliot. He had been wrong. He felt worse—much, much worse. He had warned Mrs. Clay that he might not return for her, believing that he could muster the strength of mind to leave her behind. But to leave her behind when he knew she would be blamed for the debacle—accused of being immoral herself! That was another thing. And he had been paid for his wickedness, too. *Like Judas*, he thought bitterly. And yet what could he do? To expose his wrongs now would bring down the vengeance of Mr. Elliot on himself—and who would believe him? Mr. Elliot could twist the story to his own advantage. Even if Mrs. Clay verified what he said, there was no assurance that she would be believed, either. He could only hope that Wentworth would not jump to any hasty conclusions.

"*For I will declare mine iniquity; I will be sorry for my sin.*" The words from Sunday's Psalm came back to him. "*Declare mine iniquity*"—to whom? Who was there to listen to his confession? Dawn was breaking before he thought of an answer to this question: he would go to the rector. The rector might be able to speak for him to the Elliots, and be listened to. He would give the man Mr. Elliot's guinea to be handed over to some poor person. *"I will be sorry for my sin."* Surely, not keeping the money would show his sincerity. He would go to the rectory as soon as Mr. Elliot was dressed for the day.

Never had his morning duties dragged on for so long. Mr. Elliot changed his mind twice about the coat he wanted to wear and found fault with the way his cravat was tied three times. His snuff box needed refilling and his watch had been mislaid. At long last his master left his bedroom for breakfast. Borlock slipped quietly down the servant's staircase and out the kitchen door.

The rector was surprised to find a visiting gentleman's valet at his door at such an early hour. He was more surprised still at the tale Borlock poured into his ears. The Reverend Mr. Darnell, a man in middle age who had long despaired of having any influence on most of the inmates of Kellynch Hall, could not but be heartened by a penitent who required no rebuke or admonishment to bring him to repentance, but professed himself already eager to right a wrong—nay, many wrongs. Just how the wrongs were to be righted was a little less clear, and the path ahead for Mr. Borlock was, at present, completely obscure.

"If it were a simple matter of telling the truth to Captain Wentworth," said Mr. Darnell after meditating on the problem for a few minutes, "there would be no question as to the best course. However, as you say, your word may not be believed. The trap has been laid very carefully and we will need proof in order to be convincing."

"You will help me, then, sir?" said Borlock hesitantly. "I did not come to you with any such idea in mind—only to confess my guilt and ask for your advice."

"I will help, of course. You say that Mr. Elliot has a grudge against Captain Wentworth because of his ship being confiscated. That must be a matter of public record which could be verified."

"No doubt it could," agreed Borlock, "eventually."

"I will start enquiries today," said the rector. "I have a friend in London who will find the record of the event if I ask him. I will also visit Sir Walter, to warn him that I believe there to be a slanderous story concerning Miss Anne in circulation. That ought to put him on his guard and enable him to contradict any lies that are told to him. No doubt he can calm Captain Wentworth's fears, if he has been worried by your deception last night."

"And what shall I do?"

"I think you ought to return to Kellynch for today, as if nothing has changed. It would not do to put Mr. Elliot on his guard, which your disappearance would do."

A knock was heard on the sitting-room door, and a housekeeper came in.

"I beg your pardon, sir, but little Mary Finch is here, saying her father is worse and Mrs. Finch wants to know if you will come."

"Oh dear, poor man," said the rector. "Tell her I will come immediately." The housekeeper curtseyed and departed, and Mr. Darnell said to Borlock, "It seems that I will have to postpone my visit to Sir Walter. I will, however, write him a note before I go and have it sent to Kellynch directly. That will safeguard his peace of mind, whatever happens."

"I will leave you now," said Borlock, rising from his chair. "I cannot thank you as you ought to be thanked for your help, but please know—"

"All right, that is enough," interrupted the rector. "I need no thanks for trying to establish the truth! And do not despair," he added. "I daresay if you search your memory you will remember some portions of Scripture which will comfort you. You have probably heard 'A bruised reed shall he not break, and the smoking flax shall he not quench.' You may meditate upon those words for a little while."

~

Captain Wentworth did not appear at breakfast. The scene at Anne's window had dominated his thoughts all night, along with the conversation with the masked man at the ball who had hinted at such a thing, and the warning letter he had received. Only a fool, he thought, would trust his own estimation of a woman in the face of so much contrary evidence. He would do nothing until Mr. Elliot had confirmed the story with his acquaintance in the village, but until then, he intended to stay alone in his room, thinking.

Shortly after the noon hour, Mr. Elliot knocked on his door.

"I am sorry to say," he said when he had been admitted to the room, "that you were right in your assumption last night. The man I spoke with is a servant who was dismissed from Kellynch a few months ago. He says that everyone in the village knows Anne has been meeting a man. I am grieved for you, and ashamed that it is my family who has brought this calamity on you."

"I must thank you for your efforts in finding out the truth for me," said Wentworth with difficulty. "I am certain you never wished to start a scandal."

"Better to find out the truth now and make a small stir about it than to marry first and then have a public scandal in a criminal conversation trial!"

"Very true," said Wentworth shortly.

"I will leave you now," said Mr. Elliot. "I am certain you will need time to decide about how you ought to respond to this betray—I mean, to this fault." He bowed and left the room.

Betrayal! That was the right word, thought Wentworth. Anne had presented herself as a pure, innocent, and even shy woman, and she was none of these things. He wondered if Sir Walter knew of his daughter's behavior. Could it have been a fraud perpetrated on him by the entire family?

He was growing angry; he could feel the wrath rising in him. It would be a mistake to say anything to the family now. He could not spend the entire day in his bedroom, neither could he be in the company of the Elliots all day pretending like nothing had happened. He would go for a ride—a long ride. He would leave a note for Croft and slip away.

He was soon riding toward Taunton—not because he had any business there, but because the road was well-kept and sign-posted and he need not worry about where he was going. He had only been gone for a quarter of an hour when he heard a horse galloping behind him. He turned to see Croft chasing after him.

"What on earth are you doing?" Croft bellowed at him as he drew near.

"Going for a ride. I left you a note."

"Yes, I received your note. But where are you going? You said you would be gone for hours."

"I wanted to think. Elliot confirmed the story, you know."

"And you believe it all?"

"Do not you?"

"I have not enough evidence to make up my mind," said Croft. "For one thing, no one has asked Miss Anne if there is another explanation."

"Anne!" Wentworth sputtered. "As if she could be trusted!"

"You have made up your mind, I see."

Wentworth set his jaw and looked straight ahead.

"You always were so hasty, Frederick," sighed Croft.

"Well then, leave me to myself," said Wentworth.

"No, not in this mood you're in. Who knows what you might do? Sophia would never forgive me if I leave you to your own devices now! It is the theft of the sugarplums all over again."

The letter that the rector had written was dutifully brought to Kellynch hall by his manservant. It was delivered to a footman, who gave it into Sir Walter's own hands.

Sir Walter had been in the midst of a daydream about the coming dinner that evening. Besides Lady Russell, three couples were coming to dine: the Alticks, the Harrises, and the Wiltons.

How awe-struck they would be by his naval heroes! How they would admire him for giving these brave men a respite from care at his noble estate! And how envious that he had a daughter actually engaged to one of them! He had just started to make a mental list of the stories he would wish Captain Wentworth to regale his guests with, when the note came and diverted his attention.

"Who is this from?" he asked the footman.

"It came from the rectory, sir."

"Ah. No doubt a missive asking for a preferment for his nephew, or some such thing. I shall read it in due course." Sir Walter tucked it into his coat pocket and forgot all about it.

Anne had awoken still feeling tired. She was surprised that Captain Wentworth did not appear at breakfast, but it was not in her nature to be suspicious, and when Benwick told her that Admiral Croft had informed him that he and Wentworth were going for a ride, she did not worry unduly. It was a little odd, to be sure, that he had said nothing to her about it, but no doubt he would explain when he returned. As the afternoon wore on and there was still no sign of the two officers, she did entertain some fears that they had lost their way. The fears increased when the dinner guests arrived and still they had not come.

Sir Walter also became uneasy. He had particularly wanted to make a good impression on the Wiltons, and he had no desire to present a future son-in-law who wandered the countryside instead of being in good time for dinner.

At long last there was a bustle at the door of the drawing room, where the guests had gathered before going in to dine, and Croft and Wentworth came in. Sir Walter's relief turned to horror, as he realized that they were still dressed in the clothes they had ridden in, a solecism he could not excuse. They looked very solemn.

"Something is wrong," said Benwick to Louisa, who had

insisted she felt well enough to join in the dinner party. "I have seen that look on Wentworth's face before; I was his First Lieutenant on the *Laconia*. This is his look of outrage."

Louisa turned wondering eyes to the captain; she had never imagined he could look like *that*. Anne, too, was stunned to see the cold, proud expression on his face; his eyes once met hers, but he did not smile or make any sign of recognition.

Sir Walter felt the awkwardness of the moment, but he had no thought but what the officers' grave demeanor was due to their inappropriate clothing; they must be mortified to appear in such garments for dinner. The only explanation, to his mind, was that they had not wanted to make the assembly wait even longer for their dinner while they changed their clothes. Misplaced concern on their part, but pardonable.

"Ah, here they are at last," he announced, and the conversations among the guests died away. He cleared his throat for his speech. "This dinner is in honor of the betrothal of my daughter Anne to Captain Fredrick Wentworth."

"No." Captain Wentworth's voice was harsh. "The betrothal is dissolved. I came to this house in all good faith. I had no idea that I would be used in such a fashion."

Sir Walter gaped at him for just a moment. "In what fashion, sir?" Sir Walter had some idea that this might be a joke; jests were frequently hard for him to understand.

"That woman." Wentworth pointed at Anne, seated next to Lady Russell on the sofa. "That woman has betrayed me. She has been secretly meeting men in her bedroom." Shocked gasps from the guests covered Anne's feeble cry.

"Careful," murmured Croft behind Wentworth. "You said you would ask for her side of the story."

Wentworth swung around to face him. "You still think there is some doubt? Very well, then. Miss Elliot!" He took a step nearer to where she stood, face ashen. "What were you doing in your bedroom last night when you left us in the drawing room?"

Anne tried to speak, but no sound came.

"Anne?" said Sir Walter, still perplexed but convinced at last that no one was joking.

"I went to sleep," Anne managed to say faintly. "I was very tired."

"That," said Wentworth loftily, "is a lie. We saw her at her window—Croft, Mr. Elliot, and I. She kissed a man, and then he climbed down the trellis outside her window."

There were exclamations from several of the women, Mrs. Clay's cry of horror among them. She alone knew that it was a terrible mistake. She opened her mouth to protest, but caught herself. How could she announce to this gathering of the gentry that she had been kissing a man—a servant!—in the bedroom of a sleeping woman? Unthinkable! And would it endanger Mr. Borlock to confess it all? He had told her that he could not explain everything to her, and she had promised to say nothing. Oh, but he could not have foreseen something like this!

"Ridiculous!" Lady Russell's voice was shaken but indignant. She clasped Anne's hand.

"I fear it is true," said Admiral Croft. "I would not have had it announced to this assembly, but—" he gestured a little helplessly toward Wentworth. "We did indeed see such a scene last night."

With a little moan, Anne fell sideways onto Lady Russell's lap, paper-white and unconscious.

"Anne!" cried out Elizabeth, hurrying over to her. "Anne, are you all right?"

There was a babble of voices now, wondering, questioning, and expressing shock.

"I will take my leave now, Sir Walter," said Wentworth above the noise. "If you did not know of your daughter's character, then I am very sorry for you. If you did, then your disgrace is well-deserved." He turned abruptly and left the room, Croft at his heels.

Sir Walter was pale. "Lady Russell, Elizabeth, what is to be done? I am distracted! I do not know what to think!"

It was Admiral Baldwin who answered him. "Let her be taken

up to bed," he said. "I, or Captain Benwick, can carry her there. Someone should fetch her maid and ask her to bring smelling-salts."

"Yes," said Elizabeth, "of course! You should carry her upstairs. I will go up with you."

In a moment they were gone from the room. Lady Russell looked at Sir Walter who seemed about to faint as well, and took command.

"My dear friends," she said, "I know not what has occurred, but I would more easily believe every man on earth a liar than Miss Anne a dissipated female. I vow we will discover the mystery shortly, and Miss Anne will be proven innocent. Therefore, I beg you, say nothing of this to anyone. You will have your reward when the truth is known and your faith in her virtue justified."

There were murmurs of assent from those gathered, including Mr. Elliot. He looked appropriately grieved, and Sir Walter, whose mind had almost ceased to form rational thoughts, noted and approved the dignified way he effaced himself.

Wentworth's manservant was in the servants' hall with Borlock when the bell for Wentworth's room rang. "At last!" he said. "I could not believe he had not yet returned from his ride!" and left to attend his master. He reappeared in a few moments and spoke quietly to Borlock.

"He is determined to leave within the hour," he said. "I have never seen him like this before—never!"

"What is it? Why does he leave?"

"He did not say, exactly—only something about betrayal and women. Admiral Croft was there, advising him to be calm and consider what he was doing, but he would not listen. No doubt we will be gone soon. I must go now—I only came downstairs to collect his linen from the laundry-room. Goodbye!"

"Goodbye," said Borlock to the man's retreating form.

Gradually the house grew quiet. Wentworth and his servant had departed, the other guests had returned home, and Sir Walter had gone to bed. Lady Russell sat with Anne, who had regained consciousness but was utterly broken by the false accusation. Baldwin paced on the terrace, wondering how he could serve Miss Elliot now. Formerly he had thought her at times lacking in sisterly affection, but she had shown tonight a warm devotion to her sister. The anxiety on her face as Baldwin had laid Anne on her bed was etched on his memory. Would that he could relieve that fear! Alas, he knew no more than she did about what could possibly have given Wentworth and the other men the idea that she was a loose woman.

The morning room windows opened out onto the terrace, and as darkness had now fallen, he looked into the lighted room. Elizabeth was there, sitting in a chair, with her face covered by her hands. Inexorably, his feet moved toward her until he was standing before her. He knelt and touched her arm.

"Miss Elliot, have you wept all this while?"

"Yes," she said, sniffling into her handkerchief, "and I will weep a while longer."

"Surely, I do believe your sister is wronged."

Elizabeth looked up at him then, gratefully. "I thank you. I have no doubt there has been some mistake. But Captain Wentworth has slandered her—slandered her to our friends!"

"It was wrong of him, very wrong. I wish—Miss Elliot, I wish I might show myself your friend in this hour."

"You are too good, Admiral Baldwin. Your unselfishness and kindness are much more than I deserve."

"Oh, Miss Elliot," said Baldwin softly, "I do love nothing in the world so well as you. Is not that strange?"

Elizabeth looked at him, the wonder on her face matching that on his.

"As strange as for me to say that I love nothing so well as you.

But you must not believe me," she added quickly. "Although I do not lie—I think I am out of my senses with sorrow, therefore do not take heed to anything I say now."

"Upon my word, Miss Elliot. You do love me!"

There was a moment of silence. "I cannot deny it," she said quietly with her eyes downcast.

"Elizabeth."

She looked up into his face and the expression she saw there stopped her heart. Love and joy were shining from his eyes.

"But I am afraid," she went on wretchedly, "that you will say you love me and then deny it later ... like Captain Wentworth."

"Then test my love," he said boldly. "Ask me to do anything for you."

"Anne should be avenged," said Elizabeth. "But my father would never— And I have no brother. Therefore, it must be you. You must fight Wentworth for my sister's honor."

He drew back in shock. "I cannot—not Wentworth!"

"No, I thought not." Elizabeth sank back in her chair. "It took very little time for you to retract your love. Such a villain tells lies about my sister and you refuse to call him to account?"

Baldwin looked at her steadily. "My love—so I will call you, for so you are—you know not what you are asking."

"Perhaps not." She pulled her hand away from his. "Anne shall no doubt die of grief, and I will follow her soon after. You may shed tears at our graves and think that you valued sentiment over love and honor."

"I wish you could see into my heart," said Baldwin, "for you would find your name written there." Elizabeth made no response. The thought of losing her now, just as he had gained her heart, was unbearable. "Very well," he said quietly. As nothing else will serve to satisfy you, I will challenge him to a duel."

Chapter Seventeen

Baldwin sat on his horse looking at the peaceful village of Kellynch in the morning sunlight. Wentworth, Croft said, had removed last night to The Nag's Head in the village. There were guests in various stages of removal from Kellynch this morning: Mr. Elliot was preparing to leave the Elliots to flounder in their sorrow, and so was Mrs. Clay. This was right and proper, according to Lady Russell: it could only add to the turmoil in the house to have so many people staying there. She had passed an indifferent night at Anne's bedside: Anne was conscious, Lady Russell reported to the others in the morning, but she had some reason to fear that her senses were disordered.

Baldwin acknowledged to himself that there was no good reason to delay his errand: he ought to ride directly to the inn, find Wentworth, and issue his challenge. Still he stayed where he was. Despite his love for Elizabeth and his being convinced that there was a mistake somewhere, he was reluctant to take this step. Wentworth was a good man in spite of his impulsiveness—and a good shot. He had little wish to wound him—or worse—and he had even less wish to die at his hands. If only he could delay the meeting! Surely some fact would come to light that would explain the apparent debauchery.

A delay—that was what was needed. If, for example, he did not find Wentworth until the afternoon, and then if he could delay the duel for another day or two ... it was worth trying. Anything would be better than meeting him tomorrow at dawn with pistols! He tugged on the bridle to turn the horse away from the village and spurred him to a trot.

Mrs. Clay was desperate to communicate with Borlock and ask him what she should do. Surely she ought to say something to the Elliots about the mistake that had been made. It was unthinkable that the error might be left uncorrected and cause untold ruin! Very early in the morning she wrote a note to him and sent it by her maid, promising her a shilling if she could get it to Borlock in secret. But although the maid said she had delivered it, no reply was forthcoming. By late morning, the maid reported that Mr. Elliot was leaving as soon as his carriage could be made ready.

Penelope considered going into the servants' quarters to find him, but she could hardly converse with him privately there. She had a notion that she might find him out of doors, making the carriage ready, and concluded that it was her best hope of getting an audience with him. She went outside and stood near the front door, watching the groom and Borlock load Mr. Elliot's luggage onto the carriage.

Borlock started on seeing her, but he made no sign of recognition. She remained there while Mr. Elliot said his goodbyes to Sir Walter, who, although he was in great affliction, could not dispense with the propriety of seeing off his heir in person. Borlock climbed onto the bench outside the back of the carriage. As it started moving down the drive, he turned to look at her; the expression on his face reminded her very much of her sons when they were detected in wrongdoing.

She watched until the carriage was out of sight. He was gone, and without a word. Unless ... She turned and walked slowly through the estate grounds until she came to the folly. There was little chance that Borlock had left her a message, but she needed to make sure. She bent down to reach into the crack, and her fingers touched paper. With a trembling hand she pulled out the note. On it was written only two words: *Forgive me.*

She sat down limply on the folly steps. It was all a lie. There was some plot against Anne—why, she could not imagine—and she had been duped into taking part in it. Borlock's words of love, his promise to reform—all of it had been false. No, not all: he had claimed that he had a bad character and that, at least, was true.

Borlock had not been present, of course, at Captain Wentworth's denunciation of Anne, but word had seeped through the ranks of the servants, and Mr. Elliot had given him a masterly description of the event when he had attended him at bedtime. Evidently the rector had never sent a note, Borlock thought, or it had not been read: Sir Walter had obviously heard the accusation without any preparation.

The news that Mr. Elliot was to leave Kellynch was heard by Borlock with joy. As soon as he could, he would invent some excuse to make a journey and then he could see what the rector was about not to have written a note after he had promised to! After that, he would find a new situation and begin life anew.

He managed to slip away to the folly to leave his message of apology for Mrs. Clay, but he hoped to leave Kellynch without seeing her. If she would keep quiet until he could return to set things to rights—it might be a week or more, but he would do it —he could explain his actions to her. He could not *excuse* his actions, and he dreaded the change that would come over her face when she realized that he was not a gentleman thief, but merely a villain.

He was almost undone when he saw her as they were loading the carriage. His self-control held good, and his pounding heart was not reflected on his impassive face. But as he mounted the bench outside the carriage and let himself see her as the carriage moved away, his heart broke. She was suffering and it was all his own doing.

Kellynch village was only two miles away, and they passed through it at a slow pace. A flock of turkeys being driven across the road caused the carriage to stop for a moment, opposite the bookshop. Through the window he could see the rector talking to someone inside. Suddenly he knew what he should do.

Stealthily, being careful not to jar the carriage in any way, he moved to the end of the bench, and used the moment when the carriage went into motion again to cover the joggle of his sliding down to the ground. He half expected to hear the coachman or even Mr. Elliot call after him, but they never looked back. He nipped into the bookshop and found Mr. Darnell on the point of departure. It took a moment for the rector to place him.

"My dear fellow!" he said genially, "Have you any news?"

"Yes, sir—but all very bad."

The rector's face clouded with dismay. "Then come with me to the rectory where we may talk in private."

Once seated in the rectory parlor, it did not take long for Borlock to tell all he knew.

"I should have gone myself," said Mr. Darnell, shaking his head. "I was intending to call on Sir Walter today—very shortly, as a matter of fact—but I ought to have gone last night. I trusted too much to my note, which may have been put aside unread as something of little importance."

"You cannot be blamed, sir," said Borlock. "I, on the other hand, was an important participant in the plot. The culpability is mine."

"There are many to blame," said Mr. Darnell, "but assigning it to one or another is an endeavor for another day. I will go to Kellynch now."

"It may be too late, sir. Captain Wentworth is gone off and I do not know where."

"Never mind; there will be someone at Kellynch who can get a message to him, I am sure. I think you ought to wait for me at The Nag's Head; here is a shilling for your dinner."

"You are very good, sir," said Borlock.

The rector chuckled. "It is but part of the guinea you gave me yesterday. Now, let us be off!"

"And you think the fellow is to be trusted? This valet?" said Sir Walter. He sat transfixed in front of the rector. The rector thought that it was perhaps the only time he could remember Sir Walter actually paying attention to what he was saying.

"I do. I am awaiting confirmation of Captain Wentworth's part in capturing Elliot's ship, which would constitute a very plausible reason for his taking such revenge."

"Scoundrel!" said Lady Russell. "I have never liked him, *never*. I had little thought that he would do such a harm to my poor Anne, but I am not at all surprised to hear that he is wicked."

"Where is Mrs. Clay?" was Sir Walter's next question. "Will she confirm this story?"

"I will find her," said Lady Russell, rising. "She was awaiting her father's carriage to come and carry her home, but I do not think it has come yet."

Penelope was discovered beside Anne's bed, tears coursing down her face.

"Miss Elliot asked me to sit with Miss Anne," she whispered. "She has been given a sleeping draught and is resting, but Miss Elliot did not want to leave her alone."

"She can be left alone for a few minutes," said Lady Russell, equally low. "I need to speak to you."

Penelope rose and followed Lady Russell out of the room. She had thought her heart too heavy to feel more dread, but she had been mistaken. She could hardly move her feet across the hallway into an empty bedroom.

Twenty minutes later, Lady Russell returned to the morning room. "Mrs. Clay confirmed your story, Mr. Darnell. She was unaware of the plot, I hardly need say, although to take up with a servant like that—! Women can be *such fools*," she added bitterly.

"We can all of us be foolish," said the rector. "But where is Miss Elliot?"

"She was sleeping an hour ago," said Lady Russell. "She was awake all night, watching over her sister, and I told her that she must sleep a little."

"Go and wake her," said Sir Walter. "The family honor has been restored—it will cheer her."

Elizabeth, struggling to wake up enough to understand Lady Russell's words, was not as cheerful as Lady Russell expected her to be when she finally understood.

"Are you saying Captain Wentworth was *tricked*?" she asked. "And by Mr. Elliot?"

"Yes. It was all done very cleverly, and although I think Captain Wentworth is very much to blame for jumping so hastily to believe the worst, he did have some reasonable grounds for his assumption."

"Good heavens!" said Elizabeth, sitting bolt upright. "And Admiral Baldwin has gone to challenge him to a duel for his slander! He left hours ago—they might be dueling at this very moment!"

Admiral Baldwin was at that moment entering The Nag's Head. He had delayed as long as he felt he dared, and he was still unhappy as he saw Wentworth consuming his mid-day meal at one of the tables. Neither of them saw Borlock, mostly hidden behind a draft-inhibiting screen finishing off his own meal.

"Baldwin!" said Wentworth. "Come and join me. Have you had enough of the Elliots, too?"

Baldwin slowly approached the table.

"I thank you, no," he said gravely. "I come on an altogether more unpleasant errand."

"Oh?"

"I issue a challenge for the honor of Miss Anne."

Wentworth's mouth opened in surprise. "You are not serious?" he said after a moment.

"I am. I have loved you as a brother-in-arms for too long to make this anything less than grievous, but I am convinced that Anne is slandered by you and will be ruined if nothing is done."

"Come, now, Baldwin, you cannot believe such a thing!"

"Not only I, but Miss Elliot, too."

"Oho! She has put you up to it, has she not? I would not trust anything an Elliot says. You are a simpleton."

"I will trust to my own wits, thank you," said Baldwin, thinking that if he must fight, Wentworth was making it much easier to bear the thought of dispatching him.

"Very well, then," snapped Wentworth. "I will meet you when and where you will!"

"I beg your pardon, sirs," said Borlock. He had risen and was coming over toward them. They looked at him in surprise.

"Borlock!" said Wentworth. "What do you do here? Is Mr. Elliot here?"

"No, sir, he is gone. I came to confess my part in the plot to make Miss Anne look guilty."

At three o'clock that afternoon, Admiral Baldwin found Elizabeth pacing in the rose garden. With a little cry of gladness she ran to him and he clasped her in his arms.

"Never did I think to see you running to me, my dear Miss Elliot," he said with a glimmer of humor.

"You are unharmed!" she said. "I was so afraid." She pulled away from him. "Is Captain Wentworth also well?"

"We did not fight, if that is what you are asking. The servant,

Borlock, who was instructed by his master to perform this ruse, interrupted us while I was issuing my challenge to Wentworth and told us the truth."

"It was Mrs. Clay in Anne's room," said Elizabeth.

"Yes. Wentworth knows that now. I have never seen a man more broken over his mistake. And how does your sister?"

"Very ill."

"And how do you?"

"Very ill, too." She began to amble along one of the paths, and Baldwin followed her. "I do not know if Anne will recover. She was so grieved and shocked by the accusation that she may never be the same."

"That is very bad," said Baldwin. "Do you think that when she knows that all now believe her to be innocent she will recover? Wentworth is as eager to marry her now as he was before."

"I do not know. She—she loved Captain Wentworth very much. That he believed such things about her … is it not natural that she should doubt him? I begin to think he is not worthy of a lady like Anne."

Baldwin saw a dead flower in one of the bushes he passed, and paused to pinch it off. "I understand you. I do believe he is worthy of her, but he has made a terrible blunder—the fault of his hasty temper! He knows it and would do anything to make amends."

Elizabeth shook her head. "I know not what he could do to prove himself. My father has already sworn that he shall not be joined with the Elliot family."

"That is a great pity, but I cannot say I blame him."

Elizabeth reached up to brush a tear from her cheek. "It is all very hopeless."

"No." Baldwin spoke with decision. "No, it is not hopeless at all. Things were far worse when I encountered the *Coquelicot*. She was an eighty-gun frigate, and we were in the Bay of Naples with a supply ship—" He stopped and looked down at her. "That will be a story for another day. The principle point is that there are in this house two admirals and a captain, all of us accustomed to making battle plans and carrying them out. This is about saving Captain Wentworth as well as your sister—and for my part, I would rather marry into a house unclouded by scandal and trouble. Which brings another point to mind—I have not yet asked you to marry me, have I?"

Elizabeth smiled at him with misty eyes and shook her head.

"That will be remedied, and shortly," he said. "But I think it is best to wait until this little matter is dealt with."

"Hurry, then," whispered Elizabeth.

There was a meeting in the drawing room that night; Wentworth could not help thinking of it as a court martial. His fellow navy-officers were there, as well as Sir Walter, Elizabeth, and Lady Russell. Louisa was above stairs, sitting with Anne. Wentworth had not been allowed to see Anne, in spite of his entreaties. She was too ill to be agitated in that way; the physician had prescribed perfect quiet, and Wentworth had submitted. He had made heart-felt apologies to Sir Walter and Elizabeth, groveling in a way that Croft had not imagined he could. He only wished Sophie could see it.

"We have heard your apologies," said Sir Walter in a most majestic manner, "and we are inclined to think you sincere. However, there has been much injury done. The physician is by no means convinced that Anne will make a good recovery."

"I beg you, sir, let me make amends," said Wentworth hoarsely. "I am very much at fault. Even if I had been tricked but yet not made so public a denouncement, the sequel would have been very different."

"I am glad you take that view of the case," said Lady Russell. "How is it you propose to make amends?"

"Would that I could think of a way!" cried the captain. "If I were a knight of old who could be sent on a quest to prove my true repentance, I would go to the world's end! Even if—" he faltered. "Even if I may never marry Anne, I will still do anything you name to make what recompence I can."

"What think you?" said Sir Walter to Admiral Croft. "Shall we tell him of the opportunity that has arisen?"

Croft glanced at the other officers and, receiving their nods of approval, said, "Yes. I think it is the best plan."

"Very well," said Lady Russell. "There is an old woman living in Bath who wishes to travel to France—to see her daughter, at present living in Dijon with her husband. Now that the war is ended, my friend Mrs. Thorogood wants to travel to see her daughter and grandchildren. She has no relative to travel with her, but she would be grateful for the escort of one who is an officer in His Majesty's Navy. Will you lend her your escort? I know not how long she will stay; you would be expected to remain with her family until she decides to return home."

"I will do it."

"Even knowing that you might never marry Anne?"

"Yes."

"Very well," said Lady Russell. "I shall write to her immediately. I daresay she will wish to travel straightaway; she has been longing to see her daughter for several years. Can you be ready to go within a fortnight?"

Wentworth bowed his head. "I am at your service."

"It is settled, then," said Sir Walter. "Honor is satisfied. When you return—if you have not met with a French beauty that you desire to marry instead—we will see if Anne is well enough to consider marriage, and if she will consider you as a possible suitor."

"I will never marry another," said Wentworth. "If Anne will not have me, I will not attempt to find happiness while she is still alone. I will have Anne as my wife, or no wife at all."

"Do you swear it?" asked Admiral Croft.

"I do."

"Well, then," said Croft to Sir Walter, "you can rely on that. I know Frederick—if he swears an oath, he will keep it."

Sir Walter nodded. "We have one other matter to discuss, then, and that is what to do with my heir, Mr. Elliot. He is the author of this calamity, and thus far he has not been punished."

"You may have recourse to the law, Sir Walter," said Benwick, speaking for the first time. "You could bring a lawsuit for damages done to your daughter's health; or *you* could bring one, Wentworth, for breaking up your engagement through deceit and trickery."

"I cannot think it desirable," said Lady Russell. "To have all the details of the event published in the newspapers for everyone to read! Mr. Elliot might be forced to pay damages, but you would all be punished."

"Very true," said Elizabeth. "One cannot wish that the humiliating affair be made generally known." She gripped the handkerchief in her lap in frustration. "The thought of Mr. Elliot inheriting the title and the estate is galling," said Elizabeth. "And yet, what can be done? The estate is entailed to him, and as long as he lives, he inherits."

"Are you suggesting that I arrange a fatal accident for him?" said Admiral Baldwin, who felt that this remark was aimed at him.

"No," said Elizabeth, "as convenient as it would be, I cannot conspire at such a thing."

"If only I had had a son," fretted Sir Walter. "The entail would have gone to him."

"Well, sir," said Captain Benwick humbly. "If you will pardon my effrontery, you might marry again and produce an heir still."

Sir Walter took in this suggestion in a slightly dazed manner. He had gone from believing that his naval guests were the very embodiments of honor to deciding that one of them was the most vile person on earth. His faith had been a little restored by the discovery of Mr. Elliot's trickery, but it was still tarnished by the fact that Wentworth had allowed himself to be fooled. Now Captain Benwick seemed to him to be the cleverest man he had ever met.

"Marry again!" he said, delighted. "Why, that would solve

every difficulty! I have remained single for my dear daughters' sake, but there is no need for me to do so any longer." He turned to Lady Russell. "Do you think Lady Eleanor Ludlow would do to become the next Lady Elliot?"

Lady Russell coughed. "Perhaps, Sir Walter, we would do better to discuss the matter later."

"Yes, yes, of course," he replied, and fell into a daydream.

Chapter Eighteen

"How is your sister this afternoon?" said Baldwin. He and Elizabeth were alone in the morning room. Louisa had gone back to Uppercross, although not until Captain Benwick had read all three volumes of *Waverley* to her. It had been nearly a week since Anne was struck down by shock and sorrow.

"Better, I think. Stronger. She is now chafing at being confined to her room. I think her only solace is watching him pace on the terrace from her window. I'm afraid she has become one of those females who pine."

"So she has forgiven Wentworth?"

"Completely. She has always rated her claims very low, and he does seem to be sorry for his errors."

"Yes, that he is. He has not talent for subterfuge, and you may trust to his sincerity."

"Anne trusts him. I confess I would not have trusted him again so soon."

"You are a spitfire, my dear," said Baldwin, grinning at her.

"So I am—rather like you. Did you succeed in applying for a marriage license for Captain Wentworth and Anne?"

"I did. And I spoke to the parson, too; he is ready to marry them next Friday. He looked a little askance at the elaborate hoax

Lady Russell has contrived—that story about Wentworth atoning for his sins by accompanying some old woman to France! He seemed to think it less than honest."

"And so it is."

"Yes, but I represented it as a form of joke. It is an untruth which is serving a purpose and will last only a few more days."

"I am glad," said Elizabeth softly. "He is being tortured—thinking Anne still too unwell to see him, thinking he must go off to France for months, perhaps, without seeing her. He has devoted himself to Borlock."

"Yes, poor fellow. They both have lost the women they love through their own weaknesses."

"Yes, well, I am less certain that Borlock ought to have loved Penelope. She is not a gentlewoman, of course, but to fall in love with a valet ...!"

"Ah, but he was not always a valet, my dear. He may be sleeping in the servants quarters now, but he was born the grandson of a knight. I do not say that he would be a good match for, say, Louisa Musgrove, but I think he was not being unreasonable for thinking of Mrs. Clay."

"I see. And do you often make matches?"

"I? Heaven forbid! I have been spending the last few years trying to convince my fellow men, as well as myself, to remain bachelors."

"You were afraid no one would have you, I daresay."

"Not a bit of it. I have been flirted with from Cork to Gibraltar."

"Is that so?" said Elizabeth with an edge to her voice. "I suppose you were the most sought-after bachelor in the Navy."

"Well—"

"And you held yourself too much a prize to condescend to marry any of them?"

"Elizabeth," said Baldwin, "Will you marry me next Friday?"

Elizabeth laughed at the suddenness of the question. "Admiral Baldwin, are you proposing in the middle of an argument?"

"You and I are too wise to woo peaceably," he said. "And I hope you will agree to it, for I have already applied for the license."

"A little precipitate, are you not?" she tried to sound affronted.

"I am. But while I was on the way there it came to me that I did not want to make *another* journey to talk to the bishop. And moreover, Elizabeth, the thought of seeing Wentworth standing up in front of the church to marry Anne and have his heart's desire while I still have not mine ... well, I could not bear the thought."

"Very well, then," said Elizabeth. "I will marry you next Friday. But by this light, I take you for pity."

"That," said Baldwin, "Is enough talking from you." He took her face between his hands and kissed her.

The next day, confirmation came from the rector's friend in London: the ship which Captain Wentworth had intercepted and then commandeered was indeed owned by Mr. Elliot. Lady Russell lost no time in visiting the Alticks, the Harrises, and the Wiltons to apprise them of the conclusion of the shocking scene they had been witness to.

Friday morning dawned. Wentworth packed his trunk, said a sorrowful goodbye to his fellow officers and a formal one to the Elliots. The Elliot carriage transported him to Lady Russell's house, where he was to meet an old lady named Mrs. Thorogood, in order to accompany her to France. He alighted from the carriage in a stoic frame of mind and was met by Lady Russell.

"Captain Wentworth, you have come."

Had he really noticed her, she would have seemed in an odd humor. There was an air of suppressed excitement about her that would be hard to attribute to his forthcoming journey with Mrs. Thorogood.

She escorted him into the house. "Come here into the drawing room and meet your companion."

He followed her into the drawing room. There was a woman dressed for travel, wearing a bonnet and pelisse, standing by the window, facing outward. She did not turn around when they entered.

"I bid you good day, ma'am," he said, crossing the room toward her. "I am at your service."

She turned around then., and he looked into the face of his beloved.

"Anne!" He looked as though he had seen a ghost. "Am I dreaming?"

Anne put out a hand as if to steady him.

"No, you are not. It is indeed I."

"Yes," said Lady Russell. "Your penance has ended, Captain Wentworth. Sir Walter is satisfied that you have made amends by your willingness to do whatever arduous task he set you. There is no old woman waiting for you to escort to France, there is only Anne for you to wed."

"If it pleases you," added Anne conscientiously.

"Anne!" His voice was only a whisper. "It pleases me—Oh, I cannot tell you how it pleases me!"

Anne was lost to Lady Russell's sight as she was embraced by the captain, who had not taken off his travelling cloak. The moment was prolonged.

"I hate to interrupt you at this interesting time," said Lady Russell, "but your presence is required at the church. The rector is waiting to perform your wedding, as well as that of Elizabeth and Admiral Baldwin. They are as impatient to be married as anyone could well be, and I will be in their black books if I do not speed you on your way to Kellynch church."

∼

While the happy couples were joining their hands and their hearts in marriage, Borlock walked to the home of Mr. Shepherd, Penelope's father. When he had arrived, however, he hesitated. He had not enough courage—yet—to knock at the door and ask if Mrs. Clay was at home to visitors. He feared a cold reception, and the repudiation of all that had passed between them, and he could not blame her if she met him thus. However, he could not go away forever without an attempt to see her. And so he found a large rock not far from the house where he could sit and gather up his courage to face the possibility of that door being shut firmly and finally in his face.

"Mr. Borlock."

He jumped. Penelope had evidently been out walking, and she had come up on him without him hearing her.

"Mrs. Clay!"

"And so you are returned." Her expression was hard to read.

"As you see." He took a deep breath and plunged in. "I have no excuse for my behavior," he said. "I ought to have risked Mr. Elliot's wrath and refused to aid him in his plan, but I was a coward."

Penelope said nothing. He swallowed and continued.

"I could not go away forever without informing you that much of what I told you was the truth."

"I know," Penelope said. "The rector told us that you are the grandson of a knight, and also that Mr. Elliot was using you as a tool in his schemes."

"Did he also tell you that I do love you?"

Her face flushed a becoming pink.

"Because I do," he went on. "When I promised to reform, I meant it. And when I told you that I love you, that was true as well. I have nothing to offer you but myself—and I am a very poor bargain. I have been dismissed from two situations and have run away from a third. I have no money and no property—what few possessions I did own are in Mr. Elliot's house in Bristol. I will not blame you if you send me away ..." his voice drifted off as Mrs. Clay drew near to him and put her hand in his.

"I am a poor bargain, too," she said simply. "I have no money of my own, I have two children already, and my birth is humble."

"But you have character, my dear. I have none."

"I would not say that, exactly," A smile lurked behind Penelope's eyes. "It was your confession to the rector that began to put everything right. It would have been easier for you to leave it all alone, at least until you had gone back to Bristol and retrieved your things. I think that shows some character."

"It is a start, perhaps."

"And I think that my father will find it proof enough of integrity to let you assist him in his work. You have a good education, I hear."

"Would he hire me? I hardly think he would trust me so soon. I can scarcely believe that you would trust me at all."

"I believe he will. He has heard from Sir Walter how you attempted to make things right as soon as you had done wrong."

Borlock shook his head. "It is too much. How could I thank him?"

Penelope squeezed his hand. "Serve God, love me, and mend."

The wedding breakfast was as lavish as Sir Walter could obtain with only two weeks' notice. He sat next to Lady Russell, watching the others eat the celebratory meal with only half his attention.

"My dear sir," said that lady when she had tried three times to get his attention, "what thoughts can be so absorbing to you?"

"I was thinking of how difficult this month has been—the excitement, the stress, the grief and the joy. Tell me, are there not lines about my eyes? I thought I noticed some in the mirror this morning."

"Sir Walter! You are fifty-four years of age. Sooner or later a wrinkle may appear."

"But I must be in my best looks to woo the next Lady Elliot. There is no one eligible in this neighborhood. I shall have to travel to London for the season. Or remove to Bath, I suppose."

"Oh, Sir Walter, that is exactly what you need. You ought to go to Bath—this week, if you can. It is just the place for you; the society is genteel, there are concerts and assemblies to attend, and the cost is so much more reasonable than London."

Sir Walter's mouth twitched at the mention of money—he did not want to consider such a thing.

"Furthermore," continued Lady Russell, "I believe I can introduce you to the next Lady Elliot."

"Oh?" Sir Walter looked at her with interest.

"She is a young woman of my acquaintance, at present residing in Bath to nurse a disappointed hope. She is very well-looking and is handsomely dowered. Moreover, she would be very pleased to be the wife of a baronet."

"And her name?"

"Her name," said Lady Russell impressively, "Is Caroline Bingley.

The End

About the Author

Barbara Cornthwaite lives in the middle of Ireland with her husband and children. She taught college English before "retiring" to do something she loves far more; her days are now filled with homeschooling, trying to keep the house tidy (a losing battle), and trying to stay warm in the damp Irish climate (also a losing battle). She is surrounded by medieval castles, picturesque flocks of sheep, and ancient stone monuments. These things are unappreciated by her six children, who are more impressed by traffic jams, skyscrapers, and hot weather.

facebook.com/BarbaraCornthwaiteAuthor

twitter.com/BCornthwaite

bookbub.com/authors/barbara-cornthwaite

amazon.com/Barbara-Cornthwaite/e/B00J47TTZM

The Bachelor of Lambton

MUCH ADO ABOUT PERSUASION BONUS STORY

BARBARA CORNTHWAITE

Chapter One

Major Knowles was nicknamed "the bachelor of Lambton" exactly as if he were the only single man in the village. He was not, of course; there were several men of various ages who had never taken the plunge into matrimony. He was, however, the most languished after. A tall, handsome fellow with a respectable fortune, there had been little reason to wonder at his single state while he was in the army. But when peace came, and he bought Ivy House—a fine dwelling with a large garden—the good people of Lambton rather expected him to find a wife and settle down with her in it. He was invited to every party of note for miles around and introduced hopefully to every single female under the age of thirty. He obligingly danced with them all and was civil even to the plain ones, but contrary to their expectations, he remained a bachelor. At thirty-five, only the most stubbornly optimistic spinsters held out any hope of him asking for their hand.

Major Knowles enjoyed his garden, which he tended himself. He had a housekeeper, a cook, a manservant, and a maid, but refused every suggestion of hiring a gardener.

"And I will say this for 'im," said his housekeeper to her

bosom-friend Mrs. Finch, "he has a way with vegetables as much as he does with roses. I've never seen such marrows as he grows."

"Ah, those roses!" said Mrs. Finch. "'Ave you ever seen the like? I daresay Robbins up at Pemberley wishes he had the same luck with *his* roses as the Major does!"

Mrs. Silver (for that was the Major's housekeeper's name) allowed herself a small smile at Mrs. Finch's allusion to Pemberley. Her daughter worked there as an upper housemaid, and Mrs. Finch was bursting with pride about it. Her conversation was littered with references to the great estate, and any information about the Darcy family that Alice told her mother was sure to be passed around the village by Mrs. Finch. Mrs. Silver was not in a mood to hear more about the roses being grown at Pemberley, and she promptly changed the subject.

"Mrs. Wimbourne says the cottage next to Ivy House is let. She didn't know who is takin' it, but I'll be glad to see it occupied. Them cottages get so damp with no fires in them."

Mrs. Finch swelled with self-importance. "I know all about the cottage being let," she said. "Alice heard Mrs. Darcy tell Miss Georgiana as how it was her friend who was coming to live there. A widow with two wee girls, she said, from someplace in the south of England. Mr. Darcy owns that cottage, you know."

"Yes, I know," said Mrs. Silver, and was tempted to add that the entire village, if not the entire district, was already well-aware of that fact. A former servant of Pemberley had resided there, a pensioner of Mr. Darcy's, until death had claimed him a few months before. "A widow, you say! Well, that'll make a change. Old Simon was a recluse, o' course—hardly saw anything of 'im in the last year, except for at church. A widow with two little girls will be much more lively. Not that Major Knowles will notice, really. He keeps hisself to hisself."

A week later Major Knowles came in from the garden and told his housekeeper that there was smoke coming out of the chimney of the cottage.

"Ah, that'll be the new tenant," she said.

"New tenant? Who is he?"

"It's a lady," said Mrs. Silver, now full of facts gleaned by Alice and duly passed on to Mrs. Finch. "The widow of the parson that had Mr. Darcy's aunt's parish, and the parson was Mrs. Darcy's cousin. I suppose she had nowhere to go, poor thing, and the Darcys invited 'er to live here."

"Hm. Very kind of them," said the Major, but he was secretly annoyed. A widow was likely to stir up all kinds of gossip and trouble. He had known a widow in his youth, a Mrs. Cotton, who was large and loud and meddlesome, and no matter how many thin and mousy widows he had met in the years since, the word always conjured up a vision of Mrs. Cotton. Why could not the Darcys have installed another recluse there, like Old Simon? This widow would no doubt try to give him advice on his garden, or decide to find him "a nice little wife." Well, he would just have to ignore this lady, that was all.

Charlotte Collins first entered the cottage on a rainy day in March. It was smaller than the vicarage at Hunsford, but it was clean and in good order. Elizabeth Darcy had offered to come with her to see the place, but Charlotte had demurred.

"The Darcy carriage will make a stir in the village, and I would rather see my new home quietly," she said.

"My dear Charlotte, everyone in Lambton already knows that Mr. Darcy owns that cottage, and therefore anyone residing in it must have some connection to Pemberley. You will be an object of interest whether I come or not."

"I know I can never live anonymously in this district, but I would rather not have an audience to my first sight of the cottage —and I will, no doubt, if the Darcy carriage is sitting in front of it."

"Charlotte, you do realize that the cottage is not in the middle of the village, do you not? It is a full half-mile past the last house.

You will have only one near neighbor, and that is Major Knowles at Ivy House."

"Yes, you said so in your letter. Still, I would rather go alone."

"Very well," said Elizabeth, squeezing her friend's hand. "I will not press you. Would you like to take your girls on this occasion or leave them here at Pemberley to play with Fitzwilliam and Jane?"

"The latter, I think. The nurserymaid has promised to take them all to the stables to see the puppies, and I think Maria and Catherine would be broken-hearted to miss that."

Elizabeth nodded and said, "Indeed, and I think Fitzwilliam and Jane would not enjoy the excursion half so much if your girls were not with them. I wish you would stay longer—it has been so pleasant for us to have you here."

Charlotte shook her head. "It is very kind, Lizzy, but when my things arrive from Kent, I wish to settle into our new home."

"At least you will be nearby," said Elizabeth, "and our children can play together sometimes as you and I once did."

"That is a great comfort to me," admitted Charlotte. "I did not wish to go back to my parents' house with my children, and still less did I want to remain in Lady Catherine's parish."

Elizabeth shuddered. "No indeed. I hope you will not be lonely," said Elizabeth. "And if you are, you must come to Pemberley to visit us. You will always be welcome."

Charlotte did not think she would be lonely. In fact, she was used to spending her days alone with her children, even when she was married. Her husband, a harmless but rather silly man, was not the sort of companion she could tolerate for long. She did not really miss his presence now, but she missed the security he had represented. His death had been a shock, not only because she had to leave the parsonage at Hunsford, but also because it meant that her husband would not inherit the Longbourn estate upon Mr. Bennet's death. If the Collinses had had a son, the estate would have been entailed to him, but with only daughters, Charlotte would never be mistress there and her future was suddenly much more perilous.

Now as she stood looking around the cottage for the first time, she was content. Mr. Darcy was letting the house to her for a very low rent. It was a favor to him, he said, to have someone dependable residing there. Charlotte was not deceived, but she accepted the terms of rent for the sake of her daughters. It would have been difficult to bring them up in the home of her slightly vulgar parents or under the all-seeing eye of Lady Catherine. Now she could raise them in the comfort and simple elegance of her own home and with a connection to Pemberley. Elizabeth would make sure they had friends among the gentry of the area. Security was what she had feared losing with the death of her husband, but Providence had seen to it that her future was still secure.

Charlotte's little girls, Catherine and Maria, were entranced by the puppies at Pemberley and wretched at the thought of leaving them behind when they moved to the cottage at Lambton. Catherine considered that at six years old, she was well able to have a pet dog, and she timidly broached the subject with her mama, but all Charlotte would give were vague promises to consider it sometime in the misty future. Starting her life again in a new place with two small children was daunting enough; she felt that a dog would be more than she could manage.

The furniture arrived from Kent, and Charlotte, with the help of her new maid (a sturdy girl recommended by Elizabeth), moved to Lambton and began to get the cottage in order. The cottage had a large garden, a little overgrown, and Catherine and Maria went out every day to explore it. Charlotte, busy with housekeeping, was thankful for the stone walls that surrounded the garden so that she had no fear of them wandering off. All was peaceful and serene for the first month of their tenure there. It was the advent of the dog that started all the trouble.

~

Charlotte caught a cold at the beginning of May. She ignored the headache that developed during the morning and pressed on with her work, but it soon developed into a sore throat, a fever, and bouts of sneezing. She took to her bed and left the sturdy maid, Betsy, in charge of the house and the children.

Betsy was a capable girl; she finished her work and then took the children for a long walk in order to keep the house quiet so Mrs. Collins could rest. The sun was shining when they set out, but the clouds were more treacherous than they looked, and it began to rain before they got home. At first it was only a light shower, but as they got closer to home it was a true spring downpour. They scurried up the path through the garden in front of the cottage. There in front of them was a dog, shaggy and dirty, cowering in the rain by the door.

"Oooo, doggie!" said Maria, and before Betsy could stop her, she stooped down to hug the dripping dog. The dog wagged its tail and flattened its ears deprecatingly.

"Poor little dog!" said Catherine.

"It's not a *little* dog," corrected Betsy. "Must be lost. We'd best chase it off."

Both girls wailed at this.

"You mustn't drive off the poor dog," said Catherine. "He wants food and someone to dry him off. And look—look at his front paw!"

Betsy looked and saw a paw with matted blood on it. The dog stood, but kept weight off the paw.

"Mama says we must be kind to animals," said Catherine. "We need to help him and give him a home."

Betsy rather doubted that Mrs. Collins would think it her duty to give a home to such a draggled wretch of a dog, but she was soft-hearted and did not relish the thought of driving the dog away. At least, she thought, she might be able to give the dog a meal and see about that paw before sending it off somewhere.

"All right," said Betsy. "We'll take him around the back of the cottage and put him in the scullery. I'm not saying you'll be giving him a home—your mama will likely say she don't want a dog— but we can clean 'im up a bit and see what the matter is with his paw."

The girls squealed and opened the door to the cottage. The dog followed them in, limping, but wagging its tail violently. They shut it into the scullery.

"There now," said Betsy. "The pair of you are a sight—soaked to the skin. We'll get you changed into dry clothes first and then I'll deal with the dog."

The girls begged to help with bathing the dog, and Betsy regretted changing them into dry clothes before the feat was attempted. After the dog was given a wash in the scullery, the wounded paw was dusted with basilicum and bound with clean linen.

The little girls were delirious with delight. "Isn't he handsome?" said Catherine, watching the dog gnaw at the bone Betsy had been saving to make soup with.

"It's a she," said Betsy, who had made investigations during the bath, "and she *is* looking much better now."

"I shall call her Lady Jane Grey," said Catherine, no doubt inspired by the silver hair of the dog. "Mama said Lady Jane Grey was a very good lady, only I forget what she did or why she was good. The dog will be happy to be named for her."

"Oh, dear," said Betsy. "No, don't name the dog. Your mama hasn't said you could keep it—nor is she like to."

But the girls found their way to their mother's bedside in the course of the evening and pleaded their case. Their case was helped quite a lot by the fact that Charlotte was feverish and a little confused, and had formed the impression that she was dreaming. When the girls said that they had found a dog named Lady Jane Grey and they were nursing it back to health, it sounded very much like the sort of thing one hears in a dream. And when they asked if Lady Jane Grey could sleep in the scullery forever and ever, that seemed to confirm the idea that she was dreaming, and she murmured, "Yes, yes, I'm sure she will be very comfortable there."

Of course, two days later when Charlotte was recovered enough to leave her bed, she was shocked to learn that she had become mistress to a shaggy dog whose paw was healing, but who had no intention of leaving the warm and comfortable cottage. Betsy had made enquiries around the village, but no one knew where the dog had come from or remembered seeing it before.

"I know where it came from," said Maria solemnly. "I prayed that God would send us a dog, and He did." In her mind, the dog had been dropped straight from heaven.

"I suppose we must keep the dog," said Charlotte to Betsy. "The girls have lost enough—let them have this one thing they wish for."

That was at the beginning of May.

By the beginning of June, Lady Jane Grey was loping all over the garden with the little girls running after her. It was also discovered that she had a propensity to dig.

"Thank goodness you had nothing planted this year, ma'am," said Betsy to Charlotte as they surveyed the holes in the garden. "But if you plant a garden next year, something will have to be done."

Lady, as the dog was nicknamed, was an active animal. The girls played with her almost constantly, and she obligingly allowed them to dress her up in a bonnet or drape flower chains around her neck. So long as the girls were outside, Lady stayed close to them ("she's protecting them," asserted Betsy), but when they went inside the cottage and left Lady out, Lady dug or explored. One day she went over the lowest part of the stone wall, which was hidden behind a large shrub, into Major Knowles' garden.

Major Knowles had just been weeding the vegetables that morning, and when he went out in the afternoon and saw a dog digging furiously in his strawberry bed, he was understandably exasperated.

He erupted into the kitchen and demanded, "Mrs. Silver, where did that dog come from?"

"Ah, that must be the dog from the cottage—them little girls took it in. They're ever so attached to it."

Major Knowles sighed and chased the dog out of his garden, urging it back over the wall with a stick. It took him the rest of the afternoon to repair the damage the dog had done—for it had also dug where some lettuces were just coming up—but he told himself that it was not really anyone's fault, and that he must not turn into an ill-tempered man, at least not under the eye of Mrs. Silver. She had made a comment the other day about an old bachelor she knew that had turned cantankerous as he grew older, and he had a suspicion that it was her way of giving him a warning. For some reason, she thought bachelors were more likely to be cross than married men—a ridiculous notion! Still, there was nothing to be gained by a reputation for grumbling.

A few days later the dog appeared again. This time she rooted around one of the flower beds, digging up some of the tulip bulbs that were resting nicely in the earth after blooming spectacularly in the spring. He looked grimly at the dog, now joyfully snuffling around the tender shoots of peas, and looked around for a handy stick to chase it with. "If that widow cannot keep control of the dog then she ought not to have it," he said to a non-existent auditor. "Besides, she oughtn't have a dog like that anyway—a working dog that belongs on a farm! She should get a little pug if she must have a dog; something that would sit quietly on her lap."

The dog surmised from the stick and the determined step of Major Knowles that her time in his garden was being cut short, but she circled twice around the rose beds before she agreed to go back over the wall. It took several hours to repair the damage, and even then some of the plants could not be salvaged. Major Knowles did the best he could and then wrote a brief note to Mrs. Collins, asking her if she could please keep the dog out of his garden, as there had been some damage done to his plants. He remained her obedient servant, & etc.

Mrs. Collins wrote back that she was very sorry, and she begged his forgiveness. She would make sure that it did not happen again, she said. Major Knowles read the note and said aloud, "I hope that means she is giving the dog to someone else."

And indeed, Charlotte thought about doing so. She talked very seriously to her daughters about Lady Jane Grey's faults, and the havoc she had caused already to the Major's garden. It might be best, she said, to find another home for Lady. The little girls were at first shocked and then overwrought and inconsolable. They would watch over her, they pleaded. They would keep her from leaving their own garden.

Charlotte allowed herself to be persuaded, at least for the time being. The girls, to their credit, watched Lady carefully, making certain that she was in the house unless they were outside with her. For a week Lady was guarded and hovered over, and Maria even stood outside in the rain with the dog for an hour rather than let her exercise unguarded. This was her own idea, and when Charlotte discovered what she had done, she scolded her for such imprudence.

"But Betsy said this morning that Lady is getting fat because she hasn't been outside as much. I thought she ought to have exercise, even if it was raining."

Charlotte looked from the dripping child to the dripping dog. It did seem that Lady was much more plump than she had been two weeks before. A suspicion entered her brain at that moment, and she confided it to Betsy when the girls were not within earshot. Betsy examined the dog and confirmed the notion. A litter of puppies would be born shortly at the cottage.

Charlotte groaned. How would they manage? The cottage was not large, and there were no outbuildings for the dogs to go into. Perhaps it would be best to have Lady Jane Grey taken away somewhere—even to Pemberley, if need be. She would think about it and make some kind of decision tomorrow.

But when tomorrow came, Maria was ill and feverish.

"I was afraid some ill would come of her being out in the

rain," said Charlotte to Betsy as they were working in the kitchen after breakfast.

"It may be, ma'am," said Betsy, "but I must say I feel rather ill myself." Charlotte looked and saw flushed cheeks and heard a sniff.

"You do look ill, and ought to be in bed," said Charlotte with authority.

"I thought I might ask if I might lie down after the dishes and the ironing."

"No, you must lie down now, for I cannot have you take seriously ill, Betsy. I can manage on my own for today, but I do not care to be without you for days on end. I would be lost without your help."

Betsy smiled faintly, and went to her bed.

That was the beginning of two very trying days at the cottage. Betsy and Maria both became more ill, their fevers climbed and their appetites diminished. Charlotte considered letting Elizabeth know they were ill, but she had determined that she would not take undue advantage of the Darcys, and she shrank from asking for their help.

Charlotte had not often felt overwhelmed in the course of her life, but on the morning of the third day she was sorely tried. She had been awake nearly all night with Maria, and although she was not a woman prone to panicking, she was beginning to be worried about her fever. Betsy was still quite unwell, and between caring for Catherine, preparing meals, and nursing the sick, Charlotte felt utterly incompetent and weak. *And even now*, she thought, *Lady Jane Grey might be giving birth to a large litter. What would I do then?*

She wondered, idly, where the dog was at that moment. Catherine had gone out with her in the morning after breakfast— no doubt she was back in the scullery now. She was rising to make sure of this when there was a knock at the door. It took her a moment to remember that Betsy was ill in bed and therefore she must answer it herself.

She opened the door and saw Major Knowles standing there on the doorstep, scowling.

"Mrs. Collins," he said, with as slight a bow as civility could sanction, "Your dog has been digging in my garden again, in spite of your assurance that you would not allow her to do so anymore. If you cannot keep your word, you ought not to keep animals, either." His voice was harsh, as he felt that he had been badly used. His garden had been ravaged thrice, and he had shown remarkable patience the first two times. Now, however, the animal had dug up his hollyhocks past any repair, and the kitchen garden had lost a good many carrots and cabbage plants. His wrath could not be contained any longer.

Charlotte's face grew pale during this tirade, and her voice shook a little as she said, "I beg your pardon, Major Knowles. I was distracted today and forgot to be sure the dog was secure."

"I have little wish to have my garden ruined because you are *distracted*, madam. If you cannot control the dog, then I will have no recourse but to go to the magistrate and tell him of your dog's destruction of my garden."

Major Knowles had been carried along by the force of his righteous anger and had not really envisioned what the response might be to his outburst. Nothing could have prepared him for what did happen: Mrs. Collins burst into tears. For a minute they stood just as they were, Major Knowles rooted to the spot in surprise and consternation, and Charlotte weeping in the doorway.

"There now," Major Knowles said eventually, feeling more awkward than he had since he had first joined the army and floundered at drill. "There now, don't weep so, Mrs. Collins, I beg you. I did not mean to cause you distress—I daresay I did speak too severely to you. Please, do stop crying."

"Oh," gasped Charlotte, trying to quell the sobs that shook her. "It is my fault for not being more careful. My maid and my child are both ill, and I had little sleep last night. If you will tell me how I might pay for the damage to your garden, I will be sure to recompense you for the destruction." On the last word her face twisted, and she began to cry again. She had not cried before another person since her nursery days, and the humiliation of doing so before a near-stranger made her cry all the more.

Major Knowles felt wretched. He had known women who were practiced criers, who could conjure up tears at will in order to sway others. Mrs. Collins was manifestly not this sort of woman: she wept almost as if she had never done it before. He offered his handkerchief and was thankful to find it accepted. When the sobbing grew quieter, he said rapidly that the dog was only behaving as dogs do, and she ought not to mind his angry words, for after all, the damage had been slight. He begged pardon again, bowed briefly, and bolted back to Ivy House where he spent the afternoon in the garden doing what he could to repair the damage and trying to forget the distressed face of Mrs. Collins.

Two weeks later, Lady Jane Grey had her puppies. By then Betsy and Maria were both well again, and the girls would hardly leave the scullery, for that was the place where the Blessed Event had taken place. Charlotte had recovered her poise and was thankful to know that only Major Knowles had seen her at her most vulnerable—the Darcys were unaware that there had been any crisis. She was kept awake at night by her thoughts for a few days, wishing that she had not made such a bad impression on Major Knowles. He must think her completely incompetent—unable to keep her dog out of his garden even after she promised to do so, and then weeping uncontrollably when he came to remonstrate. She did once wonder if she would have cared so much if he had not been so handsome and masterful, but really it made no difference. She scuttled unobtrusively out of his way when their paths crossed—which was not often—and tried to dismiss the matter from her mind.

She was not the only one who feared they had made a poor showing of themselves. Major Knowles had only to close his eyes to see again Mrs. Collins bursting into tears, and he berated himself endlessly for being so brutal. Dogs were dogs—you could not keep them contained completely, and she must have done her best, poor thing, to keep that shaggy creature close to home. He did not know about the puppies, of course, and thought that the fact that the dog had not come again must mean that she was wearing herself out to see that the dog did not bother him. He almost wished the dog would come, so that she could see him extend tolerance and forbearance. He often saw her from a distance at church with her two little girls, who were always neatly dressed and well-behaved, but she never seemed to come near enough for him to tip his hat to her or greet her in a friendly way. Every time he saw her, he found more things that he admired about her. There was a simple elegance in her dress and her bearing. She seemed to be drawn to women of good character instead of the gossips and complainers. And although she must be a friend of the Darcys if she was renting that cottage, she did not appear to flaunt her connection with them. He had unjustly berated a most worthy woman, and it galled him.

In early August the beets and cucumbers were ready for harvest, and as Major Knowles looked over the baskets of gathered vegetables, he was seized with inspiration.

"I think," he said as casually as he could to Mrs. Silver, "that we ought to share a little of our bounty with our neighbors. Perhaps you would be good enough to bring some of these over to Mrs. Collins at the cottage?"

Mrs. Silver caught the over-careless note in his voice and smiled to herself.

"As you wish, sir. They'll be most grateful for it, I don't doubt."

They were grateful. Mrs. Collins wrote a sweet note acknowledging the gift, and Major Knowles read it over frequently in the following days. The next week, radishes and cauliflower were ready to be harvested, and again, a gift was sent over to the cottage. A note of thanks was returned, as effusive as the writer would allow herself to be.

A few days later, Lady Jane Grey, tired of the society of her five active pups, escaped for a few minutes into the garden of Ivy House once again. The major spied the dog from his window, and just as he got out into the garden, he saw Mrs. Collins at the wall, calling to the dog. She started guiltily when she saw him.

"I beg your pardon, Major Knowles," she said rather desperately, "Lady got away from me just now—truly, she came over the wall just a moment ago."

"Ah, yes, there she is," said the major pleasantly. "I'll send her back to you."

Determined not to seem angry, he dared not shout at the dog or speak harshly to it, and he could not pretend to throw something at it either. "Come here, Lady," he crooned. "Good girl. Go along home, now." Anything less commanding could hardly be imagined. Lady took his cheerful tones to mean that he wanted to play with her, and she galloped around the garden happily, wagging her tail and barking at intervals.

"Oh, no," moaned Charlotte, seeing the dog race through the famous beds of roses. "Lady, come here!"

"Wait there, Mrs. Collins," said the major, "I have a little bit of food that ought to entice her. I'll go into the kitchen and get it."

He hurried into the kitchen and shocked Mrs. Silver by demanding a piece of beef.

"Beef, sir?" repeated Mrs. Silver. "I'm sure I don't have any except for that cutlet Cook was to serve you for your dinner."

"That'll do excellently," said the major. "Just trim off a piece for me." He brought the piece out and took it over to where Mrs. Collins was obediently standing by the garden wall. It came up to her waist and she was bending over it as far as she could, attempting to persuade the dog to leave off digging in the cornflower bed.

"Here, Lady," said Major Knowles in as sweet a tone as he could manage. He dangled the piece of meat in front of him. "Come and get this lovely bit of steak!"

Lady Jane Grey paused in her digging. She cocked her head as if considering the offer, but it is doubtful that she would have been won over if Catherine had not appeared next to her mother, holding one of the puppies in her arms. "Mama, where is Lady?"

The puppy whimpered, and that drew Lady Jane as nothing else had. She ran to the wall, leapt on top of it, and jumped down again on the cottage side. Catherine let the puppy down, and after a minute of sniffing, licking, and tail-wagging, mother and pup scampered back toward the cottage.

Major Knowles felt a little silly, still standing there with the piece of meat in his hand. He held it out to Mrs. Collins, saying, "For the dog," and then he felt more awkward still. As if she would think he meant that she and her children should eat it! She did not seem to notice his discomfiture, and her words of gratitude sounded sincere. He was afraid that she would excuse herself and leave, and so he struck up a conversation with the child.

"Hello there," he said to Catherine with a slight bow. "How do you do?"

She curtseyed very prettily and said, "Very well, I thank you, sir."

"Are there many puppies at your house?" he asked.

"Yes, sir, five."

"Five, is it? Quite a litter!" he said, and out of the corner of his eye he saw an anxious expression on Charlotte's face. Correctly surmising that she was afraid he was envisioning six dogs shortly jumping over the wall and ravaging his garden, his only thought was to lay her fears to rest. "I don't suppose," he said, "that you would let me keep one of them, when they are old enough, would you?"

"But—" said Charlotte.

He turned to face her. "Yes, Mrs. Collins?"

"I beg your pardon, sir," she said, "but are you *quite* sure you want one? The puppies are certain to dig as well."

"Quite sure," he said, even though he had given the proposition no thought at all. The relief on Mrs. Collins' face was worth a dozen ruined flower beds.

"In that case," she said, "You may certainly have one. I will ask Mr. Darcy if we might put up a fence next to the wall so that the dogs will not come over it any longer."

"I beg you will not do any such thing," said the major. "I have not had many visitors of late, and certainly none so lovely as the present ones. If there is a wall, I might never have such callers again, and then where will I be?" He said it as if to Catherine, who smiled at his nonsense, but it was not lost on him that Mrs. Collins blushed.

"The puppies cannot be given to anyone for six more weeks," said Catherine knowledgeably. "They need to stay with their mama until then. Will you be very disappointed to wait that long?"

"I will try to be patient," said Major Knowles. "Patience is a virtue I have been known to disregard, and I am seeking to amend my character. Six weeks of waiting is just the sort of practice I need." He ventured a look at Mrs. Collins and saw that she understood him. There was a faint smile on her face—one of the first he had ever seen. It erased the worry-lines on her forehead and brought out the warmth of her brown eyes.

He knew an impulse to say all that was in his heart and suppressed it. He had already acquired a dog through rashness; who could tell what other injudicious acts he might commit if he remained talking to the Collinses? He had best leave them. "I must be going now," he said. "I bid you good day, ladies." He reached up to tip his hat to them as he bowed—only to discover that he was not wearing a hat and that his fingers were grasping at the empty air above his head. He was too embarrassed to see what the reaction of the females was.

~

Charlotte went into the house with her cheeks glowing and her heart beating erratically. There had been no mistaking the look in the major's eyes. It was startling and gratifying all at once.

Major Knowles spent the rest of the day in a very distracted frame of mind. Mrs. Collins was not averse to him, he was sure. Whether she would welcome his advances at this time remained to be seen, but he was certain that she did not hold any grudge against him. He wondered how soon he might call on her. He wished it might be the very next day, but that did seem a little too precipitate. By the time he retired to bed that evening he had come to a decision: he would wait three days. Then he would go to the cottage bringing flowers—for the little girls, he would say—and he would announce that he had come to choose which puppy should be his when they were weaned. Surely Mrs. Collins would ask him to sit and talk with her for a little while, and he would contrive to win her heart. How? He did not know, but he was determined to do it.

Three days later Charlotte received a letter from Lady Catherine DeBurgh. She waited until the girls were immersed in attempting to bedeck all the puppies with ribbons and little capes, and then sat at the writing desk in the parlour and began to read it.

My Dear Mrs. Collins,

I thought it my duty to write to you and enquire after your health. Your late husband was, after all, the vicar here for several years, and I would not like to be remiss in attending to his widow—in spite of the fact that you did not follow my advice and take the cottage in Hunsford that I recommended to you. It could have been repaired for you, you know; the roof had only fallen in on one end, and it would have been very little trouble to make it sound again. If you had stayed here in Kent you would have had the very great benefit of my guidance and advice. What is more, your little girls would have had so many advantages! They might easily have attended the school in the village and perhaps one day become governesses. And then, too, the food is so much better here. Only last week the gardener told me that the kitchen garden had an abundance of marrows, and I ordered them to be dispersed among the deserving families of Hunsford. If you had been here, you would have received your portion.

As it is, I fear you must be in a very bad way—no doubt you are friendless and even hungry. And your poor little girls must be miserable so far from Rosings. I only hope they will not resent your removing them from a place of comfort and plenty to your present situation of want and penury.

Charlotte paused her reading as Maria entered the parlour with one of the puppies.

"See, Mama, how fine she looks? Only she keeps trying to take the ribbon off her ear."

"She does look very pretty, my love, but puppies are not very interested in fashion. I think she will be happier if you take it off of her and gave her a bone to chew on instead. That is what she really likes."

Maria sighed at the perverseness of the puppy's inclinations, but nevertheless untied the ribbon and left the room with the dog to beg Betsy for a bone in the kitchen. Charlotte smiled after her, thinking of how happy the girls were here, how well fed they all were, and how many friends they had. And then there was Major Knowles ...

She turned back to the letter.

And if which I fear may be the case, you have not survived and are now in your grave, I hope you will always remember that you ought to have followed my advice, and it is due to your own obstinacy that your girls are now motherless.

Charlotte laughed. It felt good to laugh—it had been a very long time since she had done so. Lady Catherine was so absurd. She read the letter over again and it was even more humorous the second time. By the end of it she was laughing so hard that her eyes streamed with tears and her shoulders shook. She put her head down on the desk and gave herself up to merriment.

"My dear Mrs. Collins!" said a voice from the doorway. "Whatever is the matter?"

It was Major Knowles, who had been admitted to the house by Betsy. Betsy had been distracted just as he entered by one of the puppies dashing out of the open door. She had pursued the puppy, who was running with all his might down the path, saying over her shoulder, "If you will wait there for a moment, sir, I will announce you!"

Major Knowles had had every intention of waiting patiently by the door, but a howl of what seemed to be anguish came from the parlour. Instinctively he went to the door, which was not quite closed, and opened it to see Charlotte apparently weeping uncontrollably.

Charlotte suddenly knew how it must look, which made it that much harder to stop laughing. In three strides he was across the room and his hand was on her shoulder, and he was saying helplessly, "Please, please stop weeping. Whatever the matter is, I will help you! I swear it!"

The tone of his voice was so tender that it pulled Charlotte up short, and she was able to gasp and say, "You are mistaken, sir." She wiped her eyes and attempted to regain some composure.

"No, no," said Major Knowles, still uncomprehending. "I *will* help you. I love you, you see," he said simply. "I want you to be my wife. Then there will be two of us against whatever the trouble is. Say you will accept my hand, my dear."

After that, of course, there was no way that he could retract his proposal, even when Charlotte was able to speak rationally and explain what had happened. It was a good thing, then, that he had no desire to withdraw his offer, and was in fact grateful that his misapprehension had sped along a courtship which he thought must have been attended by much awkwardness, unpracticed as he was at wooing.

Charlotte was grateful as well, for having discovered the state of her own heart, she had no desire to spend tedious weeks waiting to see if her earnest wishes would be fulfilled.

Lady Catherine, when she heard of this second marriage of Mrs. Collins, was most seriously displeased. She had decided that Charlotte, having spurned her advice in the matter of living arrangements, must be miserable and filled with regret. It was hardly to be borne that she should find love and happiness. She most pointedly did *not* wish Charlotte joy in her upcoming nuptials and comforted herself by thinking that this must have the effect of humbling Mrs. Collins. Charlotte, it must be said, did not even notice.

The little girls begged that Lady Jane Grey be allowed to attend the wedding, as she had been the one to introduce the bride and groom to each other. The rector could not allow a dog inside the church, he said, but he suggested that she instead be given a piece of the cake as a reward for her labors. Lady Jane Grey was quite content with that.

The End